You Said Forever

Susan Lewis is the bestselling author of thirty-eight novels. She is also the author of *Just One More Day* and *One Day at a Time*, the moving memoirs of her childhood in Bristol. She lives in Gloucestershire. Her website address is www.susanlewis.com

Susan is a supporter of the breast cancer charity, Breast Cancer Care: www.breastcancercare.org.uk and of the childhood bereavement charity, Winton's Wish: www.winstonswish.org.uk

Praise for Susan Lewis

'A gripping story of love, uncertainty and betrayal . . . a guaranteed tear-jerker that will keep you at the edge of your seat.' *OK!*

'A master storyteller.' Diane Chamberlain

'Spellbinding! You just keep turning the pages, with the atmosphere growing more and more intense as the story leads to its dramatic climax.' *Daily Mail*

'Utterly compelling.' *Sun*

'Expertly written to brew an atmosphere of foreboding, this story is an irresistible blend of intrigue and passion, and the consequences of secrets and betrayal.' *Woman*

'Sad, happy, sensual and intriguing.' *Woman's Own*

ALSO BY SUSAN LEWIS

Fiction

A Class Apart
Dance While You Can
Stolen Beginnings
Darkest Longings
Obsession
Vengeance
Summer Madness
Last Resort
Wildfire
Cruel Venus
Strange Allure
The Mill House
A French Affair
Missing
Out of the Shadows
Lost Innocence
The Choice
Forgotten
Stolen
No Turning Back
Losing You
The Truth About You
Never Say Goodbye
Too Close to Home
No Place to Hide

Books that run in sequence
Chasing Dreams
Taking Chances

No Child of Mine
Don't Let Me Go

Behind Closed Doors
The Girl Who Came Back
The Moment She Left
Hiding in Plain Sight

Series featuring Laurie Forbes and Elliott Russell
Silent Truths
Wicked Beauty
Intimate Strangers
The Hornbeam Tree

Memoir
Just One More Day
One Day at a Time

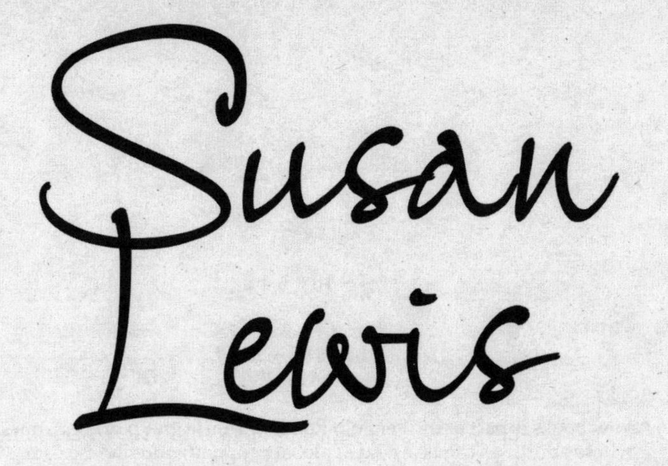

You Said Forever

arrow books

3 5 7 9 10 8 6 4 2

Arrow Books
20 Vauxhall Bridge Road
London SW1V 2SA

Arrow Books is part of the Penguin Random House group of companies whose addresses can be found at global.penguinrandomhouse.com.

First published in Great Britain by Century in 2017
First published in paperback by Arrow Books in 2017

www.penguin.co.uk

A CIP catalogue record for this book is available from the British Library.

ISBN 9781784755591
ISBN 9781784756741 (export)

Typeset in 12.39/15.91 pt Palatino LT Std by Jouve (UK), Milton Keynes
Printed and bound in Great Britain by Clays Ltd, St Ives Plc

Penguin Random House is committed to a sustainable future for our business, our readers and our planet. This book is made from Forest Stewardship Council® certified paper.

To my dear friends of more
than twenty-five years,
Vanessa and Richard Owen

Chapter One

'May I ask how Chloe is?'

Though Charlotte had heard the question she kept her eyes down, giving the impression her mind was elsewhere.

'I've always said,' the woman chatted on, undaunted, 'that it was a wonderful thing you did. Very courageous.'

Charlotte attempted a smile, but her hand was tightening on the bottle she was holding, not to smash it against a wall. She'd never do that in front of a customer, indeed had never done it, but this woman was making her tense. 'As you can see,' she said, pouring a soupçon of pale lemon-coloured wine into a clear glass, 'our Pinot Gris has a delicate tinge of green . . .' She broke off as a random kick of emotion stole her words, but her movements remained fluid as she poured another sample of the vintage into a second glass and handed one each to the woman and her husband.

Swirling the wine to release the bouquet, the man put his nose to the rim and inhaled deeply. 'Pear,' he declared, inviting contradiction and receiving only a friendly nod of agreement from Charlotte. Frowning curiously, he added, 'With a hint of . . . ginger?'

Charlotte's sea-green eyes showed approval. He'd missed out the trace of citrus blossom, but who, other than a seasoned professional, would have picked up on that? She only knew it was there because Will, their winemaker, had told her.

'Cellaring, three to five years,' the man murmured, reading from the tasting notes Charlotte had handed him.

These visitors were English, Charlotte could tell from the accent, though she had no idea if they were tourists or residents of New Zealand.

She was doing her best to ignore the woman's scrutiny, but it was so powerful, invasive, it might go right through her skin. Whoever she was, she clearly wasn't interested in the wine, but at least her husband was making a good show of it.

'Am I right that she's called Chloe now?' the woman asked, apparently not bothered by Charlotte's discomfort, or simply not noticing it.

Once again Charlotte bypassed the question. 'As you can see from the notes,' she said to the man, 'our philosophy is to make artisan wines that are food friendly, have texture . . .'

'Is she here?' the woman wanted to know,

attempting to peer past the walls of floor-to-ceiling wine racks and chalkboards to the hidden office beyond. She turned around, as though her quarry might be creeping up on her from behind.

With the frontage of the tasting room, known as the cellar-door area, rolled wide open there was nothing – and no one – between the tasting counter and courtyard, where guests were welcome to sit under the jacarandas while sampling Tuki River wines. If they came at the right time of day they might also be served a small tray of canapés, courtesy of Rick's Bistro across the way. Although each table was covered in a crisp white linen cloth, it was easy to see they were fashioned from barrels – puncheons in fact – and the empty wine bottles acting as candleholders all bore the Tuki River Winery label. Earlier, on her way from the house, Charlotte had gathered some sprigs of lavender to liven up the tables, but a gently insistent breeze wafting in from the ocean had soon carried them off.

'You can see she's not here,' the husband muttered under his breath.

The woman turned back to Charlotte.

'She's at school,' Charlotte said, trying to sound friendly while feeling resentful. *For heaven's sake,* she wanted to shout at the woman, *the girl is eight years old, so where the heck do you think she is?*

'Of course,' the woman smiled, seeming to think the notion sweet. 'And how's she doing?'

Starting to wonder if this apparently random visitor was actually a reporter, Charlotte picked up another bottle to continue the tasting. 'Perhaps you'd like to try the Reserve Chardonnay,' she suggested. 'It's a 2014 vintage, and we don't have much of it left now . . .' *If only that were true.*

'Mummy! I'm home,' an excited voice called across the courtyard from the parking area.

The woman spun round immediately to find Cooper, Charlotte's almost four-year-old son, hanging out of a car window, all wayward dark curls, dusty face and sky-blue eyes. Behind the wheel of the car was Rowan, his nanny.

'Have to go to the bathroom,' Cooper announced, giving a telltale shiver as Rowan drove on.

'Oh, he's adorable,' the woman cried, clasping a hand to her chest. 'And how wonderful that Chloe has a brother now.'

She also had a sister – Elodie, aged eighteen months – but Charlotte wasn't about to confide that. 'The Reserve Chardonnay,' she continued, 'was left in barrel, on full yeast . . .'

'Do you get your oak barrels from France?' the man interrupted, apparently wanting to show off some knowledge.

'Of course,' Charlotte replied.

'They're the best,' he informed her, as though she might not have known.

'Could I get a photograph with you?' the woman

asked, taking out her iPhone. 'You're quite a celebrity back home, you know. I expect you are here too.'

'Yvonne, we're here to taste the wine,' her husband growled.

'Of course, but . . .'

'Excuse me,' Charlotte said as her mobile rang, and seeing it was her half-brother, Rick, she eagerly clicked on. He was nothing if not an expert at coming to her rescue, even when he had no idea she was in trouble. 'Tuki River Winery,' she announced, making it sound like a business call.

Twenty minutes later Charlotte watched, with no small relief, as the couple wound their way through the still-empty tables across the courtyard to the rustic, herb-bordered parking area beyond. They'd bought three bottles, two Pinot Gris and a Chardonnay, which she'd packed up in a smartly branded carrying box and tied with a dark green ribbon. It was important to give the appearance of being successful and upmarket, even if they were struggling to stay afloat.

Gathering up the used glasses, she put them in the sink behind the beechwood countertop and turned on the tap. Images of Chloe were fluttering out of the past: Chloe shrieking with joy as she ran into the waves; her eagerness to help build a beach fire; eyes lighting up at the prospect of a surprise; delight at being accepted into a poi dance class; laughter as she and Charlotte practised the dance moves at home; pride on receiving a gold star at school; hanging limply in Anthony's arms as he carried her to bed.

How was it possible for Charlotte's heart to melt and freeze at the same time?

Melt with love; freeze with fear of the way Chloe had changed in the last year.

She gave a small gasp, taking in the air of now, returning herself to the task at hand.

The irritating English couple – the woman anyway – could well prove the last visitors of the day, although Charlotte sincerely hoped not, since Tuki River Winery could do with selling a whole lot more of 2014's vintage than they were currently managing. Not that random drop-ins, or even sizeable tour groups were ever going to sort the problem. However, there was never any knowing who might be amongst them, disguised as a tourist but with the purchasing power to change Tuki's fortunes completely.

It didn't happen that way, and she knew it, but clutching at straws was one way of keeping her hopes alive as she tackled the hectic, chaotic demands of each and *every* day. Another was to carry on believing in her dynamic and undaunted husband, who owned and ran this idyllic – scenery-wise, anyway – vineyard in the Special Character Zone of New Zealand's Hawkes Bay.

The original plan, almost five years ago, had been

to move from England and buy a vineyard near Charlotte's mother and stepfather in the Bay of Islands. Unfortunately, that had fallen through at the eleventh hour, almost crushing the dream, until her stepfather, Bob, had put them in touch with Kim Thorp and Andy Coltart, the owners of Black Barn Vineyard, a multi-award-winning estate in the heart of Hawkes Bay. Kim and Andy had more or less brokered Charlotte and Anthony's purchase of this two-hectare vineyard, now renamed Tuki River Winery. The modest twelve parcels of vines were spread randomly and hopefully amongst endless acres of fruit orchards, cornfields and thousands upon thousands of hectares of long-established vines belonging to some world-famous estates.

It had never been anyone's intention to use Charlotte and Chloe's 'celebrity' to help pull in the punters. It wouldn't even have crossed the minds of the serious businessmen involved in getting them started; for them it was all about the product, as it was for Charlotte and Anthony. However, that wasn't how the average tourist, or even some locals saw it. For them, the cellar-door area of Tuki River Winery was a golden opportunity to get a look at the mother and daughter who'd been all over the news almost five years ago.

It was rarely they got to see Chloe; she was either at school or up at the house, which was a good fifteen-minute walk from the cellar door through a lush two-acre parcel of reserve Chardonnay vines. Charlotte, on the other hand, was almost always to be found organising wine tastings at the cellar door, or checking in guests who'd come to stay at one of Tuki River's three holiday retreats nestled around the estate.

Four years might have passed since they'd come here, and Hawkes Bay might be a good seven hundred kilometres from her mother's home town of Kerikeri, but Charlotte's sensational arrest for child abduction in Northland, followed by the forced return to England, apparently remained a source of deep fascination. It was shocking just how intrusive and insensitive some people could be. It was as though, because Charlotte and Chloe had been on their TV screens and in their newspapers, not to mention all over social media, they felt entitled to know all the details of their lives. Charlotte Nicholls, joint owner of Tuki River Winery, was the same Charlotte Nicholls, social worker (known at the time as Alex Lake), who'd snatched a child from an abusive family in the UK and *got away with it!* That was how a lot of people put it, *got away with it,* and Charlotte couldn't argue with that because she *had* taken a child, namely Chloe – although she'd been called Ottilie back then – and she *had* got away with it. This wasn't to say she hadn't been tried for the crime, with a very strong chance of being sent to prison at the end of it. As it turned out, the jury had gone against all the evidence that proved her guilty, and set her free. To them all that had mattered was Chloe, the small child of four, who'd been so badly abused by her father and neglected by her mother that she'd only started to speak when Charlotte had come into her life. Chloe needed Charlotte perhaps even more than most children needed their mothers. Charlotte – and Charlotte's mother Anna – were the only people the sweet, but terribly damaged little girl had the confidence to relate to, so who in their right mind was going to send Charlotte to prison and condemn Chloe to a life in care?

As soon as her freedom was assured Charlotte had applied to the family courts for an adoption order, so Chloe was now legally hers and no one, but no one, could tear them apart.

Since thinking about Chloe could cause her to feel breathless, and often brought dark butterflies to her heart, Charlotte did what she usually did when the world seemed to be closing in on her; she buried herself in work. This wasn't difficult, for there was always so much to do. Consequently she was hardly seeing anything of her children these days, and could only thank god for Rowan, her stepfather's twenty-three-year-old niece, who'd come down from the Bay of Islands to help out. Without her Charlotte's family might well have fallen apart by now, although Charlotte kept telling herself that no matter what, she'd never let that happen. If it came right down to it, she'd turn her back on the business and tell Anthony that he had to find someone else to help run it. The thought of doing that made her feel sick, for she wanted, with all her heart, to support him, to be able to put him first and be at his side when they managed to turn his dream into a dazzling reality. Tuki River Winery meant the world to her too, but not more than her children – or her marriage. The trouble was they were all so tied up in each other that she hardly knew where one began and the other ended.

Going to her laptop, in a niche below the chalkboard she updated each morning with the special offers of the day, she was about to check on their Internet orders – please god let there be some – when Rowan pulled up in the old Range Rover and a scrub-faced, barefoot Cooper came tearing across the courtyard, his angelic little sister in wobbly pursuit.

'I made cakes at kindi today,' Cooper cried as she swung him up in her arms. 'They're not real so you can't eat them, but they look real so we could pretend and see if we can trick Daddy.'

Laughing, Charlotte planted a smackeroo on his cheek and stooped to gather up Elodie.

'Mummy,' Elodie beamed, her adorable little smile spreading all over her pixie face. She was proving much slower in talking than Cooper had, and didn't seem to exude his boundless confidence, but she was still a baby and the reasons behind her delayed development didn't necessarily have to be as sinister as Charlotte sometimes feared. Certainly the doctor had found nothing to concern him, not on the physical front anyway. On the psychological front . . . That was something Charlotte couldn't bring herself to go into. Not yet, but she would, as soon as things calmed down a little, and in the meantime she was doing everything in her power to make sure Elodie knew how much her mummy loved her.

'You don't suppose your attachment to Elodie has something to do with the fact that she looks like you?' Anthony had teased when it had become evident that Elodie was going to stay blonde like her mother, with the same aquamarine eyes and delicate features. She didn't have freckles yet, but with her creamy fair skin she would undoubtedly develop them soon enough, while Cooper, with his father's olive complexion and inky dark hair was, according to Anthony, a little demon amongst the vines.

Chloe bore more of a resemblance to Anthony and Cooper, though her eyes were a velvety chocolate brown, while theirs were varying shades of blue or grey depending on their moods. Her hair, russet-brown and curly, cascaded halfway down her back and was almost as impossible to brush as it was to tame into slides or elastics. She was a strikingly pretty young girl who'd lately become alarmingly unpredictable and far too worldly for her years.

'So where are you all off to?' Charlotte asked, as Cooper whizzed across the yard to the children's playground where he'd spotted his uncle doing something to a swing. Rick's Bistro was sprawled across a small north-facing slope the other side of the playground, and was a popular eatery for both locals and tourists. Out of loyalty Rick and his partner Hamish always encouraged clients to choose a Tuki River wine with their meals. If it weren't for the bistro a whole week could go by without Charlotte and Anthony selling a single bottle.

'Are you going to answer Mummy?' Rowan prompted Elodie. Rowan was a sweet, round-faced girl, part Maori, part Kiwi, with a shock of coppery curls, unevenly set brown eyes and a colourful tattoo of a butterfly on her left shoulder that fascinated the heck out of Elodie. Chloe was so desperate for one too that she'd tried inking one on herself, until finding it impossible she'd decided to draw one on each of Elodie's cheeks instead. That would have been bad enough, but being Chloe she'd had to add a moustache and spectacles, and all in indelible ink. Chloe and Cooper had hooted for days, which was as long as it had taken for the mask to be washed off without taking Elodie's tender skin with it.

(She had looked funny, but Charlotte and Anthony hadn't dared to let Chloe know they thought so or she'd be sure to do it again – and no doubt worse.)

'We're going to pick up Chloe from school,' Rowan reminded Elodie.

Elodie turned to her mother, and as though suddenly tired she dropped her head on Charlotte's shoulder.

Wishing she could keep Elodie with her, Charlotte said to Rowan, 'Does Chloe have ballet today?'

'Swim club,' Rowan corrected. 'I'll drop her there then take these two for ice cream in the village while we wait. Do you need anything while we're out?'

'You could pick up a few things at Bellatino's,' Charlotte replied, reaching for her purse. Thank goodness the retreats were providing an income, albeit small; if it weren't for them they really would be struggling to put food on the table.

Grabbing her mobile as it rang, she saw it was Anthony and clicked on.

'Hi, it's me,' he told her.

'No kidding,' she responded wryly.

He wasn't listening, something was already taking his attention, and a moment later he said, 'I'll call back.'

As the line went dead Charlotte handed Elodie to Rowan. 'Why don't you stay and watch Chloe until she's finished at swim club,' she said, preparing a list for the deli, 'then take all three of them for ice cream?' Chloe liked ice cream and surely wouldn't want to miss out.

Perhaps Chloe didn't like ice cream today. For all Charlotte knew it could be the new poison. Or maybe there had been an incident at the ice-cream shop that Rowan hadn't mentioned for fear of getting Chloe into yet more trouble.

'I would if Chloe wanted us to stay,' Rowan was saying, 'but this morning she said she didn't. I'll see if she's changed her mind when we collect her, but I was hoping to get them home, fed and in bed by eight so I can meet the girls at Pipi's for a glass of wine and dessert.'

Knowing this was what many of Havelock North's young mothers did once or twice a month – eat with the kids, put them to bed, then leave the husbands or nannies in charge while they met up with friends – Charlotte tried not to mind that she wasn't a part of it. She'd do better simply to feel thankful that Rowan's devotion to the children allowed her, Charlotte, to work late when she needed to, which was just about every night and a big part of the weekends.

Almost before Rowan had driven off Charlotte was back at her computer, about to log into the Wineworks portal, when a call came from Francis, the cellar-door manager at the Black Barn Vineyard. 'We've just sent a tour bus your way,' he told her. 'About forty on board, from one of the cruise ships, so brace yourself. If you need a hand shout and I'll send someone over.'

Knowing she'd never cope with so many alone, Charlotte said, 'I'll find out if Rick and Hamish can come. If not you'll hear back from me.'

Eternally grateful for how supportive everyone was at Black Barn, Charlotte was about to call Rick when she spotted him heading her way. With his tight, wiry frame, close-cropped hair and electric-blue eyes he was as handsome as he was plucky, kind and intuitive – and she couldn't have loved him more if she'd known him her entire life.

'Just the person,' she smiled as he stopped to straighten up one of her tablecloths and brush away a fallen jacaranda pod. It was a pity the vibrant lavender-blue flowers were starting to fade now, for with their dense and exotic fern-like foliage they provided the most beautiful and romantic canopy for the cellar-door courtyard. That alone should have made people want to come, especially in the evenings when the candles were lit and soft music was playing.

Sadly it had yet to happen, at least in a significant way.

'It's my turn to ask a favour,' Rick reminded her, tidying up the tasting notes she'd left awry on the counter. 'Heidi's just called in sick, so we're short of a server tonight. Any chance?'

Not in a million years, however what Charlotte said was, 'I've got a group of forty on the way for a tasting. You come help me with that, and I'm all yours between eight and ten thirty.' That should give her half an hour after finishing here to spend with the children while wolfing down a sandwich and sorting out whatever needed doing at home. *Half an hour, was she kidding? Please just let Chloe be in a good mood or she really would have to let Rick down.*

Anthony, who still hadn't rung back, was in Wellington putting on a tasting for an Australian distributor and wouldn't be home until sometime tomorrow.

Sinking at the thought of that and all it entailed – *later, Charlotte, don't think about it now* – she merrily high-fived Rick to seal the deal.

'How are things here?' he asked, starting to set out glasses ready for the tasting at which almost no wine would be sold, because cruise-ship tourists rarely bought more than a bottle per couple, if that.

'Still waiting for the big order,' she admitted. 'If it doesn't come soon . . .'

'Think positively,' he admonished.

'Or practically,' she corrected. 'We have to know what we're going to do if we can't shift the 2014 stock before the 2015 vintage is bottled and this year's fruit is harvested, or it'll be like trying to stuff ten thousand gallons into ten pint pots. We don't have the space, or the wherewithal to buy more storage.'

'There's still plenty of time.'

Irritably, she said, 'It's February, Rick. That gives

us a couple of months, max, to sell the twenty thousand bottles of wine we've failed to shift in a year.'

Stopping what he was doing, he came to give her a brotherly hug. 'It'll work out,' he said softly. 'Zoe's got everything in hand. You need to put your trust in her.'

Only wishing she could get past the unease she felt around their new publicity and marketing adviser, Charlotte said, 'Zoe Reynolds has been working with us for over three months now and we've yet to see any results.'

'You will, but these things take time, and half of that three months was taken up by the Christmas break. No, listen, just look what she did for the bistro. She put us on the map, and I promise, she'll do the same for you.'

'PR is one thing; sales are another.'

'They go hand in hand, and she has some serious contacts in the gourmet world. Isn't she with Anthony in Wellington now, introducing him to the Australian guy?'

Hoping that was all Zoe was doing with Anthony, Charlotte said, 'Do you seriously think this man is going to buy our entire stock?'

'I don't know who he is, so I can't answer that, but if he's a major Aussie distributor there's a chance. And let's not forget that you've got some good vintages, the Reserve Chardonnay in particular, it just hasn't been marketed right. And that's what Zoe will take care of. I wouldn't have recommended her if I didn't have so much faith in her, not at the rate she charges. It'll be worth it in the end, you'll see. Now tell me, have you spoken to your mother recently?'

Frowning as she thought, Charlotte said, 'Why?'

'She's worried about you.'

'Which means you've spoken to her.'

'Actually, I had a call from Dad and inevitably the subject of you came up.'

'I hope you told him there's nothing to get worked up about. Mum's got enough on her plate with your sister going through chemo and your dad's foot still in plaster.'

'That's what I told him, because I knew you'd want me to, but I have to admit I worry about you, Charlotte. You need to ease up a bit, take some time off . . . OK, OK, I know you're going to start shouting at me about cashflow and not being able to afford extra staff and never having enough time to brush your hair never mind have a bath . . .'

'I never said that. I shower every day.'

Laughing, he said, 'You need to take some time with the kids. It's what you want, so do they. They need you, especially Chloe . . .'

'Don't,' she protested, putting up a hand to stop him. 'You're not telling me anything I don't already know, so let's leave it there and talk about how many you've got booked in for this evening.'

Regarding her darkly, he seemed on the verge of saying more, until finally he took out his mobile and began sending a message. 'I'll have Hamish email over the menu so you can get early answers to anything you don't understand.'

'Is anyone else working the tables?'

'Yours truly.'

'I'm not washing up,' she told him forcefully.

Laughing as he connected to his partner, he wandered back across the courtyard, appearing as relaxed as a multimillionaire enjoying his favourite hobby. Since this was exactly what he was, thanks to the sale of his and Hamish's Auckland-based advertising agency to a multinational company headquartered in New York, Charlotte could only feel pleased for him that things were turning out so well with the new venture, namely Rick's Bistro. Envious too, of course, in fact madly so, since Anthony's several millions acquired from the sale of his house in London's Holland Park, and various other investments, had been sunk in their entirety into buying and regenerating the vineyard. And she shouldn't forget the sensational home on the hill that they'd designed and had built when they'd truly believed they couldn't fail; nor the renovation and expansion of the holiday retreats, which, it had to be said, were always booked out. Sadly, though, they didn't provide anywhere near enough income to make even a noticeable contribution to the two hundred thousand dollars a year they needed simply for vineyard overheads.

Watching miserably as a glossy red tour bus full of Oriental cruisers pulled into the car park, she tried raising her spirits with a reminder of how much she'd loved it all at the beginning. It could be like that again, she kept telling herself. Something would happen to prevent them having to go to the bank for a loan they might never be able to repay. They weren't going to lose their home and everything they'd worked so hard for. Something would come good before the harvest, because it had to. And as soon as it did she would bring someone in to help run the cellar door, accounts, online orders, special offers, holiday retreats and staff rostering, so she could spend more time with her children.

Her husband too, of course, presuming he wanted to spend time with her.

Chapter Two

It was just after seven by the time Charlotte finally closed up the cellar door, having sold twenty-two bottles of mostly Pinot Gris to the Orientals and three more to a local who often dropped in, as much for a chat as to stock up his chiller.

With no cars available – Anthony had the Volvo in Wellington, Rowan was using the old Range Rover and Will had the pickup – she began the fifteen-minute uphill trek through the vines, her mobile in one hand and laptop in the other. Although her mind was swimming with worries, and her heart longing for something so big, so out of reach it seemed that she couldn't even put it into words, the feel of the evening sun on her skin, the peachy light it was casting over the ripening fruit and tangled foliage, the sense of being hidden in the heart of nature, was as soothing as allowing herself to believe that everything was right with the world. Even now Anthony was shaking hands on a deal with the Australian distributor that would see Tuki River wines in half the supermarkets throughout the land. They'd raise a glass to celebrate the occasion, and as soon as he was able Anthony would call to give her the good news.

Keep telling yourself that, Charlotte, and somehow you might will it into reality.

In truth, she'd be satisfied with a call from Anthony whatever he had to say, but since the brief connection earlier she'd heard no more and if she rang him she knew she'd very probably be told it was a bad time.

She'd fallen into a habit, it seemed, of picking bad times.

Over the past year she'd come close on several occasions to asking him if he still loved her, if he regretted marrying her, wished he'd never come to New Zealand, but in the end she always shied away. After all, what the heck was she going to do if he confirmed her worst fears? Where would that leave them? How could they possibly go forward knowing that they had somehow got themselves into a mess, and they had no idea how to begin getting out of it?

For the children's sake it was best to continue the way they were, at least until some decisions had been taken about the vineyard and whether it was going to survive. It was hard to imagine Anthony accepting defeat – in part it was what she loved about him, his confidence and tenacity – but he had no more money to sink into the business, and what little she'd once had had been used up long ago. It was no wonder they'd lost the spark between them, the breathless, insatiable passion that had once made it impossible not to believe in the future. Back then they'd found it so easy to laugh, and dream and make love every day, because back then there had been no pressures and everything, just everything, had seemed possible.

More than two months had passed since the last time they'd been intimate, and with the way things were she was afraid it wasn't going to change any time soon. Maybe it was her fault. Having Zoe Reynolds around was gradually eroding her confidence. With Zoe's supermodel looks and glamour-girl figure, not to mention the razor-sharp business brain and easy charm, she made Charlotte feel diminished and incapable. Charlotte just couldn't feel comfortable around her, in spite of how friendly Zoe was towards her, while Anthony clearly had no problem with her at all. In fact he appeared to enjoy her company far more than anyone else's. He was impressed by the woman, and willing to put his trust in her, as Rick had advised. Added to this, she provided Anthony with an escape from the house, from Chloe.

Don't go there! It's wrong to blame Chloe; she's a child with problems – oh god does she have problems – but she has nothing to do with the fact that Zoe Reynolds is Anthony's type.

Charlotte had thought that from the moment she'd set eyes on Zoe. The dynamic bombshell from Sydney didn't only have beauty and brains – and one of the sexiest figures nature had ever created – she came from the kind of world that Anthony knew well. Her family had money, land and influence in places Charlotte only ever read about in magazines or saw on TV. According to Rick she had a husband, but since Charlotte had never seen him, or heard any mention of him, chances were they were no longer together. This meant Zoe could be on the lookout for a replacement, and who, in their right mind, wouldn't want Anthony? They even looked good together, being of a similar height and colouring, and the only time Charlotte saw Anthony laugh these days was when Zoe gave one of her wicked twinkles.

Yes, she could definitely see them together, because before giving up everything in Britain to fulfil a dream to own a vineyard Anthony had been a prominent QC who'd moved in all the right circles, with contacts right up to Number 10. He'd never been married, but only because his fiancée, a successful businesswoman who'd hailed from an aristocratic family, had been killed in an air crash at the age of thirty-five – two years before Charlotte and Anthony had met.

Charlotte was convinced now that Anthony had still been grieving at the time his sister, Maggie, had introduced them. The only reason Charlotte had known Maggie was because Maggie was a foster carer, so Charlotte, in her then capacity of social worker, was occasionally at Maggie's home. She'd happened to be there one day when Anthony came in and all but took her breath away. He might have looked fierce (still did), with his intense dark eyes and firmly set mouth, but the instant he'd smiled it was as though he was lighting up every last part of her. Even now his smile was able to turn her heart into fluttery chaos. In fact she only had to think of it for its effect to work its magic, and make her long with all her being for everything to be right between them again.

Why didn't he ring?

He'd been gone all day, surely he wasn't going to let the sun set on the argument they'd had this morning over how long he was going to be in Wellington.

'Why do you have to be away overnight?' she'd demanded, stuffing Cooper's feet into his jellies.

'I don't want to wear these,' Cooper protested, kicking them off again.

'I told you,' Anthony said, 'the meeting's not until five. If it goes well we'll want to take him for dinner, so it'll be too late to make the three-hour drive back.'

'Where are you staying?'

'At the Bolton.'

'We can afford that?'

Sighing, he grabbed Cooper as he made to escape, sat him down and put his shoes back on. 'Here's my girl,' he smiled, holding out an arm as Elodie toddled happily towards him.

From there he'd taken over the morning ritual, had even, as far as Charlotte was aware, taken Chloe to school (after Chloe had punched Charlotte for trying to pull a brush through her hair) and Cooper to kindi. Charlotte, still furious with Chloe, had gone to check some guests out of one of the retreats.

Now, Charlotte looked up ahead and felt an unsteadying wash of emotions coasting over her heart. The house was in view, the beautiful, architectural sprawl of a home that she and Anthony had created together and that she loved almost as though it were a living part of their world. It had started life as an abandoned wooden fruit siding that they'd found beside the railway station in Hastings. Apparently for many years it had been the main dispatch area for all Hawkes Bay apples. Now, having been transported here in pieces, it had been radically recut and restyled to enjoy its new incarnation as a family home. The wood was all stained black, the door and window frames were white and the original corrugated roof had been transformed into a series of dramatically elegant structures resembling shade sails.

Though the place had turned out far bigger than

they'd intended, with their growing family and so many visitors – her mother and stepfather from Kerikeri, her sister Gabby and Gabby's family from Devon, and Anthony's sister Maggie and her husband Ron from Kesterly – they were already running out of space. It didn't matter, there was enough wood left over to extend the place when they were ready – or for someone else to if she and Anthony were forced to sell.

Sidestepping that as swiftly as she sidestepped so much these days, she left the vines and crossed the lawn – home to a netted trampoline, see-saw, slide, swings and a playhouse – to the wide stone terrace that ran the entire width of the house. It was shielded from the sun by four striped canopies, all of which were open, and was cluttered with toys, chairs, cushions, shoes, a pair of Spiderman pants, various bits of food and a small bicycle. There was no sign of anyone, nor any sounds coming from inside the wide-open doors, though she guessed Rowan was putting the little ones to bed while Chloe would no doubt be watching YouTube clips on her iPad mini somewhere, or sulking over something that had happened at school that couldn't possibly have been her fault, because it never was.

Look on the bright side, Charlotte, at least all hell isn't breaking loose (although Chloe usually reserved the seriously heated dramas specially for her mother). *For all you know she could be helping Rowan, or getting ready for bed, or preparing something for school in the morning*. She wouldn't be at a friend's, because she wasn't invited any more, and no one ever came here.

Thinking of how lonely Chloe probably felt underneath all the attitude and bravado, of how very different she was now to the sweet, shy little girl Charlotte had adopted, Charlotte could sense how easy it would be for her to feel engulfed by failure. If anyone had told her back then that such an angel could turn into a monster at times, that an eight-year-old could be a baby one minute and like a violent teen the next, she'd have . . . What would she have done? Refused the adoption? Of course not, she'd never have done that, and it wasn't as if she hadn't known that children who started out the way Chloe had went on to have problems later. So much of her time as a social worker had been spent trying to help those children and their families – the big difference was, she hadn't lived with them, hadn't been on the inside experiencing just how difficult, how heartbreaking and even impossible it could be. She was having the first-hand experience now, and she knew she really had to try harder, find a way to reach Chloe for both their sakes before something happened that they'd all end up regretting.

Checking her phone in case there was a message she'd missed, she found no one had rung, or texted since one of the retreat guests had been in touch to say how much they'd loved the place.

'These retreats are adorable,' Zoe Reynolds had gushed when Charlotte had shown her around the estate. 'You did them up yourself?'

'With the help of a builder, and my mother,' Charlotte had replied, feeling proud of her efforts, and vaguely embarrassed that Zoe's approval was pleasing her.

'We can definitely use them for promotion,' Zoe told her. 'Are they on the website?'

'Of course.'

'I must take a look at that, make sure everything is being maximised to its full potential. I'm expecting a photographer to turn up any time now, so if you can let me know when it'll be convenient for him to go into the retreats that would be great.'

Three weeks had passed since that conversation, and as far as Charlotte was aware no photographer had shown up yet. He ought to be here now, she was thinking, as she paused to gaze out across the vines she'd just walked through down to the vast swathes of fruit orchards beyond their property, and on to the far horizon where the glassy blue Pacific and early evening sky were streaked with red by the setting sun. To the right, past the olive farm next door, and out of sight from here, was the Tukituki River, relaxed and stony in these hot summer months; a bubbling, dangerous torrent when winter came. To the left were more vines belonging to the Te Mata Estate, and beyond them, a kilometre and a half away on the road into the village, was the Black Barn Vineyard.

Starting as her mobile rang, she was flooded with relief to see it was Anthony and quickly clicked on. 'How's it going?' she asked, starting to pick up some of the debris left behind by the children.

'Hard to tell,' he replied. 'He seemed interested, but he's going to get back to us tomorrow.'

'Did you discuss quantities?'

'He knows how much we have available; we didn't need to get into detail, not yet, anyway. How's everything your end?'

'OK. I've just got back. Have you spoken to the children yet?'

'About five minutes ago. Chloe asked if she can sleep in our bed with me being away for the night, so I said it was OK.'

Trying not to sound irritable, Charlotte said, 'You should have asked me first.'

'Why? What's wrong with her sleeping in our bed?'

'It's like a reward for something, and you know very well she doesn't deserve it. Besides which I'm working at the bistro tonight. I don't want to wake her when I get in. Did she tell you how school went today?'

'She said it was OK. Cooper's made some cakes, I hear.'

'He's saving them for you.' Why wasn't she smiling?

'So I believe. Elodie blew me a kiss down the phone.'

'You make it sound as though she's never done that before.'

He fell silent.

Wishing she hadn't sounded so sharp, she said, 'So where are you and Zoe going for dinner tonight?'

'I've no idea. I might just grab room service.' Before she could say any more he added, 'I'm getting the impression that nothing I say right now is going to make you happy, so I think it's best I ring off.'

'OK. Don't forget to email me with the wines you want to offer for tasting tomorrow, unless you want to keep them the same as today.'

'Speak to Will about that.'

'And the special offers we discussed at the weekend?'

'We can deal with that when I get back. Has the new website guy been in touch yet?'

'Not with me.'

'OK, I'll get Zoe to chase him up. Hope it goes well at the bistro tonight,' and he was gone.

Wondering what had happened to their closeness, why nothing ever seemed to feel right between them, Charlotte forced herself to carry on clearing the terrace, doing her best to keep her breathing steady and focus her mind elsewhere until she was ready to deal with the children. There was nothing she could do tonight about him being in Wellington, with Zoe – did she really need to worry about that? Didn't she already have enough on her mind?

'Mummy!' Elodie whooped cheerily as Rowan brought her on to the terrace.

'Sweetheart,' Charlotte smiled through her tears, and taking her into an enveloping embrace she kept her face buried in the wonderful baby scent of her, not wanting Rowan to see she was upset. 'Why aren't you asleep?' she asked Elodie, kissing her nose.

'She almost was,' Rowan replied, 'but then Daddy rang.'

'Daddy,' Elodie echoed.

'And you blew him a kiss?' Charlotte smiled.

Making a kissing sound, Elodie let her head drop on her mother's shoulder and twisted a finger around Charlotte's hair.

'Where are the others?' Charlotte asked, following Rowan into the house. To the left was an enormous kitchen with bar stools all around the countertops and large French doors to the side, opening to a newly installed sandpit, trio of boxwood swings and a barbecue. To the right was the spacious sitting room where a vast stone fireplace dominated three cosy sofas, an assortment of beanbags, a small desk belonging to Cooper, a table and chairs belonging to Elodie and a hammock that was Chloe's and generally found in the garden, but for some reason had been brought inside. Between the two rooms was the vast, double-height entry hall, home to a large oak dining table complete with ten non-matching chairs, a driftwood chandelier with a sock and a paper aeroplane hanging from it, and a sideboard full of anything anyone could manage to stuff inside.

'Cooper's asleep, would you believe,' Rowan replied, 'and Chloe's in your room playing games on her iPad. Apparently Anthony said she could sleep there. Shall I go and put this one down?' she offered, taking Elodie back.

Though Charlotte would have liked to do it herself, Elodie was already half asleep and she really needed to see Chloe before she drove down to the bistro.

'How did it go at school today?' she asked Rowan quietly.

'Pretty good, I think,' Rowan replied. 'She came out on time and no one said anything to suggest things hadn't gone well.'

'And swim club? Did she let you stay and watch?'

'No, but Logan Fry's mum kept an eye on her and apparently she was as good as gold.'

Relieved beyond words, Charlotte said, 'Three days back at school and no bad reports. Do you think we're turning a corner?'

'I hope so.'

Willing it with all her heart, Charlotte wolfed

down a discarded Marmite crust from the children's tea table and ran upstairs to the master suite, which should have been her and Anthony's private domain but rarely was.

'What are you playing there?' she asked, going to sit on the bed next to Chloe.

'Lego Nexo,' Chloe answered, keeping her eyes on the tablet. 'It's so cool.'

In spite of knowing it was rated 10+ Charlotte simply said, 'How are you getting on with it?'

With a sigh, Chloe said, 'It's kind of dumb, but I like it.'

There were moments, Charlotte thought, when Chloe seemed so confident, so certain of who she was and what she wanted, that it was as though she didn't need parents at all. However, Charlotte rarely forgot that deep down inside there was still the small child who'd had to deal with far too much already in her short life. It was the child Charlotte loved, and who had loved Charlotte with all her heart, whereas the skinny girl lying on the bed seemed to be growing into a stranger in front of Charlotte's eyes. It was impossible to know what was really going on with her, because Chloe refused to talk to anyone about the atrocious tempers, rages even, that had started about a year ago, but they surely were a reaction to her terrible early years. Or maybe they were simply a part of Chloe growing up and testing boundaries.

Boundaries? Don't make me laugh. It's like she wants to bring the entire world crashing down round your ears.

Ignoring the inner voice, Charlotte said, 'Fancy a chat before I go out?'

Chloe shrugged. 'I need to finish this. Dad said I could sleep here, by the way.'

Charlotte watched her face, so young and tender and yet so oddly, unnervingly remote at times. 'I'm waiting for an apology,' Charlotte told her. 'You punched me this morning and you know very well . . .'

'All right, I'm sorry, I'm sorry,' Chloe broke in irritably, 'but you shouldn't have pulled my hair. It really hurt.'

'I was trying to make it presentable for school.'

With a sigh Chloe cast aside the iPad and rolled on to her back. Everything about her demeanour emanated insolence, apart from her eyes; they appeared more inquisitive than challenging.

What on earth was going through her mind? What did she see when she looked at her mother? How did she feel after she'd hurt her brother or sister?

'What did you do at school today?' Charlotte asked carefully.

Chloe shrugged again.

'You must have done something.'

'PE. Maths. I can say "want any dessert?" in Maori. *E hiahia ana koe ki etahi purine?* So do you think Uncle Rick will give me a job at the bistro?'

Charlotte was about to reply when Chloe suddenly said, 'Have you been crying?'

Charlotte frowned in surprise. 'No. What makes you say that?'

'You look like you have. Have you had another row with Anthony?'

'He's Dad to you, and no I haven't.'

'He's not my dad though, is he? He hasn't adopted me.'

'But he will as soon as everything's straightened out here.'

'I don't think he wants me.'

Having been through this before, Charlotte stifled a sigh as she said, 'That's just nonsense, and you know it. He loves you every bit as much as I do . . .'

'But not the same way he loves Cooper and *Elodie*.'

Disliking the way she said Elodie, Charlotte caught Chloe's hands between her own and stared hard into her eyes. 'You're trying to create problems where there are none,' she told her forcefully. 'Now I have to go, Uncle Rick's expecting me in twenty minutes.'

Chloe blinked in amazement. 'So who's going to be looking after us, if you're not here?' she demanded.

'Rowan, who do you think?'

'But Rowan's going out with the kindi mums.'

Charlotte's insides lurched as she remembered that was indeed the plan. Oh dear God, what was she going to do? She couldn't let Rick down at this short notice, but nor could she ask Rowan to give up a rare night out, and she sure as hell couldn't leave the children on their own.

Fifteen minutes later, having apologised to Rowan more times than either of them could bear, Charlotte was driving down to the bistro with Chloe's anger still ringing in her ears.

'You didn't even read me a story,' she'd yelled as Charlotte left the house. 'You're mean and wicked and I hate you.'

Swallowing yet more guilt, while praying Chloe didn't start breaking things as she sometimes did when things weren't going her way, Charlotte took out her phone and connected to Anthony. 'Hi,' she said softly into his voicemail, 'I just wanted to say I'm sorry about earlier. I guess I was feeling a bit stressed, but I shouldn't take it out on you. Hope everything goes OK with the meeting tomorrow. I'm working at the bistro tonight, but give me a call later if you can.'

It was just after eleven by the time she returned home shattered, and far more upset than she wanted to admit. Anthony hadn't rung or texted, which meant he either hadn't got her message, or he had and simply hadn't wanted to call.

'I'm still awake,' Chloe whispered as Charlotte let herself into the bedroom.

Sinking inside, Charlotte said, 'Then you shouldn't be. It's late and you've got school in the morning.'

'I don't want to go.'

'You have to.'

'Who says?'

'I do. Please Chloe, I'm very tired so I don't want to get into an argument now.'

Chloe fell silent, but only until Charlotte came back from the bathroom. 'I didn't mean it when I said I hated you,' she murmured, as Charlotte lay on the bed next to her.

'I know,' Charlotte said.

'I love you really.'

'And I love you.'

'Always and forever?'

'Always and forever.'

Feeling Chloe's arms go round her neck, Charlotte pulled her small frame in close to her and held her tight. She remembered only too well the torment and confusion of growing up in an adoptive family, never quite believing she was wanted, always certain her adoptive mother didn't really love her. She'd felt convinced that her real mother, the one she'd later found and loved so dearly now, simply hadn't wanted her. She'd do anything to prevent Chloe feeling like that, but in her heart she could tell that on a level Chloe didn't yet understand, she already did, and this was simply the start of it.

Charlotte shot out of bed. The noise was deafening, thuds, crashes, screams coming from Cooper's room. She dashed across the landing, pushed open the door, terrified of what she was going to find.

Cooper was lying quietly in his bed, fast asleep. No one else was there.

Realising it must be coming from Elodie's room she raced next door, fear thudding so hard in her heart it was part of the uproar.

Elodie was asleep in her cot, the mobile over it swaying gently in a breeze from the open window.

Charlotte's hands flew to her ears. The noise was still there, banging inside her head like it was trying to break her skull.

'Chloe,' she gasped, and rushing across the landing she stumbled in through Chloe's open door expecting to be hit by a flying shoe or toy, but the room was empty. The bed hadn't been slept in; nothing was out of place. Where was Chloe?

As she remembered that Chloe was sleeping in her bed, she stumbled back to her room and found her on Anthony's side of the bed, fast asleep with Boots, her precious bear, right next to her.

Realising a nightmare had bled out of her subconscious to trick her into believing it was real, she sank down on the edge of the bed and dropped her head in her hands.

'It's all right,' she whispered shakily to herself. 'It was just a dream. Everything's fine. No one's been hurt.'

Chapter Three

'You're not looking your best, sweetie,' Rick declared when Charlotte turned up just before nine the next morning to find him picking agapanthi from the overflowing borders around the bistro.

She was far from it after her disturbed night, for she'd got almost no sleep after thinking, *believing*, Chloe was attacking the little ones. It had felt so real.

'I hate that you're not on top form,' he told her.

'Funnily enough, I hate it too,' she replied, 'but until we start getting some good news around here . . .'

'Oh no, please don't tell me Anthony didn't get the order?'

'He's still waiting to hear. Which means he's still in Wellington, with Zoe, and I'm here looking and feeling crap, as you so kindly pointed out . . .'

'But we can do something about that,' he cut in with a flourish, as his partner appeared. 'Hamish, I've decided my sister can do with some spoiling, and we're the ones to make it happen. Shopping? Lunch? A day at the beach?'

'Why don't you let her choose?' Hamish suggested, his gentle eyes made larger and somehow kinder by the thick lenses of his glasses.

'I don't have time for any of it,' Charlotte protested.

'Which is why we can't let her decide,' Rick told Hamish, and taking out his mobile he connected to Visage in the village, spoke to someone he apparently knew, and managed to book her in for some kind of exotic facial and massage and a glamorous beach-wave hairdo that was going to transform her into a surf-babe sensation.

Of course, she felt madly guilty an hour later as she left Rick in charge of the cellar door and turned out of their drive on to River Road. Apart from knowing very well that it was Rowan who deserved this treat, she felt terrible for not taking advantage of this unexpected free time by spending it with Elodie and Cooper. With Chloe at school she could whisk the little ones out of kindi for the day and spend some time in their world without having to worry about their sister doing something to spoil it. Perhaps she'd skip one of the treatments and call Rowan to tell her to take it instead.

Perfect, that was exactly what she'd do, and when Rowan had finished being spoiled Charlotte could return to the cellar door, for the mountain of demands that were piling up on her desk and computer were making her head spin even to think of them.

The drive into Havelock village was along a straight, pretty road with lots of palms lining the way and colourful flower beds gleaming so bright in the February sunshine they almost didn't seem real. She passed the grand Te Mata Estate and stylish Black Barn Vineyard, Summerset in the Vines retirement village, the turning towards Arataki Honey, the Woolshed apartments, feeling oddly as though she hadn't seen them in months, when it had surely only been a few days.

Eventually, she took a left at the public pool and decided to park outside the library.

It was the most perfect summer's day – no wonder everyone was smiling. It would be such bliss to imagine that she didn't have a care in the world, so for the next couple of hours she might try to do just that.

Moments after getting out of the car her phone bleeped with a text.

Sorry only just realised you left a message last night. Should be me apologising. Missing you and kids. Will call when on way back. Ax

They always used to end their messages with *love you* but that hadn't happened in a while. Still, at least he'd said he was missing them, which was something, provided it was true.

Trying not to vex herself with why he hadn't

realised there was a message until now, she texted back, *Any idea what time we should expect you?*

Not yet, but have a dinner arranged at Craggy Range with Kim and Andy from BB.

In other words he wouldn't be spending the evening at home.

Deciding not to answer, she put her phone in her bag and headed deeper into the village, forgetting for a moment why she was there. It didn't matter, it would come back to her once she'd reminded herself that it wasn't unusual for him to spend time with Kim and Andy. As the owners of Black Barn they'd become his mentors as well as good friends, and no doubt something had come up in the past couple of days that he wanted to run past them.

She just couldn't help wondering why she hadn't been invited to the dinner.

Because Zoe was going?

Realising she was in danger of becoming obsessed with Zoe, and that if she carried on the way she was she'd end up pushing them together – if it hadn't happened already – she took out her phone as it rang, desperately hoping it was him and experiencing a jolt of shock when she saw it was Zoe.

A dozen horrific reasons for the call were already ripping through her mind by the time she said, cheerily, 'Hi, Zoe. How are you?'

'Hi Charlotte. I'm good thanks. Keeping my

fingers crossed for this deal. We should know by the end of the morning.'

'How hopeful are you?' It was amazing how friendly she could sound when she was feeling something else altogether.

'Well, if his phone calls last night are anything to go by,' Zoe replied, 'then he's definitely keen to make it happen, but I know him, he drives a hard bargain, so I've warned Tony that we might not get the price we'd hoped for.'

Gritting her teeth at the Tony – no one but Zoe ever called him that – Charlotte said, 'We're prepared to be flexible.'

'Of course, but we don't want to end up feeling cheated. Oh, hang on a sec . . .'

As she went off the line Charlotte turned into Joll Road with its stylish boutiques and trendy pavement cafes, and found herself so drawn into the pleasure of it all that she began wishing she had time for a leisurely shop and girlie lunch. The latter would be easier if she had any friends. Any of it would be easy if she had the time.

'OK, I'm back,' Zoe announced. 'So, to the real reason for this call. Do you remember the photographer I mentioned a while ago?'

'I do.'

'Great. He's just been in touch to say that he can fit us in for a couple of days at the end of the month, so if you can let me know when it would be OK to go into the retreats I can start drawing up a schedule. How would you feel about the children being photographed?'

Startled, since this had never been mentioned before, Charlotte said, 'Have you asked Anthony about that?'

'Not yet. I thought I'd come to you first, mainly because of Chloe. You two are a great selling point, I'm sure you realise that, but I'm not into exploitation, so if you say it's off the agenda that's what'll happen.'

'I'm afraid it is off the agenda,' Charlotte told her.

'That's fine. How about you? With Tony? It's going to be important to put faces to the vineyard . . .'

'Exactly what are these photographs for?' Charlotte asked, going right past Visage and plonking herself down at a table outside the Olive Tree cafe.

'I've got this great guy in Auckland who's going to put a glossy brochure together for us at cost. He owes me. I want this brochure to tell the story of Tuki River Winery in beautiful pictures, and seductive text. We can use it in all sorts of ways, send it out with press releases, tasting invitations . . . Actually, I've been talking to *Cuisine* magazine about running a feature on you guys and they're very interested to hear more. If I can show them some shots taken by Frank Ingershall they might just end up sending their own reporter to come and check you out.'

Since publicity in *Cuisine* was something of a holy grail for people in the wine trade, Charlotte could only feel impressed. 'If you really think it'll help for me to be photographed,' she said, 'then of course I'll do it.'

'Thanks,' Zoe said warmly. 'I'll make sure you've got all the support you need, hair, make-up, and we can go through your wardrobe together. It has to look natural, so your regular clothes will be just right, but you'd be a braver girl than I if you'd forgo hair and make-up.'

Unable to imagine Zoe ever needing such backup, Charlotte could almost hear Rick cheering as she said, 'I'm happy to put my trust in you. You just tell me where I have to be and what I have to do. Meantime I'll get you the schedule for the retreats.'

As she rang off, with five minutes to spare before her first Visage appointment, Charlotte quickly called up her emails, making a rapid search for orders, and felt her head throb when she found none. She'd really hoped that the special offer they'd introduced on the website this morning might have yielded some results, but it hadn't. At least not yet, but it was still early, and who knew what might happen in the hours to come.

Did she have time, she wondered, to go on to Polly Greenborough's blog? She didn't know the woman, she even suspected the name was made up, but like her Polly was the adoptive parent of a traumatised child. The family lived in Oldham, Lancashire. It was clear that Polly and her husband were facing the same sort of challenges with their eight-year-old daughter, Roxanne, as Charlotte and Anthony were with Chloe, and Charlotte could only wish that the blog wasn't four years out of date. There was still a lot to read, so she had no idea yet how things had progressed in the Greenborough family, though Roxanne must be twelve by now, and Polly's other children six and eight.

The same age gaps as those between her own three.

Deciding to leave Polly's next instalment until later, she gathered up her bag and started towards the salon, coming to a sudden stop when her phone rang and she saw who it was.

Te Mata School. How she'd come to dread seeing those words on her screen.

'Hello,' she answered dismally, 'Charlotte Goodman speaking.' What a dreadful mother she was to hope that her child was sick rather than in the kind of trouble Chloe had been in for most of last year.

'Hello Mrs Goodman. It's Mike Bain here,' the voice at the other end told her.

She tensed all over. If the principal was calling it had to be bad. He was a lovely man, adored by all the children.

'I'm afraid,' he said, 'that we've had to take Chloe out of class for the third time this week . . .' Third time? This was only the fourth day back, and how come she was only hearing about this now? '. . . and in light of what's happened this morning,' he was saying, 'I'd be grateful if you could come and pick her up.'

Wanting to sink to her knees in groaning despair, she said, 'Is she all right?'

'Yes, she's fine. A deputy principal is with her at the moment.'

'What did she do?'

'I think it's best we don't discuss it on the phone. Is your husband around?'

'No, he's in Wellington, but I'll come right away.'

After dropping into the salon to cancel her appointments, she ran back to the car calling Anthony on the way. Before he could answer she rang off. Problems with Chloe would only have the usual effect of causing more tension between them.

Less than ten minutes later she was waiting outside the school for the electronic gate to slide open, and praying with all her might that Chloe wasn't about to be excluded. It was possible, given all the trouble she'd caused last year. She was spiteful, disruptive, argumentative, and hadn't even been allowed to see the last term out. Mike Bain had said it might be a good idea for Chloe's Christmas break to begin early. It would give her some time to reflect, he'd said, and perhaps they could start the new year with a clean slate.

It was more than Chloe deserved, considering how difficult she could be, but Mike Bain wasn't someone to give up easily on a child, especially one who'd had as challenging a start in life as Chloe. He'd even been in touch during the Christmas break to find out how she was doing, and Charlotte hadn't exactly been lying when she'd said that Chloe was behaving well. For the most part she had behaved well, so Charlotte hadn't felt it would be helpful to start getting into how Chloe was never invited to friends' houses for playdates or sleepovers, and none of Chloe's invitations to the vineyard were accepted either. Over Christmas that hadn't mattered too much since her cousins from England had been staying, and Nana and Bob had come down from Kerikeri, but as busy a house as they'd been with Anthony's sister and brother-in-law there too, it hadn't stopped Charlotte noticing that Cooper's friends had also started to stay away.

Was that because of Chloe?

She could only presume it was, because Cooper was constantly being invited to his friends' homes, it was just the other way round that seemed to be a problem.

And then there was Chloe's behaviour towards Elodie. Pushing her over, breaking her toys, rasping at her in an ugly voice . . .

As Charlotte pulled into a parking space her mobile rang, and seeing it was her mother she hurriedly clicked on. 'I'm just about to go into the school,' she said. 'There's a problem with Chloe.'

'Oh no,' her mother groaned. 'I thought she was having special assistance this term.'

'She is, but apparently there's still a problem.'

'Do you know what it is?'

'Not yet. I'll call as soon as I can. Is everything OK with you?'

'It's fine, but we do need to talk.'

Unsettled by the seriousness of her mother's tone, Charlotte ran into the school reception area and found the door to Mr Bain's office already open, ready to invite her in.

Oh Chloe, Chloe, why on earth don't you realise how lucky you are to be at a school like this, she was crying inside. *What's going to happen to you if they don't want you here any more?*

'Mrs Goodman, Charlotte,' Mike Bain said warmly, taking her hand and showing her to a chair on the visitor side of his desk. He was a tall, good-looking man in his mid-forties with a humorous twinkle in his kindly eyes, and such an easy and reassuring way with him that every parent for miles around wanted to send their child to his school.

After closing the door, he sat down too and fixed Charlotte with a solemn expression. 'I'm afraid,' he began, seeming to dislike this as much as Charlotte did, 'that Chloe has once again been encouraging other children, some younger than herself, to engage in . . . let's just call it inappropriate behaviour.'

Charlotte's heart was so tight it was hard to breathe. She didn't want him to elaborate, she didn't want this to be happening at all, but it was and he was already going into brief, but sensitively delicate detail of the acts involved.

'Are you sure it wasn't just show and tell?' Charlotte said desperately, as if that was any better than what he'd described.

It was. A whole lot better.

'Not this time, I'm afraid, and unfortunately it was one of the parents who's here helping out today who caught her.'

Feeling an excruciating crush of shame, Charlotte said, 'Am I allowed to ask the parent's name? I'd like to apologise.'

'There won't be any need. She's aware of Chloe's history so no blame is attached to you, but obviously we can't allow this sort of thing to continue.'

Of course they couldn't. 'I'll talk to her,' Charlotte assured him. 'I'll make her understand that what she's doing is wrong.' As if she hadn't tried that already, so many times she was running out of ways to explain, cajole, threaten, understand – whatever it took.

'I think she already knows it's wrong, and in part it's probably why she's doing it.'

It was all so difficult and harrowing and unanswerable that Charlotte could only look at him helplessly, then quickly turn off her phone as it rang.

'We've done everything we can to try and help her,' Mike Bain continued gravely, 'and we appreciate your support in our behaviour programmes; not every parent wants to admit that their child has a problem . . .'

'Well, we always knew that Chloe did.'

He nodded. 'She's a sweet girl; clever, funny, a great team player when she wants to be, but unfortunately there's this other side to her that seems to be playing a more dominant role as time goes on.' He broke off as Charlotte's eyes went down to hide her tears, and after a pause he continued more gently, 'I'm sure you're aware that because of her circumstances we've made more allowances than we might for another child, but I'm afraid that several parents have already complained.'

Charlotte swallowed dryly. 'So . . . So what are you saying, exactly?'

Sounding as regretful as he obviously felt, he said, 'I'll have to put the case to the Board of Trustees before any official action can be taken. In the meantime we have a couple of options. The first could be for you to come to school with her and supervise her . . .'

'But I can't . . . I have two other children and a business to run . . .'

'I understand that, which is why the second option, of her being educated at home through a correspondence course, might work better. We'll provide the necessary learning materials, and you'll get all the support you need from the school during this interim period, but you or your husband – or a private tutor – will need to do the teaching.'

Charlotte's head was spinning. As if they didn't have enough to do, they now had to educate Chloe, who might, or might not, welcome it, depending on her mood, and who was even more capable of causing disruption in the home than she was at school. Nevertheless, she obviously couldn't expect anyone to tolerate these . . . *episodes*, especially now they seemed to be getting more frequent. Show and tell might be a part of most kids' early experience, but the kind of things Chloe knew and had even taken part in . . . What sane parent would want their child around her?

Thinking wretchedly of her own two, Charlotte tried to come up with something to say, but Mr Bain was speaking again.

'. . . some very good child psychologists who would be able to help . . .'

'She won't talk to them,' Charlotte told him shakily. 'You know how often we've tried, but she either clams up or flies into a rage. Which obviously isn't a reason not to try again,' she added lamely.

He smiled his encouragement, and she started to

get to her feet. For some reason she found she couldn't rise.

'Sit there for a moment,' Mike Bain said gently. 'I'll go and get Chloe. Maybe you'd like to call your husband?'

As the door closed behind him Charlotte stared at the walls covered in children's drawings, awards, photographs of important occasions, and felt herself coming so close to breaking down that only the sudden wailing of a child outside stopped her.

Rushing to the door, afraid it was Chloe, she saw two receptionists and Mr Bain running into the car park where a small boy was howling for a reason Charlotte didn't try to find out. She had her own concerns right now, and they were so frightening and complex, and so potentially enormous that she wanted to howl for rescue too. Polly's blog said:

I felt at the end of my tether today when I was called in by the school yet again. They can't take any more of her, so I was forced to bring her home where she went into a frenzied rage, smashing things up, terrifying the younger two, kicking and punching me . . . Her psychologist wasn't available for me to talk to; I haven't found her to be of any help anyway and Roxanne hates the probing. She physically assaulted the last psych, so badly that there were mentions made of contacting the police. Fortunately we were able to calm things down, but the psych didn't want to see her again. I'm sure there's an expert out there somewhere who can help us, but finding that person . . . I don't want to admit to the thoughts that go through my mind, I'm ashamed of them and they upset me so much that my husband just walks away. He doesn't know what to do any more than I do, but we have to find a way. Where is Roxanne now? I should go to find her.

Chloe was sitting cross-legged on the sofa in her bedroom, her pale face turned towards the window, her eyes seeming not to blink as she stared out at the perfect blue sky.

Charlotte stood at the door, watching her. It was hard to gauge how she might be feeling when she was showing no emotion, and almost never talked about herself in the kind of detail that might have helped Charlotte to gain an insight into how much her past was driving her. It was clearly playing a part in the way she was behaving at school, at home too, but what kind of instincts or urges were behind it was impossible to tell, when Chloe wasn't old enough to understand, much less articulate, what was happening to her psyche.

Since Charlotte's professional experience of traumatised children had been to remove them from an abusive home and place them into foster care, thereafter monitoring them from a distance, she had no specialist knowledge of how to handle her daughter. Naturally she'd talked to psychologists, especially this past year, and several had been more than keen to help, but even the best wills in the world had ended up getting them nowhere. On one occasion Chloe had turned violent, on two more she'd flatly refused to engage, and the last attempt had ended in tears and hysterical accusations on both sides.

Just like Polly Greenborough, Charlotte had done plenty of research online, so she was aware that Chloe was likely to be suffering from a variety of problems such as PTSD or ADHD through to attachment difficulties and separation anxiety. How to identify any one – or more – of them in order to attempt treatment was beyond her, and would remain so until she found the right help. It should be so easy, there were so many qualified people out there willing to give their support, but even here, in New Zealand, with so much social backup, it still wasn't easy to find the right person. It had to be someone Chloe felt able and willing to respond to, and all the credentials in the world couldn't guarantee this. Charlotte sorely wished she knew how to confront the situation herself, but she didn't, nor was she going to try. Any attempt to take Chloe back to those terrible times, without the expertise to deal with what might happen if they had Chloe in their grip, would be a reckless and cruel invitation to disaster.

Of course Chloe knew she was adopted; it had

come up after Cooper was born, when she'd wanted to know why there weren't any photos of her as a baby.

Since she'd only been five at the time, and still the sweet, loving child that had won Charlotte's heart, Charlotte had explained that she was extra special because she, Charlotte, had chosen her when she was three. 'You were with a different mummy and daddy then,' she'd said, 'who weren't very good at looking after you, and because I loved you very much I went to the courts to ask them to let me be your mummy instead.'

It had been enough at the time, but later, around a year ago, Chloe had wanted to know more, so Charlotte and Anthony had told her how Charlotte had rescued her from the daddy who was doing bad things to her and brought her to New Zealand.

'I shouldn't have done that,' Charlotte had confessed, 'because everyone in England was looking for you. They thought your bad daddy had killed you, but you were safe with me and I didn't want anyone to take you away.'

'Where is he now?' Chloe had asked, clearly afraid he might come and get her.

'He's in prison being punished for what he did to you,' Anthony reassured her.

In a small, tentative voice, Chloe said, 'What did he do to me?'

Smoothing her curls, Anthony said, 'He did all sorts of things that were very wrong.'

'You don't do wrong things, do you?' she asked him.

'Not like that,' he promised.

To Charlotte she said, 'Why didn't my other mummy save me?'

'She tried,' Charlotte assured her, because it was true: as tormented and confused as Erica Wade had been, she'd managed to send an email warning Charlotte of what her husband was doing to their daughter. The fact that Charlotte hadn't found it until the morning after she'd stolen Chloe away from that dreadful house hadn't mattered, for it had gone on to provide all the evidence the police had needed to convict Brian Wade for his crimes.

'Where is she now?' Chloe asked. 'Can I see her?'

Gently Charlotte said, 'I'm afraid she died.'

'How did she die?'

How did you tell a little girl of seven that her daddy had stabbed her mummy to death the night before the police had come to arrest him – the same terrible night that Erica had sent the email and Charlotte had managed to get Chloe away? You had to tell her as much of the truth as you felt she could handle, was what they'd been advised, so that was what they'd done. Charlotte wasn't sure, at the time, just how much Chloe was registering, or how she was processing it, for she'd simply sat quietly listening, her lovely dark honey eyes moving between them as they spoke, her small hands clinging tightly to Boots, her treasured old bear.

She was holding him now as she stared out of the window; she always reached for him when she was upset, or feeling lonely and confused. She'd had him the day Charlotte had first seen her, in a park close to her awful home. She'd been just three years old then, and Charlotte's instincts had told her right away that something was wrong.

Charlotte could see that small girl now, still buried inside the eight-year-old dynamo, and was remembering how drawn she'd felt to her that day, and how Chloe had seemed to feel the same. She'd turned to look at Charlotte as her monstrous father had led her away and in that moment, or perhaps it was even before that, it was as though something quietly insistent had started to link them together.

Where was that link now? It had bonded them so tightly during Charlotte's struggle to save, then keep her, that Charlotte had truly believed nothing could ever break it.

'Are you going to look at me?' she asked, her voice conveying no emotion; she didn't yet know how to play this.

Chloe shook her head.

'Then speak to me. Tell me what happened at school today.'

'I didn't do anything. It wasn't me.' Her tone was loaded with resentment, her eyes didn't move from the window.

'What wasn't you?'

'What they're saying?'

'Do you know what they're saying?'

Chloe fell silent, and the mutinous look Charlotte had come to know well made its appearance. If only it were possible to leave it there, to go no further and pretend this wasn't happening. Such denial might prevent this developing into the kind of scene Charlotte had come to dread.

'Who was in the girls' toilets with you when someone came in?' she asked.

'No one.'

'You were in there on your own?'

Chloe turned her face further away.

'Do you understand that because of what you did you're not being allowed to go to school any more?'

Chloe's face flushed as she said, 'I don't care. I don't want to go.'

'You used to like school.' It was true, she'd loved it when she'd first started, aged five, had been a star pupil and could hardly wait to get there each day.

'I hate school,' Chloe spat scornfully. 'And I hate you. You're always picking on me and I haven't done anything wrong.'

'You know you have,' Charlotte insisted, 'and I think you love me as much as I love you.'

'No I don't, and anyway you don't love me, because NO ONE DOES!'

Flinching at the shouting, while feeling the tragedy of those words, Charlotte said, 'I love you, Chloe Goodman, and so do Daddy and Cooper . . .'

'I don't want Daddy and Cooper to love me, and anyway they don't. They just pretend to.'

'I honestly don't know where you get this nonsense from, but you have to stop believing it because it isn't true.'

Chloe mumbled something into her bear.

'What did you say?' Charlotte prompted, really hoping she hadn't heard right.

'I didn't say anything.'

'Yes you did, so could you repeat it please?'

Eyes flashing with temper, Chloe cried, 'My *real* daddy loves me.'

Charlotte felt as though she'd been slapped. What on earth was Chloe telling herself about that terrible man? Didn't she remember anything of what he'd done to her, how afraid she'd been of him? 'You've never spoken about him before,' she said carefully.

Chloe shrugged.

Bracing herself, Charlotte said, 'Do you want to talk about him now?'

'No! I want you to go away and leave me alone.'

'I can't do that when I know you're upset.'

'I'm not upset. I'm angry because you stole me

and brought me to New Zealand and I didn't want to come. I wanted to stay at home with my real mummy and daddy but you wouldn't let me.'

Oh god, oh god, oh god. How twisted everything was in her mind, how wrong and painful and horribly, tragically confused. How had that happened? They'd tried so hard to ensure she knew she was loved, that they'd fought for her, had done everything in their power to her theirs so she'd feel safe and protected and as special as she deserved to feel. But now here she was talking about being stolen and wanting to go back to her real mummy and daddy.

'You understand that your real mummy's dead, don't you?' Charlotte said gently.

Chloe's face darkened. 'That's what you say, but how do I know you're telling the truth?'

Charlotte baulked. 'Do you honestly believe I'd tell such a terrible lie?'

'I don't know. All I know is that you stole me and you shouldn't have done that when I already had a mummy and daddy.'

Realising she was creating a story that had no basis in reality, Charlotte said, 'You know that your daddy's in prison for what he did to you.'

'He didn't *do anything*.' Chloe's eyes were wild with the denial, her small chest was heaving with the force of her anger. 'I want you to go away now,' she cried. 'You're upsetting me and trying to make me believe things that aren't true.'

'Chloe, I can't just . . .'

'Go away! This is my room and I don't want you in here any more. *Go away! Go away! Go away!'* She was on her feet, fists clenched, face white with fury as a tirade of unintelligible rage began erupting through her lips. It was as if she was growling, screaming, retching, sobbing all at once; the frustration was so terrible that Charlotte tried to reach her, but Chloe thumped and kicked her way free. 'Get out! Get out!' she yelled. 'You're a liar and a thief and you're always blaming me when it's not my fault. I hate you! I don't want to be here any more.' She began throwing things around, smashing a mirror, tearing her clothes, pushing over her dressing table, still shouting and raging.

Charlotte covered her head, knowing better than to fight, for when she was like this Chloe was an unstoppable force.

In the end, Charlotte got to her feet, winced as a shoe thudded into her back, and closing the door behind her she stood against it trying, and failing, to detach from the uproar. Inside she was reeling, though not so much from the violence, she'd seen it before; it was the way Chloe had spoken about her birth parents. It was clear from what she'd said that she had no proper understanding of what had happened to her, or to them.

Going downstairs, she connected to her mother and took the phone out on to the terrace. 'We must have handled it all wrong,' she said after bringing Anna up to speed.

'It's hard to know a right way, given her background and age,' her mother sympathised, 'but take it from me, you've done a fantastic job of bringing her up this far. There were always going to be problems. You knew that at the outset.'

'Did I? If I'd stopped to think about it I'd probably have known, but I wasn't thinking about it then. It all happened so fast, me taking her, bringing her here, adopting her . . .' She took a breath, trying to steady her nerves. 'If you saw her tempers . . . I know you have, but if you knew what they were like to live with . . . She's got us all on edge, fearful of what she might say or do next and it's getting worse. One small child and she can fill up the whole house with the anger and frustration going on inside her.'

'You need professional help.'

'Of course, but you know how well that's gone so far. And even if she'd agree, how long is it going to take to straighten her out? Will it even be possible? And what will we all have to go through while we try? I'm already afraid of the impact her behaviour is having on Cooper and Elodie. She steals things from them, she's cruel to them . . .' She didn't add how worried she was that certain other things might have happened; she had no proof that Elodie's bruises had been caused by Chloe, and she knew it wasn't unusual for little boys to play with themselves, so it would be wrong to hang the blame for that on Chloe.

'Then what are you suggesting?' her mother asked. 'That you send her away to get help?'

Shocked, Charlotte cried, 'No, of course not. She's already suffered enough rejection, that would only make it worse.' Quickly checking her phone to see who was calling, she said, 'I have to take this. Can I ring you back?'

'I'll be here.'

Minutes later she was on the line to Rick asking if he could go and deal with a guest's TV problem, but apparently he had a cellar door full of people and Hamish had popped into the village. Realising she'd have to go to the guest's aid, and take Chloe with her, she was about to run upstairs to get her when Anthony rang.

'What news?' she asked, hastily clicking on.

Sighing, he said, 'Well, we've got the order.'

Frowning at the flatness of his tone, she said, 'Why am I getting the impression we're not celebrating?'

'Because it's not as straightforward as we'd have liked it to be. I'll explain when I get home, but the important thing is we can start arranging to move the stock out of Wineworks to make room for last year's vintage. Are you at the cellar door?'

'No, I'm at home, but I can go online here. What do you want me to do?'

'Actually, nothing yet. Let me talk to Will first. Have you seen him today?'

'No, but I'm sure he's around somewhere.'

'OK, I'll try him and start heading back. Who's running the cellar door if you're at home?'

'Rick and Hamish. When does this distributor want to take delivery of the wine and when can we expect to be paid?'

'Getting it to them will be more complicated than usual because it's going abroad, but I'll talk to the guys at Wineworks about that. Payment is half now, half on delivery.'

Sensing he wasn't yet ready to admit how much he'd been beaten down on price, she said, 'Well, at least we'll have some cashflow to pay Will and Rowan and the young guy Will has helping him. I was starting to worry about that.'

'Me too. And Zoe's next instalment is due any time, isn't it?'

'I'll check, but I think you're right.' Judging it wiser not to point out that this was an unnecessary expense when Zoe had obviously played a big part in getting the order, she said, 'Are you coming home before you go to Craggy Range?'

'Of course. I'll have to change first, and I need to spend some time in the winery with Will. Christ, what's that banging? Have we got work going on?'

Practically cowering from the crashing about upstairs, Charlotte said, 'I'd better go. Drive safely,' and quickly ending the call she dashed up to the landing to find Chloe hammering her tennis racquet against a radiator.

'Stop that now, or we're going to have water everywhere,' Charlotte shouted, grabbing the racquet.

Letting it go, Chloe ran towards the chaotic bed in her room and threw herself face down.

'Why were you doing that?' Charlotte demanded, going after her. 'If you wanted my attention you just had to call.'

'I did, but you ignored me.'

'I didn't hear you. So what do you want?'

'Nothing.'

Rolling her eyes, Charlotte said, 'I need you to come with me . . .'

'I don't want to.'

'You have to. You can't stay here on your own and I . . .'

'I'm not going anywhere.'

'Chloe, I'm too busy to play games. Now get up off the bed and come with me.'

'No.'

'I said, get up . . .'

'And I said no.'

Grabbing her, Charlotte hauled her to her feet and turned her to the door. 'Let's go,' she growled.

Chloe promptly sank to the floor and curled herself into a ball.

Throwing out her hands, Charlotte cried, 'One

of the guests needs me to sort out the TV. I can't leave you here, so please, Chloe, get up and come with me.'

Chloe didn't move.

'Please,' Charlotte implored.

Still no movement.

Rashly, she exclaimed, 'I'll pay you.'

After a moment Chloe said, 'How much?'

'However much you want.'

'Ten million dollars?'

'Twenty million,' Charlotte countered.

Chloe's eyes widened and to Charlotte's amazement she started to laugh.

Feeling battered and relieved, Charlotte pulled her up. 'I don't know why someone wants to watch TV on such a beautiful day,' she said, 'but I guess it's none of our business.'

'Can you take me to poi tonight?' Chloe asked as they got into the car. 'I want you to come and watch me instead of Rowan.'

Charlotte hesitated, trying to decide on the best way to handle this, for poi dancing was one of Chloe's favourite after-school classes. She'd even made her own poi sticks, but how could she be allowed to carry on as though being suspended from school didn't matter?

On the other hand, was keeping her shut up in the house any kind of an answer?

Polly's blog: *I wish I could offer advice to all of you who've responded to this blog. I hadn't realised there were so many adoptive parents trying to find their way. If you're lucky enough to find the right professional, you're definitely in with a chance. For those who haven't managed that yet, all I can tell you is to keep remembering how young and blameless your adopted child is. I know how hard it is at times, especially when you see your other children suffering. It's my biggest concern, how all this is going to affect their development. I can already see my youngest withdrawing, keeping her eyes down when she has no reason to, and my son, aged four, is starting to misbehave too. He and Roxanne had the most terrible fight last night. It took all our strength – me and my husband – to pull them apart. Everyone ended up in tears, then suddenly, out of the blue, we were laughing. What was funny? I've no idea, it's just the way it happened.*

It scares me to think of what Roxanne might be capable of.

Chapter Four

'Mummy! It's Daddy!' Cooper shouted excitedly, and zooming out across the terrace he practically flew over the lawn to greet his father, who was striding up through the Reserve Chardonnay vines with Will.

As Cooper hurled himself into Anthony's arms Charlotte couldn't help but smile to see how affectionately and effortlessly Anthony swung him into the air, before settling him on his shoulders. There was always a different feeling about the place when Anthony was there; it seemed more alive, more complete, *safer*, as though a cliff edge had suddenly retreated, or looming disasters had vanished into the hills.

How very different he was today from when they'd first met. Then he'd been a tall, suave and very good-looking lawyer, with neat dark hair, a cleanly shaven chin and the sternest grey eyes she'd ever seen. Now he was as rugged as any farmer with silver flecks in his shaggy hair, an almost permanent shadow on his chin and eyes that had seemed slightly softer since the children had been born. His muscular limbs and strong, lean face were as tanned as Charlotte had ever seen them, and in his usual khaki shorts, dusty polo shirt and leather sandals he was more attractive now than he'd ever been.

It had taken Zoe Reynolds's arrival at Tuki River to remind her of just how much she loved and desired her husband; not that she'd forgotten, but they'd been so busy building this place up. Perversely, Zoe's presence had made her anxious, and distant, as though she was punishing him for comparing her with Zoe and finding her lacking. There had been no actual evidence to say he was thinking that way, unless she counted the fact that he'd become more distant too.

Polly's blog: *I worry about the strain Roxanne's issues are putting on my confidence, but most of all on my marriage.*

Pushing the recollection aside, Charlotte instantly found herself reflecting on how rarely she and Anthony shared a smile these days. If it happened at all it was always with the children, and he wasn't with them anywhere near as often as he used to be.

'I saved you some cakes,' Cooper was telling him in a rush, as they reached the end of the vines and

Anthony tipped him on to the grass. 'I'll get them. They're really good. You can have them all.'

'Can't wait,' Anthony called after him, and either not noticing Charlotte in the kitchen, or not bothering to, he turned back to Will.

As they talked Charlotte helped Cooper find a plate and tray for the cakes he'd kept hidden in his bedroom for this very moment, while Rowan sang a Maori song to Elodie as she changed her, and Chloe lay in her hammock engrossed in her iPad. It wasn't unheard of for Chloe to go running out to Anthony too, but today she'd no doubt assumed that Charlotte had told him about the trouble she was in at school, so she was in no hurry to be scolded or lectured or told what privileges were to be removed.

She'd taken the ban from poi dancing surprisingly well, which had led Charlotte to wonder if there had been some unpleasantness there as well. It might account for why she'd wanted Charlotte, rather than Rowan, to go with her this evening.

Hearing a car pulling up outside, Charlotte stepped out on to the terrace in time to see Zoe getting out of the Volvo.

Why was Zoe driving Anthony's car?

Get a grip, she warned herself sharply.

'Hi Will,' she said, as he and Anthony came on to the terrace. The winemaker was almost as tall as Anthony, about ten years younger, and was quite a favourite amongst the ladies of Hawkes Bay with his surfer's looks and single status. What a shame he didn't seem to do it for Zoe.

'Five K of sulphur,' he was saying into his phone as he gave Charlotte a wave, 'and three hundred copper.'

'Hi, how are things?' Anthony asked her, checking his own phone as a text came in. 'Have you seen my iPad? I thought I took it with me, but I don't seem to have it now.'

'I'm fine, thank you,' Charlotte retorted. 'How are you?'

His eyes flashed as he glanced at her. 'I'll call the hotel,' he said, 'maybe I left it there.'

'You hardly ever use it,' she reminded him.

Before he could respond Zoe was saying, 'Hey Charlotte, glad you're here. I've brought my laptop to show you some of Frank Ingershall's work so you'll know we're in safe hands.'

Charlotte smiled. 'That's kind of you,' she replied, feeling miserably short and plain as the glamorous Zoe stooped to embrace her. She was looking sensational, as usual, in a short, multicoloured spandex dress that showed off her fabulously long legs to mid-thigh, and her equally beautiful arms and shoulders. In fact not very much of her slender, yet shamelessly curvy body was covered up. Charlotte had to wonder if there was anything about herself that Zoe didn't like, because from where she was standing, with those mesmerising sloe eyes, exquisite cheekbones and tantalisingly full mouth, the woman was a galling example of female perfection.

'Has Tony filled you in on details of the order yet?' Zoe asked, grimacing awkwardly as she glanced at Anthony. She even looked good when she pulled a face.

'I was just about to,' Anthony told her. 'It's the entire stock,' he said to Charlotte, 'but they . . .'

'Daddy! Here are your cakes,' Cooper cried, having carefully arranged the plate of Play-Doh confections and a glass of squash on the tray. 'You have to eat them all up, because I made them myself.'

Anthony's eyes were shining as he inspected the delicacies. 'They look too good for me,' he declared, turning one over in his hand. 'I think you should at least help me.'

'They're not real!' Chloe shouted from her hammock.

Cooper spun round. 'You're spoiling it!' he exclaimed angrily. 'Mummy! She's spoiling my trick and I kept them all specially.'

'Chloe, be quiet,' Charlotte ordered.

'I was just saying,' Chloe retorted sulkily.

'They are real,' Cooper told his father, eager to get his joke back on track.

'I can see that,' Anthony assured him, and gamely putting one in his mouth he started to chew.

'Ha ha!' Cooper cried triumphantly. 'I got you. Did you see that, Mum? Do you want one, Zoe? You'll really like them, won't she Dad?'

After emptying his mouth into his hand, Anthony said wickedly, 'She'll love them. Zoe's very fond of cake.'

Slanting him a meaningful look, Zoe took a fake cake and pretended to nibble. 'Mmm, delicious,' she told Cooper.

Delighted, Cooper leapt up and down and almost knocked Elodie over as she beat a wobbly path to her daddy.

'Here's my little angel,' Anthony laughed, sweeping her up and planting a noisy kiss on her fat, creamy cheek. 'And how are you today? Have you been behaving yourself?'

'Daddy,' she replied happily, clutching his face in her tiny hands.

Kissing her again, he turned her in his arms and told her to say hello to Zoe.

'Wee,' she gurgled messily.

'Something like that,' Zoe laughed, brushing a finger over her cheek. 'You're so adorable, I could eat you all up.'

'Not till you've finished my cakes,' Cooper put in.

Trying not to sound stiff, and failing, Charlotte said to Anthony, 'You were telling me about the order.'

Anthony's good humour drained.

'I feel terrible,' Zoe admitted. 'It wasn't what I was expecting . . .'

'But it's OK,' he assured her. 'If we have to sell as cleanskins, that's what we have to do.'

'Cleanskins?' Charlotte echoed dismally. 'Oh god, just what we didn't want. We're supposed to be building up the Tuki River brand, how can we do that if there are no labels on the bottles?'

'We can't,' Anthony answered shortly. 'But it's either that or try to fund storage for another twenty thousand bottles and that we can't do.'

'So the best part of our 2014 vintage is going to be sold in Australia as a supermarket brand,' Charlotte stated furiously. 'I'm guessing we didn't get a good price either.'

'It could have been worse,' he retorted tightly, and turning to Will he started walking him back towards the vines, taking Elodie with him.

'Is Daddy cross?' Cooper asked Charlotte.

'Not with you,' Charlotte replied, ruffling his hair.

'He liked your cakes,' Zoe told him, going down to his height.

Cooper grinned. 'Don't tell him,' he whispered, 'but they aren't real.'

Laughing, Zoe hugged him and watched as he charged after Anthony to join in the manly chat.

'Your children could make me broody,' Zoe confessed as she followed Charlotte into the house.

Forcing a smile, Charlotte said, 'Would you like a

drink? We've plenty of 2014 Pinot Gris – although apparently not for much longer.'

'I'm really sorry,' Zoe groaned, perching on one of the bar stools. 'If I'd known it was going to turn out that way I wouldn't have set up the tasting.'

'Anthony could always have said he didn't want to sell,' Charlotte pointed out, 'but as you know we're not in a position to be choosy.'

Taking the glass of wine, Zoe sipped it and said, 'It's a good vintage. It shouldn't be selling as a cleanskin, but with time not being on our side . . .'

'Why don't we just drink to its new incarnation,' Charlotte interrupted, 'and feel thankful for the money we're saving on labels and caps.'

With a wry smile, Zoe tapped her glass to Charlotte's and drank again. 'So tell me about your day,' she said chattily. 'When I called Rick earlier he mentioned you'd gone off to the beauty salon.'

Charlotte grimaced. 'As you can see, I didn't quite make it.'

'That's a shame. We all need spoiling once in a while. So what did you do instead?'

Glancing over to where Chloe was once again plugged into her iPad, Charlotte said, 'Believe me, you really don't want to know.'

'Maybe I do.'

Charlotte smiled. 'Shall we look at these photographs?' she suggested. 'I think a glossy brochure is a great idea, provided it's not going to cost us.'

'It won't, I promise. I'll just pop back to the car and get my computer. Are you coming to Craggy Range with us later, by the way?'

Feeling her insides knot, Charlotte said, 'Rowan has a yoga class so I'm staying with the children.' She still hadn't been invited.

'Of course.' Zoe smiled. 'I'll be right back.'

After she'd gone Charlotte took a large gulp of wine and put a hand to her head as she inhaled deeply. Everything was falling apart. She couldn't even speak to Anthony without things coming out the wrong way, and he seemed to have so little patience with her that simply being near him was making her feel edgy and angry. She really had to get a better grip on herself, start doing something to turn the situation around or she was going to end up losing him.

'Mum,' Chloe said, drawing out the word.

'Yes?' Charlotte replied, sipping more wine as she tried to focus on what the children were going to eat tonight.

'Have you told Anthony yet that I got sent home from school today?'

Why does she keep saying Anthony? It's getting right on my nerves. 'No, not yet,' she replied.

'Do you have to?'

Charlotte looked up. 'Of course I do. You're not going back, you do realise that don't you?'

Chloe's face tightened. 'I don't want to go back, *ever.*'

Sensing another scene brewing, Charlotte turned away, trying to think about something else. Out of nowhere she was suddenly saying, 'What you did to the other girl was wrong. You know that, so I don't understand why you did it.'

'I didn't do *anything*. It was her, not me. I tried to stop her.'

BED was what Mike Bain called it – blame, excuse, denial. Polly Greenborough had written quite a bit about that too.

Deciding she had to stop this conversation now, before Zoe came back, or before she did something rash like try to brain Chloe, Charlotte said, 'Why don't you come and help me make some tea? We can have pancakes if you like.'

Seconds of no response ticked by until Chloe decided to tumble out of the hammock and came to start taking eggs from the basket. 'I don't want to live here any more,' she stated, smashing first one, then another egg on the countertop. 'I want to go back to England where I belong.'

Pushing her aside to clear the mess, Charlotte said, 'Be careful I don't end up sending you there, because the way you're behaving . . .'

'What?' Chloe challenged when Charlotte broke off.

Charlotte's head stayed down as she clenched her fists tightly, waiting for a wave of horrible intensity to pass.

'What?' Chloe demanded again.

'Nothing,' Charlotte finally managed. 'Just make the pancakes, and try for once in your life to do it without any more of your stupid talk and backchat.'

Charlotte didn't want to read any more of Polly's blog today. She felt oddly exhausted by it, and disturbed – always disturbed – and even afraid of where it might be going, although in many ways it helped to know that she wasn't alone in the way she was feeling. There were hundreds, thousands of adoptive parents out there in her position. Had Polly found the answers? Were there going to be all sorts of helpful links and advice in the next few entries? It could be that Polly and her family were living happily together now, or at least more harmoniously. Had her husband stayed? Were her other children finally bonding with Roxanne?

Maybe she should skip to the end of the blog to find out how Polly had coped; but how was it going to help her if things hadn't worked out? What was she going to do if something terrible had happened and the Greenboroughs' lives had changed for ever?

I'm upstairs in my room now with my music blaring and the door half open, the way Mummy left it, so she can see me when she passes by.

Who wants to see me?

Justin Bieber is usually my favourite, but even though

he's playing through the iPod speakers I can't hear him because I'm listening to YouTube through the headphones plugged into my iPad. I like the funny animals videos best, but the baby ones can be cute, and Taylor Swift and Niki Minaj are really cool. There's tons of stuff to watch, from music, to dancers, to girls putting make-up on, to dangerous toys and scary tricks, to seriously weird people doing unbelievably weird things. I don't like seeing weird things very much, they make me feel scared and like I want to go and cuddle up to Mummy to feel safe, except I can't because she'd go mad if she knew I was watching them.

They shouldn't be allowed.

At the end of each day I have to hand my iPad over to one of my parents so they can check on what I've been doing, which is OK, I don't mind, or not any more, because I have Anthony's iPad now which lets me do all sorts of things they don't know anything about.

Serves them right – they shouldn't keep treating me like a baby.

Last night was the first night I had it. I spent ages watching some American teen girls talking about how to get boyfriends. It was awesome. Not that I want a boyfriend yet, I'm too young, but as soon as I'm old enough I'm going to find someone to marry and get out of here.

I got myself into some chat rooms after, which was a bit scary and amazing. I didn't say anything myself, I just 'listened' to fashion hints and all sorts of jealous, bitchy stuff, and how to get an eating disorder to help lose weight. After that I went back to YouTube and watched some videos of girls at parties pretending to be strippers. I told some of my friends about it in school this morning, which was what led to all the trouble, because they'd wanted me to show them how it was done, so I tried and they tried too, which was hilarious and I could tell they were really turned on. It would have been all right if someone's mother hadn't walked in when she did.

What wasn't fair was how I got all the blame, and as far as I know Joel Allan and Wayne Fisk didn't even get told off for being in the girls' toilets.

Later, when I'm sure everyone's in bed asleep, I'm going to close my door, put a chair against it and go on Anthony's iPad again to find out what it says about my real parents. Not that I want to see them, or be in touch with them – I can't if my mother's dead – but I wouldn't mind betting there's a lot about my creepy dad. There might even be a chat room discussing the things he did to me. I'm finding that a bit frightening, but I'm definitely going to try and find out.

For the time being though I'll just stay on my own iPad playing my games and videos so I can hand it over to Mummy when she comes in and let her think that when the light goes out Chloe is going to sleep.

I don't really think she cares whether or not I'm asleep, just as long as she doesn't have to put up with me any more today. That's OK, because I don't have to put up with her either. Or him, Anthony, who isn't my daddy but keeps making out like he is.

I think the real truth is that those horrible creepy people everyone keeps saying are my real parents stole me from some very rich people when I was born and they sent Mummy out to find me, but instead of giving me back she ran away with me and kept me.

Chapter Five

It was early in the morning with a misty rain meandering over the bay and small rabbits and quail busily foraging for food as Anthony and Will netted a large parcel of vines on Waimarama Road. Birds had been hammering the fruit for several days now, making it high time it was covered, especially with a first full yield expected from the Cabernet Franc grapes this year. When Anthony had bought the vineyard over four years ago Dave McKee, the winemaker at Black Barn, had advised him to pull out all the Cabernet Sauvignon vines as they really didn't do well in this soil. Anthony had followed the advice, and at the same time had welcomed Dave's recommendation of Will Abbots as his winemaker.

Will had done a fantastic job here at Tuki River, everyone agreed with that; at blind tastings amongst professionals his wines often came out in the top three, and thanks to him Tuki River had, in this short time, gained something of a reputation locally, if not elsewhere.

So the problem wasn't with the wine, it was with the marketing, which was Anthony's domain, and he couldn't feel more frustrated with himself that he hadn't made a better job of it. The problem was he hadn't done enough research at the outset, and just to compound matters he'd encouraged Charlotte to pour whatever money she wanted into building a dream house, restructuring the cellar door and revamping the retreats. All of that could, and should have waited until the business was properly established and all the right strategies and staff were in place to make it work.

However, it was too late to change things now, the money was spent, and since they had a home that Charlotte and the children adored, an extremely inviting cellar door and retreats that at least paid for themselves, he guessed they had something good to show for their rash investment. Of course they had the vineyard and winery too, which in fairness had taken up most of the capital, and since they were in the Special Character Zone of Hawkes Bay they really shouldn't fail.

'The first years are often tough,' Kim Thorp from Black Barn had reminded him over dinner at Craggy Range last night, 'but you're doing all the right things to push through and turn your fortunes around.'

'By selling the 2014 as cleanskins?' he'd asked bitterly.

'You've sold, that's what matters,' Kim had responded. 'OK, not the way you wanted, or for the price you'd hoped for, but sometimes it goes like that. It's happened to plenty of start-ups over the years, and a good many of them have gone on to survive, and to establish their brands. It'll happen for you is my prediction. With Will making the wine, and Zoe working on the marketing . . .'

'I'd hoped to do better than this for the first order I brought in,' Zoe told him regretfully.

'You've helped move what's left of that vintage out of storage,' Andy Coltart reminded her. 'That was your first task, and you've achieved it. Christ, we should be celebrating here. You've only been on the case a couple of months and in that time you've pulled off what no one else has managed since that vintage went into bottles.'

Anthony had felt his failings acutely in that moment; however, he wasn't someone to let past difficulties overshadow the way they went forward. With around eight weeks to go before picking began he'd be assisting Will every step of the way, but he needed to work with Zoe too, which was going to end up leaving precious little time for his family. This didn't please him at all, for as committed as he was to working the land and learning everything he could about the making and selling of wine, he loved being with the children. Nothing mattered as much as watching their simple joys and earnest endeavours; or eating with them at Rick's Bistro, or somewhere in the village. Family days out at Ocean beach, a bike ride up Te Mata Peak, or a picnic and swim at Maraetotara Falls gave him more pleasure than anything he could remember from before they were born.

However, the needs of the business had become paramount, and he was sure Charlotte would rather he didn't let them slide into bankruptcy for the sake of spending more time being a dad. It could always come later, once they were properly on their feet, by which time heaven only knew if their marriage would still be intact.

Was it his fault that he and Charlotte had lost their closeness? He'd asked himself that a thousand times, and though he felt sure it must be, trying to get her to respond to him, even physically, these days was proving even harder than getting someone to buy their wines. Still, at least a breakthrough had been made on that front, such as it was, which reminded him, before he went over to Wineworks later to discuss export, he needed to go to the bank to organise a sixty-day loan to keep them afloat until payment for the order came in.

Taking out his mobile as it rang, he saw it was Charlotte and clicked on. 'Hi. What is it?' he asked brusquely.

Just as tersely, she said, 'Can you cover the cellar door for part of this morning?'

'I'm busy. Why?'

'I have to go into school to get some things for Chloe.'

'What?'

'I didn't get a chance to tell you last night, but she's been suspended and from now on, at least for the next few weeks, we have to educate her at home.'

Stunned, he swore under his breath and turned away from the nets. 'What did she do?' he demanded.

'The same as before, but slightly worse.'

'Meaning?'

'Do you really want the details?'

No, he really didn't. What he wanted was to get hold of the perverted bastard Brian Wade, who'd sexualised his own daughter by the time she was three, and kill him. 'Is she all right?' he asked gruffly.

'I think so. Don't ask me about the other children who were involved because I don't know. I can only tell you that they've had enough at Te Mata so they're putting it to the Board of Trustees.'

'Which means?'

'Exclusion, probably. Apparently they can't do that without finding her another school first, but until then it's over to us.'

Signalling to Will that he'd be right back, Anthony wandered further along the vines. 'What are we going to do?' he asked, knowing this was far bigger than either of them was capable of handling without the proper backup.

'What we're being told,' she replied. 'I'm picking up the materials they've put aside at ten o'clock and for the rest of the morning I'll be teaching. If you could take over for an hour or so this afternoon . . .'

'Charlotte, you know that's not possible. I can't even cover the cellar door. We have to get these nets on or the birds are going to devastate the fruit.'

'I understand that, but I can't do everything myself . . .'

'Can Rick or Hamish help out?'

'They're doing breakfasts this morning until midday, then turning straight around for lunch.'

Sighing, he said, 'Then let Rowan go to the school.'

'She needs to stay with Chloe and Elodie while *I* go. I'm her mother, for heaven's sake, I can't just send someone else. Think how it would look.'

Conceding the point, he said, 'You'll have to call Black Barn to ask if anyone there can help with the cellar door for a couple of hours. If they can't it'll just have to close until you can open up again.'

'And will you make some time to teach Chloe this afternoon?'

'If I could, I would, but it just isn't possible.'

'OK, thanks for nothing,' and the line went dead.

Furious, he came close to ringing back, but even if he did the answer would still be the same. He had no more time to start home-schooling Chloe than he did to get any deeper into the argument.

As he walked back to the nets he wasn't sure who he was the angriest at, himself, Charlotte or Chloe. Since his emotions had become horribly conflicted about Chloe of late he quickly passed over them, with a reminder that she was hardly responsible for what was making her behave the way she was. How they were going to get past all the disruption and tension she was causing was anyone's guess, but they absolutely had to find a way. It was getting to a point where the atmosphere she created was intolerable, even toxic at times, and he didn't always trust her around the little ones. He felt sure Charlotte didn't either. To call her a cuckoo in the nest would have been cruel in the extreme, but he often wondered if it wasn't how she saw herself, and if she did, how much were he and Charlotte to blame for that?

After winning the trial, freeing Charlotte from a charge of child abduction, he should have stepped away for a while, given her some time to think, to decide what she really wanted. Instead, he feared he'd overwhelmed her with his feelings, swept her off her feet in a way she might not have been ready for. She'd always claimed she was, but everything back then had happened so fast – the adoption, Cooper suddenly being on the way, the wedding in the Bay of Islands on the beach where she and Chloe had lived during the time they were in hiding. Meanwhile, her stepfather was setting everything in motion for him, Anthony, to fulfil the dream of owning a vineyard, which had ended up falling through, but that hadn't deterred Bob. Within weeks he'd found this place in Hawkes Bay, unnamed at the time since all it had produced was cleanskin wines, and now it looked as though it was going to continue that way.

The point was, neither he nor Charlotte had had time to think about what they were doing, or even what they really wanted. It had all just happened and now, though he knew neither of them would ever regret bringing Chloe with them, in spite of everything they loved her too much for that, he was afraid that Charlotte might no longer feel the same about being married to him.

After several days of sorting out books, a learning schedule and various school-type materials, this was Charlotte's third day of trying to teach Chloe at home and it wasn't going well. It was a shame, because the first two days had actually been more fun than frustration. Far too much time had passed since she and Chloe had embarked on projects together, or laughed so much over silly things, and she'd loved feeling that connection again, but sadly it wasn't happening today.

Probably, Charlotte conceded, because Chloe was

getting fed up with how often Charlotte's mobile kept ringing, and with Rowan out on a hike with friends, Elodie was proving a distraction too. However, Elodie was fast asleep on the sofa at the moment, and the phone was on silent so time to press on.

'OK,' Charlotte said, doing her best to sound firm and interested as she attempted to return Chloe to the book they were supposed to be working from. 'We're coming up with adjectives,' she reminded her. 'You need to fill in the gaps . . .'

'I don't want to,' Chloe complained.

'You have to. So: the blank cat was asleep on the blank chair. Give me some alternatives for the blanks.'

After a groan of boredom Chloe broke into a mischievous grin, proving she was more engaged than she was letting on. 'The stupid cat was asleep on the disgusting chair,' she declared wickedly.

Charlotte slanted a look that made Chloe giggle, and supposing it would have to do, she pointed to the next one.

Obediently, Chloe said, 'The smelly dragon came out of the pervert's cave.'

Charlotte's head throbbed. 'That's not an adjective,' she stated.

Chloe merely shrugged.

'What made you use that word? I don't expect you even know what it means.'

Yawning, Chloe said, 'Can we have a story now?'

Still not sure what to do about the 'pervert's cave', Charlotte said, 'We've only just started this.'

'It's boring. I want to do something else.'

'How do you know the word pervert?'

'I don't know, I can't remember.'

'Do you know what it means?'

'My real daddy was one.'

Charlotte stared at her hard. Since she was monitoring Chloe's online activity she could only conclude that someone at school had thrown the joyful little epithet at her, having picked it up from a parent.

'I want to go back to school,' Chloe declared, scribbling across her exercise book.

'I'm afraid that isn't an option.'

'Ask Mr Bain. He'll say yes, you'll see.'

'He can't, Chloe, and you know why.'

Chloe's eyes narrowed angrily.

'Don't do that,' Charlotte snapped.

'Why not?'

Because it makes you look like your father and I'd rather never *be reminded of him, thank you very much.* 'Because it makes you look ugly.'

'I am ugly.'

'No you're not. Now let's do this please.'

'It's not my fault those other children made me take my pants off – and they did too, so why aren't they in trouble?'

'You know very well that no one should take their pants off at school.'

'I like taking mine off. It feels nice. And everyone else likes it too, so it's not just me.'

Though Charlotte realised it wasn't unusual for children Chloe's age to play risky games, there was no getting away from the fact that when they had the kind of history Chloe did there was nothing benign or acceptable about it.

'I only do it when they tell me to,' Chloe informed her.

'When who tells you to?'

Chloe shrugged. 'Them.'

Charlotte felt herself starting to tense. 'Who tells you to take your pants off?' she pressed.

'They do.'

'Who are *they*?'

'I don't know. They just tell me and so I do it.'

More than a little unsettled by what she was hearing, Charlotte caught Chloe's hands and held them tight. 'Can you hear people speaking inside your head?' she demanded urgently.

'You're hurting me,' Chloe protested, snatching her hands away.

Charlotte repeated the question.

'No. I can just hear you keeping on and on and on at me and I want to go home.'

'You are home.'

'I mean to my real home, in England.'

Before Charlotte could respond her mobile rang and since it was a call she had to take she clicked on, watching Chloe from the corner of her eye as she kicked Elodie's toys out of the way and made off towards the stairs.

For the next half an hour Charlotte was tied up dealing with bookings, the cleaning roster and chasing delivery of fifteen specially commissioned oak barrels from France. By the time she'd finished Chloe was nowhere to be seen and Rowan was back with Cooper, who promptly woke up Elodie.

Enchanted by how thrilled both children were to see her, she embraced them hard and continued to cuddle Elodie as Cooper babbled on about his day at kindi.

'Where's Chloe?' Rowan asked, giving the children a drink each.

'In her room I expect,' Charlotte answered, glancing at the abandoned schoolbooks. 'I'm afraid we didn't get very far today.' Should she try to talk to Chloe again, find out more about these voices that were telling her to do things? Though Charlotte realised she could be overreacting, or misconstruing what Chloe had said, she was haunted by the fact that Chloe's birth mother had been a paranoid schizophrenic. It was possible for the disorder to be passed on, Charlotte knew that, but how likely it was, or whether it might be happening here she had no idea.

To Rowan she said, 'Can I leave you in charge while I pop down to the cellar door for a while?'

'Of course. Did Chloe eat her lunch?'

'Yes, but I expect she'd like a biscuit or something now. If you find her on the iPad remind her that she's only allowed online games for an hour today and she's already had it.'

Twenty minutes later Charlotte was at the cellar door, on the phone to her mother.

'Oh Charlotte, you know what children are like,' Anna sighed, sounding tired, but not unsympathetic. 'It isn't unusual to have an imaginary friend, or friends . . .'

'But this is Chloe we're talking about and you know about her mother . . .'

'I also know that she's upset at the moment. She's been suspended from school, which is no small thing, she's uncertain about what's happening to her, how things are going to play out going forward, where the right and wrong is in what's she's doing with other children . . .'

'She knows it's wrong, but she still does it. It's like she can't help herself.'

'Whatever, I'm sure there are all sorts of things going round in her head. It doesn't mean she's becoming schizophrenic. It just means she's confused and understandably anxious about the way things are changing.'

Ready, or needing to believe her mother was right about the schizophrenia, Charlotte found herself breathing a little easier. 'But it's yet another example,' she pointed out bleakly, 'of how I jumped into taking her on without thinking it through.'

'You did what you had to at the time, what you felt was right, and there's no going back on it, so you . . .'

'What are you talking about?' Charlotte cried angrily. 'Who said I wanted to go back on it? I'm merely admitting how naïve I was when I adopted her. I suppose I presumed that she would always be the sweet-natured, shy little girl she was then, and that being with me would help her to put her past behind her. I completely ignored what the experts say about the first thousand days from conception being the most critical in shaping a child. The real damage had already been done, there was no way to erase it, which isn't to say I wouldn't have adopted her, because of course I would. I love her, we all do, and as far as I'm concerned she's as much a part of this family as Cooper and Elodie.'

'Indeed,' her mother said emphatically, 'and I can tell from your tone that what I've been hearing is true. You're overworked, exhausted, stressed . . .'

'You've been talking to Rick.'

'And Rowan. They're worried about you.'

'They don't need to be. I'm fine. Things are starting to look up, actually. We've sold the 2014 white wines at last and as of today we have some money in the bank.'

'If you were short you should have let us know.'

'Anthony would never do that. Anyway, we're not now, and I'm afraid I have to go because someone's just arrived for a tasting. I'll call again later so you can tell me how things are going with Shelley's treatment.'

As she rang off she began setting out glasses, a spittoon and Tuki River napkins, until she was startled into surprise at seeing Zoe winding her way through the tables, holding *Chloe* by the hand.

'Look who I found out on Te Mata Road,' Zoe declared with an affectionate smile.

Charlotte looked from one to the other as they reached the counter. Chloe was boldly meeting her gaze, as if challenging Charlotte to make something of this. 'What on earth were you doing on Te Mata Road?' Charlotte demanded.

Defiantly, Chloe said, 'I was running away.'

Charlotte's eyes flicked to Zoe before she asked, 'Where did you think you were going?'

'To England,' Chloe breezily informed her.

Charlotte looked at Zoe again, and almost without thinking clicked on her mobile as it rang.

'Charlotte,' Rowan cried, 'I can't find Chloe . . .'

'It's OK, she's with me,' Charlotte told her, and ringing off she went to take Chloe's face in her hands. 'You realise it's a good job Zoe saw you,' she said firmly. 'You could have got into a lot of trouble . . .'

'I don't care.'

'But I do. And so should you. You're eight years old, you shouldn't be out on the roads on your own, anything could have happened to you . . .'

'I told you, I don't care.'

Charlotte pulled her in closer. 'What am I going to do with you?' she murmured desperately. Thank god this was New Zealand and not England, less traffic and fewer perverts, but that still didn't make it entirely safe. To Zoe she said, 'Did she have a bag or anything?'

Zoe shook her head. 'She was as you see her now, heading along the road towards the village.'

Envisaging the solitary figure, barefoot, wild-haired and directionless, Charlotte said, 'How far had she got?'

'Only just past Black Barn. I wasn't sure . . .'

'Hey! Is that you, Chloe Fantazma-goey?' Rick shouted over from the bistro garden.

Chloe spun round. She adored her Uncle Rick. 'Yes, it's me,' she cried excitedly, and promptly abandoning her mother and Zoe she dashed across the courtyard to be swung up high into the trees and offered her favourite drink, a cake, an ice cream or whatever her little heart might desire.

Knowing she couldn't leave it there, but uncertain what to do for the moment, Charlotte turned back to Zoe. 'Thanks for picking her up. I don't know what she was thinking . . .'

'Oh, we all did it when we were her age,' Zoe

laughed dismissively. 'It was quite an adventure to run away, I always found.'

'I shudder to think how far she'd have got if you hadn't spotted her. Was she OK about getting into the car?'

'No fuss at all. I think she was quite relieved, if the truth be told.'

Charlotte nodded, and deciding to put it aside until she'd had more time to think it through, she said to Zoe, 'I thought you were in Auckland.'

'Just got back. In fact I was on my way to see you when I happened upon Chloe. I have it in my calendar that one of the retreats is free for me to view this afternoon.'

Going to get the key, Charlotte said, 'Have you seen Anthony today?'

'Not yet, but I'm hoping to. We've got a lot to discuss about the 2015 vintage . . . Do you know when it's being moved from the winery over to Wineworks?'

'I'm guessing the whites will go any time now, but that's Anthony's department.'

'Of course. I was just wondering if it might be worth Frank Ingershall getting some shots of it starting out on the next stage of its journey.' After making a note for herself, Zoe said, 'I should only be a few minutes at the retreat – Frank wants to see some visuals before he comes, so I'll use my phone camera. I'll bring the key back when I'm done, then how about we indulge in a glass or two?'

Charlotte blinked. 'Of wine?' she said stupidly.

Zoe laughed.

Charlotte did too. 'My treat,' she joked, amazed at how readily she'd accepted when she didn't have the time for one glass, never mind two, and clicking on her mobile she took a call from Anthony.

'How's the schooling gone today?' he asked over the hum of whatever was going on in the background.

'Not much progress,' she replied, going to brush some jacaranda pods from the tables. Should she tell him about the pervert comment, and the attempt to run away? He always hated hearing about problems with Chloe, and they only ended up causing even more tension between them.

How had Polly Greenborough's marriage fared?

'I've organised a couple of hours tomorrow so I can help out with the teaching,' he said. 'Will I know what to do?'

Amazed and thrilled, she said, 'I can show you. It's not hard, she's only eight, remember?'

With a smile in his voice he said, 'Any news from Mike Bain?'

'No, but I'm expecting to hear from a special ed psych any time. He or she will probably want to come to the house to assess how she's doing.'

'OK, we should both be there when that happens.'

Relieved that he wanted to be, she said, 'It'll make a lot of difference to Chloe if you are. She tried to run away earlier.'

'Are you serious? What happened?'

'She decided she wanted to go to England, so she crept out of the house and I didn't realise she was gone until Zoe brought her back about ten minutes ago.'

'Where is she now?'

'At the bistro with Rick.'

Sighing, he said, 'So what's all this about England? Where's it coming from?'

'I don't know, but she's mentioned it a few times lately.'

'Have you checked her online activity? You need to keep a close eye on it . . .'

'I don't need lecturing, thank you.'

'Sorry.'

'I have to go, someone's just turned up for a tasting.'

'OK. You can start serving the 2014 Cabernet Franc.'

'There's none here.'

'I'll get some to you. I won't be back until seven, by the way. Will and I are going for a tasting at Gimblett Gravels,' and the line went dead.

After making friendly chat with two couples from Holland, and selling them a bottle each of Pinot

Gris, Charlotte was about to disappear into the office to catch up on the day's emails when Zoe returned.

Minutes later they were at one of the tasting tables with two glasses and a bottle of Reserve Chardonnay between them, surrounded by trees and vines and the incessant buzz of cicadas while watching Chloe helping Rick to lay tables over at the bistro.

'I can't remember the last time I did something like this,' Charlotte sighed wistfully. 'I'm always so busy trying to sell the wines that I hardly ever have time to relax and enjoy them.'

'This,' Zoe declared, holding up her glass, 'is my favourite of yours. Actually, it's a favourite, full stop.'

Charlotte smiled. 'We haven't had as much trouble selling this as we have the Pinot Gris, but there again we don't have as much of it. Anyway, the problem's solved now, thanks to you, and before we know it we're going to be up to our eyes in the 2015 trying to sell that.'

'I promise I'm going to do my best for you,' Zoe said earnestly. 'There are quite a few ideas I'm working on already. The brochure should definitely help lead the way, but it's only a beginning. We need to take a good look at your social media profiles. I guess you don't have time to engage much . . .' She stopped as Charlotte put up a hand.

'How about we have a few minutes not about wine, other than to drink it?' Charlotte proposed.

Zoe broke into a smile. 'I'm up for that,' she replied, reaching for the bottle and refilling their glasses. 'So what do you want to talk about?'

Charlotte took a breath as she thought, although she knew the answer already. 'How about you?' she suggested. 'I know you're brilliant at what you do, because everyone says so, but who is the woman behind the professional?'

Zoe simply shrugged. 'There's not much to tell about me really. I'm an only child, grew up in Bunbury, south of Perth. My parents split up when I was twelve – Daddy was rich – mining – so Mummy got a great settlement. As soon as I set off on my Europe experience after uni she travelled as far as Italy with me and never came back. She's still in Tuscany, not far from Florence, and I generally go to see her for a few weeks during our winter, her summer. Daddy died about ten years ago and left me quite comfortably off, but the bulk of his estate went to his new family.'

Charlotte was watching her closely, thinking of what very different worlds they came from.

'I guess I'm lucky he left me anything,' Zoe continued, 'because I never used to see him. His wife didn't like to be reminded that he'd had a life before her. Still, that's wicked stepmothers for you, they can have a hell of a lot of influence and mine certainly did. How about you?'

Reflecting back to her own early years, Charlotte

said, 'I never felt wanted by my adoptive mother, but tell me more about you. Have you ever been married?'

Zoe's eyes went down. 'I still am, but we haven't been together for the past eighteen months. He found someone else and . . . Well, he broke my heart.'

Charlotte could tell by the tremor in her voice that she wasn't over it yet. 'I'm sorry,' she said. 'That's a horrible thing to go through.'

Zoe shrugged. 'Some people face a lot worse. How about you? Have you ever had your heart broken?'

Remembering how she'd once felt sure that Jason the builder was the great love of her life, Charlotte said wryly, 'I thought it had been, once, but with hindsight it was just bruised. Losing Anthony would break my heart.' Had she said that as a warning, or simply because it was true?

Zoe's eyes were on hers. 'I'm sure it would,' she agreed, 'but I don't think it's going to happen. Do you?'

Charlotte said, 'I hope not, but I'm afraid things haven't been great between us lately.' Why was she telling Zoe this? She'd barely even admitted it to her mother.

Zoe was still watching her. 'That's what he said when I asked him about you.'

Startled, Charlotte couldn't think what to say.

Anthony had discussed her with Zoe? The idea of it was making her light-headed, angry, ready to explode even, yet here she was having a similar sort of conversation. 'He told you our marriage was in trouble?' she finally managed.

'Those were not the words he used. What he said was that you've both been under a lot of pressure since taking on the vineyard, and he's afraid that you might regret it.'

Charlotte swallowed dryly.

'Do you?' Zoe prompted.

'No, of course not,' Charlotte replied hastily. 'I just wish . . . I guess I wish we had more time to spend with the children, and with each other.'

'I'm sure it'll happen once this rough patch is over.'

Charlotte took a breath. 'As long as that's all it is, a rough patch,' she murmured, and seeing Rick on his way over with Chloe she went to fetch another glass. What else had Anthony told Zoe about their marriage, she was wondering as she returned to the table. And why had the subject even come up?

As though reading her mind, Zoe put a hand on hers as she said, quietly, 'I'm sure everything will turn out fine, on *all* fronts,' and with Chloe and Rick now in earshot the subject was changed.

Anthony could hear the shouting and screaming even before he was out of the car.

'What the hell's going on?' he demanded, running

in from the terrace to find Chloe throwing anything she could get her hands on about the room.

'I don't know what happened,' Charlotte shouted, shielding Elodie and Cooper as Chloe raged and seethed and slammed fists and feet into anything she could reach.

'Chloe!' Anthony barked, signalling for Charlotte to whisk the little ones upstairs.

'Don't touch me!' Chloe yelled as Anthony tried to grab her. 'You're not my dad. You can't do anything . . .'

'Calm down,' he urged. 'Stop shouting and tell me what's wrong.'

'You are,' she screamed, 'and her and her and him,' she spat after Charlotte and the others. 'You're what's wrong,' and grabbing Cooper's bike she hurled it at Anthony with all her might.

Catching it, he thrust it aside, but wasn't quick enough to grab Chloe as she raced up the stairs after Charlotte. He was behind her like a shot, but as he reached the landing she snatched up her tennis racquet and began swinging it at him.

'Get the children in the bedroom,' he shouted to Charlotte.

'Stay away from me,' Chloe threatened, backing up.

Seizing her, he tried to tear the racquet from her hand and winced as it caught him in the face.

Wrenching free, Chloe dashed for the stairs. 'I'm

going to kill you,' she warned, 'I'm going to kill all of you,' and moments later he heard her rummaging in the cutlery drawer.

'Anthony,' Charlotte whispered.

'Go back inside,' he urged, pulling their bedroom door closed. God alone knew what he was going to do if Chloe came back armed, but as long as she didn't harm the others . . .

'I'm going to get you now,' Chloe seethed as she came to the top of the stairs. 'You're going to be sorry you were ever horrible to me.'

'Chloe, put it down,' he cautioned. 'Whatever you've got behind your back . . .'

'It's a gun.'

Knowing it couldn't be, he was about to try and grab her when she whipped her hands in front of her and shouted, '*Bang!*'

Anthony started, and stared in disbelief.

'It's a banana,' she laughed.

Whether it was shock, or plain relief that it really was a banana, he had no idea, he only knew that he was tipping over the edge into laughter too.

'I had you scared, didn't I?' she giggled.

He didn't deny it. 'Why were you so angry when I came in?' he asked, wishing his own state of mind could swing as fast as hers.

She shrugged. 'I don't know. It's just everything. I hate it here and I want to go home.'

'But this is your home.'

'No it isn't.'

'Chloe . . .'

'Bang!' she shouted, wielding the banana again.

'Please talk to me, tell me what's upsetting you.'

'Bang!'

'You know that's not an answer . . .'

'Bang! Bang! Bang!' and turning on her heel she ran into her room and slammed the door.

'I should go after her,' Charlotte said, coming on to the landing.

'Bang!' Chloe yelled at the top of her voice.

Charlotte turned to Anthony.

'What started it?' he asked, touching a hand to his bruised cheek.

'I don't know. One minute she was lying on the floor playing with Cooper and his cars, the next she was kicking his garage and him and . . .'

'She was kicking him? Is he all right?'

'Yes. Shaken up, obviously.'

'Couldn't you have stopped her?'

'I got him away,' she snapped. 'You saw the state she was in, I couldn't control her.'

Sighing, he said, 'Let's give her some time to calm down. You go and settle the others and I'll clear up the mess she made downstairs. After that we need to talk about getting some professional help.'

'Do you seriously think I'm not already on the case?' she whispered furiously. 'I've made at least a dozen calls, and these appointments aren't easy to get. There are waiting lists, kids with bigger problems apparently, and even if we get her in you know what'll happen. It'll be just as useless as before, and frankly you're not helping.'

His eyes closed as she slammed the door, and wishing himself a thousand miles away he took off downstairs to repair what damage he could.

I'm in my room with Boots listening to the others moving about, going up and down the stairs, in and out of the bathroom, putting Cooper and Elodie to bed. At least Elodie's stopped bawling now. She makes a horrible racket, waaah! Waaah! Waaah! And Cooper's no better. He shouldn't have grabbed the car off me, it just made me mad and it's not like he doesn't have fifty thousand others. What's wrong with letting me have that one?

Everything's wrong with it, because I'm a nobody who doesn't deserve any toys or treats or food or friends or any of the things other people have. The only friends I've got are in chat rooms, but I still haven't plucked up the courage to speak to any of them. I will tonight though. I'm going to find the one I was on the other night where they called my creepy dad a pervert, and make friends with them. They might know who he stole me from and then I should be able to make contact with my real parents to let them know where I am.

I'm still using Anthony's iPad and no one has asked me for it yet, so it must mean that they want me to have it. They just better not try to make me see one of those doctors again, the ones who keep asking questions and pretending like they care, when they don't know me, and even if they did they still wouldn't care. I can't stand them. I hate them so much that I hit one once, and I'll do it again if one comes near me.

I wonder if I've got any real brothers and sisters.

I wish I could go home to my real mum and dad. I've got to find a way.

Everyone was in bed. The house was perfectly still as Charlotte sat at her laptop reading from Polly's blog:

> *I'm sorry I haven't written anything here for a few months, but thank you for so many kind messages wishing me well and hoping my silence might mean that things are improving. I only wish I could say they were, but after Roxanne tried to burn the house down we had to go and stay with my parents while the damage was repaired. She was very sorry, of course, and for weeks after she was on her best behaviour, until something upset her – I've no idea what it was – and she took it out on my youngest by pushing her down the stairs.*
>
> *The broken arm is healing well, but I'm afraid the envy, or threat Roxanne feels from having another girl in the house is only getting worse.*

Charlotte's breath was short; fear was pushing her towards the edges of what she could stand. She knew, of course, that Chloe considered Elodie to be a rival, her terrible behaviour had started only weeks after Elodie was born, but it was something she'd hoped, prayed, Chloe would grow out of. And she might, but the question was, how much would Elodie – and the rest of them – have to suffer before she did?

... so social services have put us together with a highly respected child psychologist, and it has given us some hope to feel we are in an expert's hands. Sadly Roxanne's mood swings and violence still remain a problem, and I'm afraid the psychologist said something earlier this week that bothered me a great deal. This could be because she managed to voice one of my darkest thoughts ...

Charlotte knew all about dark thoughts; she never wanted to speak them aloud, but the fact that she might share them ...

... This woman, we'll call her Hayley, suggested Roxanne's craving for attention was too big for our family. In other words, we're not capable of giving Roxanne the support and understanding she needs. I could have told her that. What I needed to hear was how we could work to overcome this. Instead, she told me how she, and several "eminent members of her profession", believed that traumatised children often fared much

better as only children. This way they would be the focus of attention, wouldn't feel threatened by siblings, and, just as importantly, they wouldn't be able to cause harm to their siblings, either physically or psychologically.

Charlotte closed down the screen. She couldn't read any more. Everything inside her was so coiled and raw, and so heavy with dread, that it was hard to remind herself that this was Polly's story, not her own.

She really must stop reading this blog and find a way to lighten the darkening mood in her family, before she lost sight of who was who, and what really mattered.

Chapter Six

All was calm the following morning, as it generally was following a Chloe storm. The dust had settled, skies were blue, the world was moving on its benign, irreversible way. However, Charlotte and Anthony had been up in the night to change Chloe's sheets after she'd wet the bed. Another sign, happening more often lately, to show how disturbed she was, and as Charlotte had held her, trying to comfort her sobs, Anthony had silently urged the school and educational psychologist to be in touch soon.

They – Chloe – desperately needed more help than he and Charlotte could give alone.

Now, in the clear light of early morning, their thoughts were on other things as the household came to life in its usual noisy and random way, with Elodie banging a xylophone while Cooper, already dressed, trundled his trike about the terrace and Chloe took her time in the bathroom.

As Anthony came into the kitchen Charlotte

noticed how tired and dishevelled he looked, and guessed she didn't present a much better picture herself.

Putting his phone aside, he glanced at her and immediately frowned. 'Why are you wearing that hat?' he demanded.

'I found it in the Volvo this morning,' she replied, whisking cereal bowls from countertop to table, and transporting a protesting Elodie to her high chair. She'd intended to make him laugh, or smile at least, but she could see now that it wasn't going to happen – and anyway, was that really what she'd expected? Maybe she was trying to make a point.

'It's Zoe's,' he informed her.

'I know,' she replied. 'Cooper, come and eat your breakfast.'

'And you're wearing it because?'

'Cooper . . .'

'I'm *coming*,' he shouted from the terrace.

'Here we are, sweetie,' Charlotte said, tying on Elodie's bib and ducking as Elodie tried to grab the hat. 'Oh heck,' she cried as the milk suddenly boiled over. 'Can you feed Elodie?' she said to Anthony, dashing to the rescue.

'Where's Rowan?' he asked, pulling up a chair and twinkling playfully at his daughter. She looked flushed and watery-eyed, but was never short of a smile for her daddy.

'In bed with a temperature. Cooper . . .'

'I told you I don't want Weet-bix,' he protested, banging a hand on the table as he saw the mistake.

'Don't do that,' Anthony chided.

'Mummy, you gave me Weet-bix,' he shouted. 'I want honey puffs.'

Grabbing the honey puffs, Charlotte dumped the box in front of him and whipped away the Weet-bix.

'I need a bowl,' he called after her.

'Go and get it,' Anthony barked as his mobile rang. 'I need to take this,' he said, and pressing a kiss to Elodie's head he clicked on the line and wandered out to the terrace.

Giving Cooper a bowl, Charlotte went to feed Elodie while checking the messages on her own phone. Three more bookings for the retreats, one cancellation and a payment reminder from Wineworks. Forwarding the latter to Anthony, she removed Elodie's hands from the baby porridge and managed to get a small spoonful into her mouth before Elodie turned away.

'I need some milk,' Cooper piped up.

'It's in front of you.'

'Oh yes.' He laughed. 'Mummy why are you wearing that hat? It looks funny.'

Batting her eyes at him, Charlotte clicked on her phone as it rang.

Although she didn't immediately catch on to who was calling since it was a voice she didn't recognise with a name she'd never heard before, when she realised who it was she sat back in her chair to listen. By the time she rang off her insides were knotting tightly.

'Cooper, go and tell Chloe to hurry up,' she instructed, bringing herself back to the moment.

'I haven't finished my breakfast.'

'Just do it,' she snapped. 'Anthony, I need to talk to you,' she called to him.

He raised a hand, telling her to wait.

Now, she wanted to yell, but it would frighten Elodie, and getting worked up wasn't going to help this new situation at all.

'Mummy,' Elodie gurgled and with a loud burp she promptly threw up.

'Oh sweetheart,' Charlotte groaned.

'Ugh, yuk, yuk, yuk,' Cooper exclaimed, managing to tip a spoonful of honey puffs over himself as he clapped a hand to his mouth.

'Look at you now,' Charlotte said crossly.

'It wasn't my fault,' he cried.

'Then whose was it?'

Cooper grinned. 'Yours, because you look funny in that hat.'

Smiling in spite of herself, Charlotte mopped up Elodie, lifted her into her arms and rocked her as she whimpered a sorry little tune. 'Please go and get Chloe,' she said to Cooper. 'You can finish your breakfast when you come back.'

Obediently zooming off across the room, he began a thunderous climb up the stairs as Anthony came inside and took Elodie from her.

'I've just had a call from CYFS,' she told him.

'Who?'

'Child, Youth and Family Services,' she explained. 'Better known to us as social services.'

'Haven't you been expecting them to call?'

'Not them, no.'

'So what did they want?'

'What do you think? Someone, probably the parent of a child in Chloe's class, must have reported Chloe, so they need to come and check her out. It's the way it works.'

'Maybe the school got in touch with them?'

'Mike Bain would have told me if he had. No, this is someone trying to make mischief, I'm sure of it.'

Eyeing her closely, he said, 'Tell me why you're so worried.'

Unable to believe he didn't know, she tore off the hat and slammed it on the counter. 'We're going to be judged as parents,' she seethed, 'and if we're found lacking they might end up *putting her into care.*'

His eyes widened. 'But they've got no reason to.'

'Says you, and say I, but they might think otherwise.'

'When are they coming?'

'The day after tomorrow at eleven and they want to speak to both of us, so I hope you can make it.'

'I'll be here. Listen,' he said, going to her, 'I understand why you're upset about this, but it'll be OK.'

'You don't know that,' she snapped, turning away. 'A lot will depend on what Chloe says to them, and she's so unpredictable these days.'

As Anthony started to reply Elodie abruptly threw up again, and Cooper came running back into the kitchen. 'Mummy, Chloe's crying,' he gasped.

'Why? What's wrong with her?' Charlotte demanded.

Cooper seemed nonplussed. 'She wouldn't tell me. She said I had to go away and leave her alone and never come back again.'

Seeing how bothered he was, Charlotte went to pick him up. 'It's all right,' she soothed gently. 'She didn't mean it, not really.'

'She didn't hit me,' he whispered.

Relieved about that, Charlotte kissed him.

'I have to go,' Anthony announced, glancing at the time and stuffing Elodie back in her high chair.

'Great, don't worry about us,' Charlotte raged as he made for the door.

'I told Zoe I'd pick her up at nine,' he shot back.

'Then call and tell her you're going to be late.'

'Charlotte . . .'

'These two children here are yours as well as mine,' she yelled, 'and right now I need to go and see to Chloe.'

'Don't shout, Mummy,' Cooper cried, covering his ears.

'I'm sorry. I didn't mean to. Ssh, it's all right.'

'Are you ready for kindi?' Anthony asked him.

Cooper's eyes rounded in surprise.

'Do you want me to take you?' Anthony pressed.

Cooper lit up. 'Daddy's taking me to kindi,' he informed Charlotte, and sliding to the ground he ran to the terrace to jam on his sandals.

Going to Elodie, Charlotte scooped her up, and spotting Zoe's hat she threw it at Anthony. 'Perhaps you'd like to return that to your girlfriend,' she snapped savagely.

Temper flashed in his eyes, but he said nothing as he stooped to retrieve it.

'I take it she went to Gimblett Gravels with you last night?' Charlotte challenged.

Frowning, he said, 'What are you talking about?'

'I'm asking if that's how her hat got into your car, because she was with you last night?'

Staring at her darkly he said, 'Yes, that'll be how it got there, but that's not what you're saying, is it?'

'I'm ready,' Cooper announced, coming to take his father's hand.

'You haven't got your lunch,' Charlotte told him, and grabbing his backpack she swung it to him.

'You need to see to Chloe,' Anthony reminded her coldly.

Wanting to slap him, she turned her back and held Elodie so tight that Elodie squealed.

'Ssh, I'm sorry,' she whispered, carrying Elodie to the stairs.

'Is everything OK?' Rowan asked weakly from her bedroom door.

'It's fine,' Charlotte assured her. 'Just a hectic start to the day. You look awful. Maybe I should call the doctor?'

'No, I'll be OK. Can I do something?'

Sorely tempted to ask if she could take Elodie for a moment, Charlotte said, 'No, you should get back into bed. I'll come and check on you before I take the girls to the cellar door with me.'

Moments later Chloe was shouting, 'I don't want her in my room. Take her away.'

'Don't be silly, Chloe. She's just a baby and I can't leave her on her own. She's not well.'

'Then you go too. I don't want you in here.'

'Tell me why you're upset.'

'I'm not upset.'

'So why are you crying?'

Turning her face into the pillow, Chloe raged furiously into it.

'Chloe, please,' Charlotte implored, going to sit next to her. 'You have to tell me what's wrong.'

'Not while *she's* here,' Chloe shouted into the pillow.

Since Elodie was quiet now, and seemed on the

verge of falling asleep, Charlotte carried her into her own room and laid her down in the cot. 'I'll be back soon,' she promised. 'You have a nice little sleep till then.'

Aware of her head starting a violent throb as she went back to Chloe's room, she sat on the edge of the bed and smoothed a hand over Chloe's hair. 'What is it?' she asked softly. 'What's got you all upset this morning?'

Chloe wouldn't answer, and as Charlotte sat there, thinking about the last few awful minutes with Anthony, she felt like burying her face in a pillow too. Why had she put the stupid hat on when she'd found it, and what had she been trying to accuse him of when she'd told him to take it back? It wasn't unusual for Zoe to ride in his car, or to go to tastings with him and Will, so why had she felt compelled to throw a scene like that? Maybe because Zoe hadn't mentioned where she was going when she'd left the cellar door last night.

Suddenly Chloe threw herself into Charlotte's arms, sobbing as though her little heart would break.

'Oh Chloe, Chloe,' Charlotte murmured, holding her tight. 'Please tell me what it is.'

Gasping desperately, Chloe tried to say, 'I haven't got any friends. Everyone's got friends except me.'

Feeling devastated for her, Charlotte went on holding her, unable to think of a thing to say that might comfort her.

'I want to have friends like everyone else,' Chloe wailed, 'and I want to go to school. I don't want to stay here any more.'

'I wish you could go to school too,' Charlotte told her, 'but I'm afraid it's not possible at the moment.'

Chloe looked up at her. 'What about if I'm good? Will they let me go then?'

'Of course, but you have to prove you can be good first.'

'How?'

'Well, you have to do your lessons with me . . .'

'That's just stupid. Anyway, Anthony's better at it than you are.'

Why had she stopped calling him Daddy? Her use of his name seemed almost aggressive, as though she was trying to hurt him, or Charlotte, or maybe herself. 'Then we'll ask him to do it again,' was all Charlotte said.

Chloe's lips pursed, a warning that she was about to say something Charlotte wouldn't like. 'My real daddy is a headmaster,' she stated defiantly, 'so I should be doing lessons with him.'

Charlotte's heart sank. In fact he'd been a deputy head, but that was hardly the point. 'You really don't need to learn any more of the kind of lessons he was teaching you,' she told her.

'Why?'

'You know why.'

'No I don't.'

Her head was hurting too much to argue, so Charlotte simply lay down on the bed with her and pulled her in close. 'Guess what, I don't have any friends either,' she confided flatly.

'But you've got me.'

Charlotte smiled. 'Of course, and I'm very glad of it. You're my special friend and my special girl.'

'More special than Elodie?'

'You're both special.'

Chloe fell silent, but kept her head against Charlotte, and Charlotte's heart ached with all the dreadful confusion that was going round in her mind. Social services were in touch; that really wasn't good. Polly's experiences with a psychologist were worrying her too. Had Polly ended up handing Roxanne over to a family with no other children, therefore giving up on her, abandoning her even? It would be how Roxanne would see it, while Polly would have done it to protect her marriage and other children – if she'd done it at all.

The very idea of doing the same with Chloe was making Charlotte feel sick with fear and guilt and a horrible sense of loss, combined with failure and self-loathing. It was as though she was actually facing the dilemma, which was crazy when no one had suggested she should give Chloe up. The trouble was, she, like anyone else, wanted, *needed*, to believe that mental-health experts had all the answers; that their counselling and advice amounted to a guaranteed panacea that would work for everyone, but she knew that wasn't always the case.

In the end she said, 'There's someone coming to see us on Thursday. She's from family services and I expect she'll want to talk to you.'

'Why?'

'She'll want to find out why you do what you do at school . . .'

'I told you, they tell me to do it, so I do.'

'Who tells you?'

'They do.'

'But who are they?'

'*The other children*. They want me to do it.'

Relieved that it was children and not what she was thinking, Charlotte said, 'But how do they even know about it?'

'I don't know. They just do.'

'Because you showed them?'

Chloe welled up again. 'You're always blaming me,' she wailed.

'No, no, that's not true. I know it's not your fault; I just need you to understand that you have to stop doing it, because if you don't we're all going to be in trouble.'

Silenced by that, Chloe tucked her head close to Charlotte again and closed her eyes. After a while she said, 'Mummy?'

'Mm?' Charlotte was sinking below the thumping in her head, almost asleep.

'Will you tell me about my real mummy?'

Oh god, how was she going to answer that when Erica Wade had been a complete madwoman, and her tragic situation hadn't been helped by the drugs her husband had kept her on. 'I didn't know her very well,' she finally managed. 'We only used to meet when I called in to take you to playgroup.'

'Why didn't she take me?'

'She had an illness that made her afraid of going outside.'

'That's just silly. No one's afraid of going outside.'

'Some people are. They're called agoraphobics.'

'I thought that was when you did exercises.'

'That's aerobics.'

Chloe was quiet again, and Charlotte closed her eyes as a wave of exhaustion washed over her.

'I'm not very happy,' Chloe finally whispered.

Charlotte hugged her hard. 'I know, sweetheart,' she said, 'but once we've got everything sorted out you will be. I promise.'

'Cross your heart and hope to die?'

'Cross my heart and hope to die.'

'You're a liar!' Chloe spat, and punching Charlotte in the face, she ran to the bathroom and locked the door.

Later in the day, with Rick gamely schooling Chloe up at the house, and Elodie seeming a lot brighter as she wheeled a pushcart about the cellar door while chatting gibberish to herself, Charlotte was on the phone to Sara Munds, the mother of Olivia who was in Chloe's class at Te Mata Primary. There was no one else Charlotte could have made this call to, for she'd hardly met the other mothers; however Sara had once told her to be in touch if she ever needed anything.

So this was Charlotte being in touch and cringing her way through every minute of it. 'I'm really sorry to ask,' she was saying, 'and if you'd rather not I'll understand perfectly, but Chloe's feeling very lonely at home on her own so I was wondering if Olivia might like to come over. Or perhaps Chloe could come there.'

'Oh Charlotte, of course she can come here,' Sara Munds responded warmly. 'I realise how difficult all this must be for you both. I'll tell you what; Olivia's having a birthday party on Saturday. Do you think Chloe would like to come to that?'

'I'm sure she'd love to,' Charlotte gushed with relief, loving this woman for how kind and non-judgemental she was being. 'Is it a dressing-up occasion?'

'The girls are coming as fairies and the boys as goblins,' Sara chuckled. 'We're having a picnic on the lawn, and if she'd like to bring her swimsuit there'll be lots of pool games, completely supervised, of course, we don't want any unfortunate accidents.'

'No of course not,' Charlotte agreed, baulking

slightly at the idea of clothes having to come off for swimsuits to go on.

Just stop, Charlotte. Not everything in Chloe's world is about that. 'This is so kind of you, Sara,' she said. 'I really appreciate it. I'm sure Chloe will want to start working on a fairy outfit as soon as I tell her.'

She was right about that, for the instant Chloe realised she was going to a party she lit up with excitement, and began running around the house trying to find things to help make her dress. Throwing her books in the air Rick declared the day's studies over, and appointed himself in charge of transforming his little angel into a fairy.

'Did Olivia really ring up and ask?' Chloe demanded of Charlotte in a fever of pride and joy.

'Her mother did,' Charlotte countered. *Please god don't let Olivia kick up when she found out.*

'Everyone's Olivia's friend,' Chloe told Rick earnestly. 'She's the most popular girl in our class. I really like her. I think she should be my best friend.' To Charlotte she said, 'How do you make someone your best friend? Is there something you have to do?'

Smiling, Charlotte said, 'It usually takes a bit of time getting to know one another first, and when you find you've lots of things in common and that you always get on well, it will happen all on its own.'

Frowning as she digested this, Chloe said, 'Shall I tell her I want her to be my best friend?'

Aching for her, Charlotte gently cautioned, 'Probably not just yet. See how it goes after Saturday first.'

With a wise-seeming nod, Chloe turned urgently back to Rick. 'When can we start making my dress? I want it to be pale blue and white with lovely big wings and lots of sparkles and things.'

'Then we should head on over to JJ Crafts in Hastings right now,' he cried, standing aside to bow her out towards the car.

'Thanks,' Charlotte murmured, hugging him. 'I probably wouldn't have the time for it myself, or the skill.'

'It's my pleasure,' he assured her. 'I mean, dressing up as a fairy, I have to be your man.'

Laughing as he left, and loving how comfortable he was with his sexuality these days, given the difficult time he'd had coming out, she went to check on Rowan before heading back to the cellar door.

If the only significant date in Chloe's future was going to Olivia's on Saturday, how much easier Charlotte would have felt in her mind. However, there was the meeting with CYFS on Thursday to get through first, although whatever the outcome of that it really shouldn't have any impact on the party. After all, they were hardly likely to remove Chloe from the family home based on a first meeting.

They're not going to take her away, she told herself firmly. They're just doing their job.

Knowing how intrusive, even aggressive these

meetings could be was making her feel so wretched she could hardly think of anything else. Having been a social worker in child protection she knew very well what powers these people had, and how capricious or even illogical they could sometimes be in their judgements. Of course she was basing her fears on what she knew of rogue or lazy workers in the English system; she had no knowledge of how child protection operated in New Zealand. The CYFS website claimed its staff were passionate about caring for kids and supporting families, but they were hardly going to say otherwise, and anyway that statement alone could be interpreted in a hundred different ways. For instance, removing a child from the home could, in certain circumstances, be viewed as caring for it and supporting the family.

Reminding herself firmly that nothing like that was going to happen, she tried to focus her mind back on her work. There were no grounds for taking Chloe away, nothing at all to indicate abuse or neglect, the usual reasons for removing a child, and she must remember that the woman who was coming, Charlotte had her name written down somewhere, was simply carrying out a routine inspection. She wasn't the enemy; she was on their side, Chloe's most of all. She would see it as her duty to offer help and support if she felt it was needed, and to leave them alone if she didn't.

*

The temperature had risen to over thirty degrees and the humidity was so intense it seemed to drip from the crowding tangles of foliage Zoe and Anthony were passing through. It was a relief, Anthony was finding, to be on this leafy trail with trees towering up around them creating a patchy barrier to the sun, and the sound of the river gushing along below seemed to add a sense of coolness even if it wasn't real. The cicadas were as loud as he'd ever heard them, grating fiercely, industrious, incessant; birds flitted in and out of branches, vermilion, blue, golden. So many colours, but he had no names for the creatures themselves. This was something he should work on with Cooper, Chloe too if she was interested. There was a time when he'd felt certain Chloe would be, but he no longer felt certain of anything where she was concerned.

The prospect of the social worker's visit passed uneasily through his mind; not the kind of scrutiny he'd ever imagined his family facing. On the other hand he'd never imagined being a parent to a child like Chloe. Still, he was ready to hope that this visit might help lead the way towards a more stable and controllable little girl who was happy and content in her world. It would no doubt be a long journey, but provided they were on the right road there would be reason to hope. Charlotte was doing her best, they all were, but with the demands of the vineyard taking up so much of his time, he was afraid that Chloe had got away from him and he couldn't see a way of winning her back. It wasn't something he'd even had to think about a couple of years ago when she'd laughed at all his jokes, been excited to tell him about her day, and seemed to love spending time with him. These days he hardly even knew what to say to her. If he were being honest, and over this he never would be with anyone but himself, there were times when he actually resented her for the chaos and unhappiness she'd brought to the home, especially to Cooper and Elodie. What kind of psychological damage were they suffering, having her as a sister?

Yet, in spite of how detached he felt from Chloe at times, it still affected him deeply to see how lonely and frustrated she was. No child should ever have to start out in life the way she had, he only wished there was a way to change it, but tragically there was no method of turning back time. What was possible, however, was finding ways to make her feel special, and he really must try harder with that.

Considering how difficult the meeting with CYFS was likely to be for her on Thursday, he decided it might give her spirits a boost if he suggested they had a family day out on Sunday. It was a long time since they'd managed such a treat, and he knew already where Chloe would choose to go, for Cape Kidnappers was one of her favourites. She became comically animated when riding the sea tractor to the end of the peninsula where they could watch the thousands upon thousands of gannets whose summer home was on the spectacular cliffs. He would ask her to tell them the story of how Cape Kidnappers had got its name, which he had to admit had slipped his mind for the moment, but she'd delight in being able to remind him. It was making him smile simply to think of her excitement, such a small and innocent pleasure to bring her world in line with that of other girls her age.

Catching a glimpse of Zoe as she climbed off the trail on to mossy boulders heading towards the waterfalls, he took out his phone to check for messages. Finding none he felt only relief. Messages almost always meant problems, and with no word from Charlotte he was happy to presume things were OK with the family. No word from Will encouraged him to believe that Will's plan to be at the winery today, getting the first of last year's vintage ready for transporting to Wineworks on Thursday, was going ahead. They'd both be there when the wine arrived for the pre-bottling testing but no one was foreseeing any hiccups there either, so the vats in the winery would be empty and the cleaning could begin in plenty of time for harvest.

Feeling beads of sweat running down his back, making his shirt cling to his skin, he regretted not bringing a hat, for the sun was fiery on his head in spite of the trees' protection. Zoe was wisely wearing the hat he'd returned to her after Charlotte had thrown it at him. Just what the heck had Charlotte thought the thing was doing in the car? It wasn't like she hadn't seen it dozens of times before; Zoe almost always wore it, and as she regularly rode in the Volvo it was hardly a surprise that she'd left it behind when he'd dropped her off after dark.

The stress of everything was getting to them both, and there was no sign of a let-up in sight. He couldn't remember the last time they'd made love, they were either too tired, or there was a child in the bed, or they were too angry with one another even to try. It was as though they'd lost interest in each other, were only together because they had to be for the children. More than once he'd felt certain Charlotte was about to give up, walk away and take the kids with her, and what would he be able to do to stop her?

'So here we are! What do you think?' Zoe called out above the roar of the falls. She was standing on a rock, her arms spread wide, her face turned triumphantly towards him as he stepped off the path on to a craggy boulder.

Though he'd been here before with Charlotte and the children, he hadn't wanted to spoil Zoe's surprise so had gone along with it, in spite of knowing as soon as they'd parked where they were heading. This small oasis, nestled deep in a tropical forest, was beautiful enough to take his breath away. Vast, glittering cascades of water tumbling wildly down the cliff face, succulent webs of vegetation and any number of shadowy enclaves hidden amongst the rocks. The lake swirling about the clearing had never looked so cool and inviting; it was taking every ounce of willpower to stop himself diving right in.

'Isn't it the most perfect place for the shoot?' Zoe shouted. 'We can put wine bottles on the rocks, with glasses and napkins and grapes . . . I'm still figuring out how to dress it. Frank the photographer will come up with lots of ideas when I email him the shots I take today. Can you see it? Is it speaking to you too?'

Yes, he could see the images she was trying to conjure, and was having no problem appreciating just how sensational the shots could be in the hands of a professional.

'You're not answering me,' she told him.

Laughing, he said, 'It's perfect.'

'Yay!' she cheered, and almost slipped as she jumped in the air.

'So, are you coming in?' she challenged and without waiting for an answer she stripped off her top and shorts, stood naked for a moment, then made a perfect dive into the silky depths.

Anthony remained where he was, the image of her still burning his eyes, slaking its power as sharply as knives. Of course, he knew what this was about; had known since they'd left the car, but he'd refused to engage with it. He hadn't turned back either. It wasn't the first time she'd made herself available to him, but it had never been as explicit as this, and he had to admit that even that mere glimpse of her naked body was having a profound and unshakable effect on him.

She swam for several minutes and in spite of knowing he shouldn't, he continued to watch. The clearing seemed strangely quiet, as though, like him, it was holding its breath. It felt almost dream-like when she finally climbed, like a nymph, back on to the rocks and stood so he could see the whole of her as she shook out her hair.

Without looking his way, or speaking, she lay down on her back to dry in the sun.

More minutes ticked by. Zoe raised a knee and he couldn't tear his eyes away. He knew exactly what he was going to do, but what he had no idea of yet was how much he was going to end up regretting it.

I've made a really stupid mistake and I don't know what to do about it. I thought, last night, when I went online that I was using Anthony's iPad, but it turned out I got mixed up and I was using mine instead. I was very upset at the time, although I can't remember why now, I think I just felt like I needed to do something to pay everyone back for being horrible to me.

Luckily Mummy didn't say anything about the chat room when she gave my iPad back just now, so maybe she didn't really check it. Even if she did, at least it wasn't the other chat room I found two nights ago when I was definitely using Anthony's iPad. Mummy would have gone ballistic over that one, everyone would, but it's nobody's business if I want to be in touch with one of my creepy daddy's friends. I expect I'll get a lot more truth out of him than I will out of anyone else, or I would if he didn't keep asking about me all the time, wanting to know what I'm wearing and stuff. What difference does it make?

Anyway, I'm not really interested in him now that Olivia's going to be my best friend.

Charlotte was in the bedroom staring out at the night, a hand pressed to her mouth, an inexorable, sharp-edged thudding beating in her head as though all the terrible thoughts were colliding.

How wonderful it would be to have a mind uncluttered by fear, horror, guilt, regret – so many negative emotions she hardly knew what they all were.

The children were asleep, and Anthony had just arrived home. She could hear him calling her, and now he was climbing the stairs. He came into the room, but she didn't turn round.

It startled her when he came to put an arm around her. 'What are you doing?' she asked, pulling away.

His eyes darkened. 'What kind of question is that?' he demanded. 'I'm not allowed to put an arm round my wife?'

Flushing guiltily, she lowered her head. 'I'm sorry . . . It's just . . . It was unexpected, that's all.' Not the only thing that had been unexpected today, and she really wasn't coping well.

'And unwelcome, it would seem?' he challenged.

She didn't answer, because she didn't know what to say.

'Charlotte?' he growled.

'Please Anthony, not now.'

He stared at her so hard that she almost stepped away.

'How has this happened?' he asked gruffly. 'Is it my fault? Have I done something?'

'No, of course not . . .'

'Then what the hell is it? There was a time when we could hardly keep our hands off each other, and look at us now. So where did it go wrong?'

She started to wave an arm towards the vines, towards Chloe's room, but let it drop. Being anxious about harvests, stressed over sales, and parents of two very small children and one that was challenging had never got in the way before. If anything, working together, building a family, watching the business grow had made them closer than ever.

My husband has decided to move out for a while, Polly had blogged. *He wants to take our youngest two with him, and I don't know what to say to stop him.*

Anthony's eyes were harsh, penetrating and . . . knowing. 'What is it?' he demanded. 'What aren't you telling me?'

Charlotte's mouth was too dry to answer.

'Charlotte? I can . . .'

'It's nothing,' she interrupted and started towards the bathroom. She couldn't tell him the truth when she still hadn't worked out how to deal with it herself, so in an attempt to change the subject she said, too brightly, 'Good news. Chloe's been invited to a party on Saturday. She's over the moon. Rick's helping her to make a fairy outfit.'

She could feel his eyes still on her, and for a long moment she thought he was going to speak. In the end he simply turned away and went downstairs.

Hardly thinking about what she was doing she went after him, and found him on the terrace with a whisky. 'I'm sorry,' she said shakily.

'Me too,' he muttered without looking at her.

She turned to stare out at the night, spotting eyes in the vines as rabbits came and went, hearing the flutter of birds in the jacaranda. 'It's just with all that's going on . . .'

'You don't have to make excuses. If you don't want to make love . . .'

'It's not that I don't want to, it's just . . .' She couldn't make herself say it.

'Just what?' he growled.

'It seems . . . wrong while Chloe is in the house.'

'*Wrong*,' he repeated scathingly.

'No, not wrong, just . . .'

'She's always been in the house before.'

'I know, but . . .'

'You don't have to hide behind her. I get that it's not the same for you . . .'

'Stop putting words in my mouth,' she cried. 'You're not listening to me; you're not even trying to understand. What I'm attempting to say is that I don't feel comfortable about making love while she's . . . experiencing the sexual feelings she is.'

'And us not being intimate is going to solve it?'

'Of course not. I don't know what is; all I know is that I can hardly think about anything else and if we make love I don't want her to be in my head making me feel . . . Oh god, I don't know how it makes me feel . . .'

'Mummy?'

Charlotte swung round to see Chloe standing at the foot of the stairs. How long had she been there? How much had she heard? 'What are you doing out of bed?' she demanded. 'It's late . . .'

'I couldn't sleep. Please can I come into your bed?'

Charlotte glanced at Anthony, and could tell by the way he was holding himself how angry he was. It was making her angry too. 'I'll come and sleep with you,' she told Chloe.

Anthony got abruptly to his feet. 'So it's going to start again?' he muttered as Charlotte made to leave the terrace.

Knowing he was referring to the times she'd slept with Chloe after Elodie was born, she said, 'Do you want me to bring her into our bed?'

Knocking back his drink, he replaced the glass on the table and strode down towards the vines.

'Is he cross?' Chloe asked worriedly as Charlotte joined her.

'He's had a difficult day,' Charlotte replied, turning Chloe around and ushering her back up the stairs.

'Did you tell him about Olivia's party?'

'Yes, I did. He was very happy for you. Now go along into bed, I'll be there in a minute.'

Closing the door to her own room, Charlotte put her head against it and clasped a hand tightly to her mouth. She should have told Anthony what she'd discovered on Chloe's iPad today; it wasn't so bad really, was it? Lots of children had similar thoughts – but even if they did they weren't all as emotionally unbalanced, or as young, as Chloe.

As he strode down through the vines, still furious beyond reason, Anthony took out his phone to call Zoe. God only knew how he'd made himself resist her earlier, or how they'd managed to discuss nothing but the brochure all the way back in the car, but he wasn't up for discussing a brochure now, or for resisting her. He was going to take her in any and every way she wanted, and if she wasn't ready to let him go at the end of it, he'd stay and give her a whole lot more.

Chapter Seven

Charlotte's persistent headache didn't seem as severe this morning. Not because she'd slept well, because she hadn't, nor had she made up with Anthony when he'd returned in the early hours. It had simply dropped to a lower level that no longer blurred her vision or made her feel her head was about to explode. Nonetheless, she was still feeling anxious and edgy, and was far more irritable with Cooper than he'd deserved before Rowan, now back on her feet, had whisked him off to kindi.

She'd make it up to him later. What mattered now was that the shock of what she'd discovered yesterday on Chloe's iPad had faded into a realisation that she'd overreacted. Not that it shouldn't be taken seriously, because it should, but she'd talk to Chloe about it when the time was right; until then she'd make sure Chloe didn't go online again. Perhaps, with the prospect of Olivia's party on the horizon, confiscating the iPad wouldn't blow up into yet another terrible scene.

She could always hope.

'Would you like a coffee?' she offered, as Anthony came into the kitchen. She felt absurdly awkward with him, as if he'd become a stranger overnight, so she wasn't sure what to say.

'Thanks,' he responded, keeping his eyes on his phone.

Should she ask where he'd spent most of the night? Did she want to know? 'Are you going out before the social worker comes at eleven?' she asked, passing the coffee.

His head came up and she saw right away how strained he looked. She was responsible for that, but so was he. 'I'd forgotten it was this morning,' he sighed. 'I'm afraid I can't be there. Will just rang. His mother's been taken to hospital and Wineworks are coming to collect the Pinot Gris.'

'At what time?'

'Eleven. I'm sorry, I wanted to be there . . .'

'Doesn't Will have an assistant these days?'

'The boy's an intern. He can't handle . . .'

'It's OK,' she cut in shortly, turning away.

'I know it's not, but there isn't much I can do about it now.'

'I said it's OK.'

Sighing again, he returned to his phone and was

about to take a call when Charlotte suddenly blurted, 'Did you spend the night with Zoe?'

His eyes darkened as he let the call go to messages.

Already regretting the outburst, she struggled for a way to take it back.

'Would it matter if I did?' he countered sharply.

Aware of a horrible heat spreading through her, she said, 'Why don't you just answer the question?'

For a moment she thought he was going to avoid it again, until finally he said, 'I'll admit that I thought about it.'

Feeling as though he'd slapped her, she turned away and continued to clear up the children's breakfast dishes; the world, her thoughts, her life seemed to be crushing her. 'So why didn't you?' she asked, managing to sound as though she wouldn't care if he had.

Finishing the coffee, he put his cup down and said, 'Next time I will.'

As he reached the door, she shouted, 'So where did you spend it?'

Ignoring her, he continued across the terrace and round to the car.

'Anthony, please come back,' she cried, going after him. 'I'm sorry . . . I shouldn't have asked that . . .'

He wasn't listening. He got into the Volvo and reversed ready to drive off.

Running to block the way, she spread out her

arms and felt so strange for a moment that it was like she'd slipped into a dream. Ribbons of light were threading through her eyes, a strange noise was drowning her ears. 'Did you really think about going to her?' she finally managed.

He didn't answer, only glared at her.

Oh god, oh god. 'But you didn't go?'

'No.'

'So where were you until three?'

'At Rick's.'

Standing aside, she watched him drive away, and was still staring down the drive long after he'd gone, unable to make her mind function past the fact that he'd considered going to Zoe. It could only mean that he knew it was an option, so how *did* he know, and how long before he took advantage of it? He might even be on his way to her now, perhaps not with the intention of making love, but it could happen if he wanted it to, and she believed that he did.

'Mummy? There you are,' Chloe yawned, strolling round from the terrace. 'Is that lady still coming today?'

'Yes, she is,' Charlotte answered, turning to her. 'You need to get dressed. Would you like some breakfast?'

'Can we go to Uncle Rick's for breakfast?'

'The bistro's not open on Thursdays, and we need to do some lessons.'

'Boring.'

Following her back inside, Charlotte went to pick up her phone, wanting to send a text to Anthony, but nothing was feeling right and with Chloe chattering away in her ear she couldn't make herself think straight.

How can I kill my family and get away with it?

This was the Web search Chloe had carried out, as though the murderous act were some sort of magic trick, and inevitably she'd ended up in a chat room where all sorts of crazy and largely unworkable suggestions were being thrown about. Thankfully, there was no evidence of Chloe engaging with any of the chats, but the question had been asked, which was what mattered.

Knowing better than to bring it up before the visit from CYFS – and god forbid it should be mentioned while the woman was here – Charlotte made a note to try and find out when the psych ed was coming, before realising that if she told anyone about the Internet search there was a chance Elodie and Cooper would be removed to get them out of harm's way.

Desperate to know where to turn, she connected to Rick to make sure he was still up for running the cellar door this morning.

'Sure I am,' he replied with a yawn. 'Good job you rang, I was still asleep.'

'A late one, was it?' Charlotte asked, trying to sound wry.

'It was,' he confirmed. 'How's your husband this morning? Please tell me he also has the hangover from hell.'

So Anthony had been there. Unravelling with relief, she chatted on with Rick for a while, until remembering Chloe was upstairs and might be online again, she told him to call if he needed her and rang off.

Chloe was in her room gluing sparkles on to the dress she and Rick had chosen for her to wear to Olivia's party.

By eleven o'clock Charlotte still hadn't heard from Anthony, but rather than torment herself with what he might be doing, she made herself believe in the Wineworks collection in order to keep focused on the visit from CYFS.

The young woman, Pania Brown, arrived on time in a glossy blue pickup and wearing such bright red knee shorts and canary-yellow top that even Chloe blinked when she saw her. What a lovely face she had, all round and smiley, like she never felt anything but happy. She was just the sort of spirit Charlotte needed to lift her own, and as they made small talk over the pouring of lemonade and Chloe's offering of biscuits Charlotte could feel herself daring to relax.

It lasted only until Chloe asked Pania if she was Maori, though why that should have made her tense she had no idea, especially as Pania merely chuckled a confirmation that she was.

Chloe promptly launched into all the Maori words she knew, and even sang the *powhiri* – a Maori song to greet visitors – with Pania gamely joining in. They were getting along so famously they might have known each other for months rather than minutes, and Charlotte could only marvel at how well suited Pania was to her job.

At last Chloe was responding to someone who was here to help.

'I had hoped,' Pania said to Charlotte as Chloe refilled her glass, 'that your husband would be here today.'

'He intended to be,' Charlotte assured her, knowing that this would be a black mark against him, 'but our winemaker had a problem this morning that meant Anthony had to stand in for him.'

Pania smiled benignly.

'He stormed off in a temper last night,' Chloe informed her.

Shocked, Charlotte said, 'It had nothing to do with you, and you shouldn't have been out of bed.'

Seeming not to take much notice, though Charlotte knew she had, Pania said, 'Shall we start with how well you're getting on with home-schooling?'

'He's not my real daddy,' Chloe blurted. 'My real daddy's in England.'

'Chloe, Pania asked you a question,' Charlotte chided, furious that Chloe was doing this. Didn't she understand what problems she could be creating for herself?

'I'm just telling her my . . .'

'Yes, we got the picture, but you know that Anthony's your daddy now.'

'No he isn't.'

Charlotte looked at Pania. 'I'm sure you're fully aware of our situation . . .'

'Of course,' Pania replied. To Chloe, she segued, 'So tell me, how do you like living here in New Zealand?'

Chloe tilted her head as she thought. 'Sometimes it's all right, but other times I just want to go home.'

'Isn't this home?'

Chloe shook her head. 'England's my home.'

Charlotte wanted to interrupt again, but knew that too much interference from her wouldn't go down well.

Pania said, 'But this is where your parents and brother and sister live. Don't you want to be with them?'

She wants to kill us all. Charlotte couldn't stop the thought.

Again Chloe was shaking her head.

Charlotte watched Pania write the answer down and felt like throttling Chloe.

'I want to be with Mummy,' Chloe ran on, 'but she doesn't want to be with me.'

Charlotte's jaw dropped. 'Chloe, how can you say that?' she protested.

Chloe's eyes remained fixed on Pania.

'Does Mummy ever say she doesn't want to be with you?' Pania asked gently.

'No, but I can tell.'

Charlotte was dumbfounded. Having never got Chloe to open up to a psychologist, here she was with a social worker telling her things that Charlotte had never heard her say before. They'd have mattered a lot if they were true, but as they weren't, they mattered for all the wrong reasons.

'This mummy stole me from my real mummy and daddy,' Chloe informed Pania. 'They didn't want to let me go, but she took me and brought me here.'

Charlotte turned to Pania again. The social worker obviously knew the facts, but what on earth would she be making of this version? Knowing it would have stirred some alarm bells for Charlotte herself when she was doing the job, she said, 'I'm afraid Chloe seems to be going through a phase of altering the truth . . .'

'I am not,' Chloe shouted. 'I'm just saying what happened, that's all.' To Pania she said, 'She wanted me then, but she doesn't now.'

'Chloe, for heaven's sake,' Charlotte cried. 'Why are you . . . ?'

'It's all right,' Pania said softly, as though letting

Charlotte know that she wasn't taking this too seriously. To Chloe, she said carefully, 'Do you know where your real mummy and daddy are now?'

'I'm supposed to think my real mummy is dead, but she isn't.'

'What makes you say that?'

Chloe's eyes went down as she shrugged.

'What about your daddy?'

Chloe mumbled something and when Pania asked her to repeat it, she shouted, 'He's in prison.'

After a moment, Pania said, 'Do you know why he's in prison?'

Chloe bowed her head as she muttered no.

Pania turned back to Charlotte. 'Would you mind if I had a little chat with Chloe on her own?'

Knowing it wouldn't help if she refused, Charlotte got to her feet. She wanted to remind Pania that she wasn't a psychologist, that she was here to assess Chloe's home life, but since Pania was doing exactly that and was, at the same time, managing to get answers that only a professional behaviourist would be qualified to handle, Charlotte could hardly protest.

Upstairs in the bedroom she toyed with the idea of calling Anthony, but decided not to. If she got his voicemail she'd only think the worst, and if he answered she'd probably be told it was a bad time. It would be, if the wine was being collected. After ringing Rowan to ask her to pick up some Panadeine from the pharmacist, she tried her mother, but rang off before Anna could answer.

Realising she didn't know who she wanted to speak to, or what she wanted to say, she dropped her phone on the bed and sat cradling herself as though trying to hold everything together. It was hard to know what was scaring her the most, the things Chloe might be saying to Pania, and what could happen as a result, the fact that Chloe wanted to kill them all, or the disastrous state of her marriage.

'She was nice, wasn't she?' Chloe said chattily as Pania set off down the drive in her jaunty pickup. 'I think I'd like to live with her.'

Not rising to it, Charlotte turned her around and steered her back inside. To her surprise Pania hadn't asked to talk to her after spending time with Chloe, nor had she given any indication of when she might be in touch again. 'Do you want to tell me what you talked about with her?' Charlotte asked, as she and Chloe entered the house.

'No, I want to go and work on my fairy dress,' Chloe replied.

'You can after we've had a chat, and after you've done an hour of maths.'

Chloe scowled. 'I'm hungry,' she declared.

'I'll make you a sandwich in a minute, but first, I want to talk to you about the kind of things you're looking up on the Internet.'

Seeming not to hear as she searched amongst Cooper and Elodie's toys, Chloe said, 'It was here just now.'

'What was?'

'My iPad. Ah, here it is,' and bringing it to the table she sat down to start opening up her apps.

Taking it from her, Charlotte said, 'Why were you reading about how to kill your family?'

'Give it back to me.'

'Not until you answer the question. Why were you . . .'

'I wasn't.'

'I saw it, Chloe . . .'

'Yeah, but I wasn't reading it. I mean, I was but not because I want to *kill* anyone, I just saw it and thought I'd click on.'

Knowing it was a lie, Charlotte stared at her hard.

Chloe grinned. 'Did you really think I wanted to kill you?' she teased.

Charlotte said, 'I don't know what to think. Sometimes, Chloe, I find you very hard to read.'

'That's because you're not my real mummy. If you were, I expect you'd know everything I'm thinking.'

Feeling a tightening in her head, Charlotte said, 'I doubt it. No one ever knows for certain what another person is thinking.' She found herself wondering what might be in Anthony's mind now. How was he feeling about the way he'd driven off earlier?

'Do you know what?' Chloe said. 'On that website some people were saying that you should shoot your family, and others said you should stab them and hide their bodies.'

'It's not a joke, Chloe,' Charlotte cried angrily. '*You shouldn't have been reading it*. You must have known it was wrong even before you clicked on. Did you?'

'Of course.'

'So why did you do it?'

'Because I was angry, and it wasn't my fault I was angry. It was all of you, getting at me again.'

'And do you think everyone who falls out with their family tries to find out how to kill them?'

'How would I know? I never asked them.'

Charlotte's eyes closed as she put a hand to her head.

'Am I banned from using the iPad now?' Chloe asked.

'Yes, you are.'

'I don't care.' As she went to grab the iPad Charlotte held it out of reach.

'I only want to play a game. I don't care about going online.'

'No games until we've done some lessons.'

'I don't want to.'

Ignoring the protest, Charlotte went to get the books. 'Tell me,' she said, spreading them out on the table, 'are you really unhappy here, or is it just something you say?'

'I was unhappy before Olivia invited me to her party.'

Wishing with all her heart that could be a cure-all, Charlotte said, 'What makes you unhappy?'

Chloe shrugged. 'Everything.'

'Like what?'

'Like everything.'

'If you don't tell me what it is then I won't be able to do anything about it.'

Chloe's eyes stayed down as she said, 'You wouldn't anyway.'

'Try me.'

'No, because you'll get angry and shout at me and then I'll be upset and I don't want to be upset.'

Reaching for her hand, Charlotte said, 'I don't want you to be upset either, so if I promise not to get angry and shout, will you tell me then?'

To Charlotte's surprise a tear trickled on to Chloe's cheek. 'Do you really promise?' she asked.

'Of course, cross my heart and hope to die.' Remembering how she'd got thumped the last time she'd said that, she had to force herself not to draw back.

Chloe's mouth was trembling as she said in a small voice, 'I want it to be just you and me, the way it was before.'

Understanding that she meant before Cooper and Elodie, possibly even before Anthony, Charlotte went round the table and pulled her into her arms.

'We had some lovely times when you were little,' she said softly, 'but we still have lovely times now, as a family. I know there haven't been so many of them lately, but we'll make sure to do something about that. OK?'

Chloe didn't answer, only kept her face buried in Charlotte.

'You could be such a lovely big sister, you know, if you wanted to.'

Chloe tensed and grabbed Charlotte's phone as it rang.

Taking it from her and seeing it was Anthony, Charlotte clicked on.

'Hi. How did it go?' he asked.

'Can I call you back?' she replied.

'Sure.'

After ringing off Charlotte wrapped Chloe in her arms again and rocked her back and forth, connecting only with how much this dear struggling little soul with all her problems and tortured background really meant to her. They'd get through this, she promised herself, no matter how long it took, she'd find the right way for Chloe so that her tender child's heart and frightened mind stopped hurting her so much.

Anthony was in the winery where he'd been all morning, supervising the 2015 collection. Now he was going through paperwork, though not making much headway as he kept thinking about Charlotte and how distraught she'd looked as he'd driven off earlier. He felt dreadful for leaving her that way, but, like Chloe, he seemed so driven by anger and frustration these days that he was falling into the trap of acting first and thinking later.

Thank god that hadn't happened last night with Zoe. It had come close, that was for sure, but good sense (or a well-suppressed love of Charlotte) had somehow prevailed as he'd approached the bistro, so he'd managed to end up there instead.

Charlotte was keeping something from him, he was as certain of that as he was that it had to be about Chloe, but until she decided to confide in him there was nothing he could do. As if he ever knew what to do where Chloe was concerned. These days he had to keep reminding himself of how much he'd loved her before his own children were born, because she did precious little to make him feel that way now.

Deciding to go up to the house if Charlotte hadn't called back in an hour, he picked up a wine thief and went through to check on the barrels of Cabernet Franc. He'd got no further than tasting the first one when a voice called out, 'Hi, is anyone at home?'

Recognising it as Zoe, he shouted, 'Back here,' and emerging from the darkness he shaded his eyes against the brilliant sunlight.

'Great, I'm glad I caught you,' she declared, coming into the winery and setting her laptop down on

Will's desk. 'Has the collection happened? It smells as though it has.'

'They left about half an hour ago.'

'Great. So you have a minute? Actually, before we get started am I right in thinking the Chardonnay and Cabernet Franc will be collected in April or May?'

'Correct.'

'That's what I've got in the diary. So I'll make sure Frank, or someone, is here to get shots of the departure. A shame he couldn't make it this morning, but hey.'

Setting aside the wine thief he'd been using to draw samples from the barrels, he rinsed his glass under a tap and washed his hands.

'So, I've been setting up tastings for June and July,' she explained, opening her laptop. 'As of today we've got half a dozen in Auckland, a couple in Wellington and four in Christchurch. Of course, this is only the beginning, but having these firmed up means we ought to start looking into flights and hotels. Do you have your diary to hand?'

Opening the calendar on his own laptop, he scrolled to June and began filling in the dates she was giving him. As they worked, he was aware of how close she was standing, so he took a step away. Even if he had no intention of doing anything about the attraction, he wasn't made of stone.

Reaching for his phone as it rang he saw it was

Charlotte and clicked on. 'So how did it go?' he asked, reaching for a cloth to wipe the sweat from his neck.

As Charlotte told him about the meeting with CYFS he was only half listening; the problems of the winery, and Zoe apparently leaving when he was sure there was more to discuss, were distracting him. He wondered if he should be trying to end Zoe's contract after what had happened at the waterfall. If he did, she'd surely want paying to the end, which would turn out to be a lot of money for nothing, and how on earth would he explain it to Charlotte? *I needed to get her out of temptation's way? She behaved inappropriately and we can't let it happen again?* It would be like admitting that he didn't trust himself, and why on earth would he do that when he had no intention of betraying Charlotte? She already had so much on her plate, she really didn't need to be worrying about anything else, especially not something that wasn't going to happen. And given that Zoe had already fixed as many tastings in a month as he'd managed in the whole of last winter, that she had an impressive brochure in the early stages of production, and that she'd brokered the Australian deal, what plausible excuse could he give for firing her?

'So what do you think?' Charlotte asked.

'I'm sorry,' he said, 'I . . .'

'You weren't listening, were you?' she accused angrily. 'I knew it. You've got other things on your mind and we're just not important enough to take up your time. Well sorry for interrupting,' and the line went dead.

Charlotte would have rung Anthony back to apologise had Chloe not appeared from upstairs and, amazingly, reminded her that they were going to do some maths.

So, setting everything else aside – CYFS, Internet behaviour, marriage breakdown, even the headache – she spent the next half an hour immersed in fractions and worked through to triple totals with much success until Chloe started to get bored.

'I don't want to do any more.'

'Just answer this question, then we'll move on to the calculator.'

Chloe wasn't interested. 'Did you have a row with Anthony when I was upstairs?' she asked, doodling in the corner of her exercise book.

'It's Daddy, and you shouldn't have been listening.'

'I couldn't help it, you were shouting. Why did you say we weren't important enough to him?'

Sighing, Charlotte rubbed her hands over her face. 'I shouldn't have said that.'

'So why did you?'

'Because he made me cross.'

'So are you going to get a divorce?'

'No! Now let's get back to what we're supposed to be doing.'

'If we're not important . . .'

'Chloe . . .'

'I'm just saying if he doesn't think we're important then we should go back to England.'

Annoyed, though genuinely puzzled, Charlotte said, 'What on earth do you think there is in England that there isn't here?'

Chloe shrugged, and gouged out the smiley face she'd drawn.

Relieved she hadn't mentioned her real parents again, Charlotte tried to focus her back on the maths, but she was having none of it.

'I want to take my fairy dress to show Uncle Rick now I've put the sparkles on.'

'You can do that later.'

'I want to do it now.'

'Chloe . . .'

'All right, but can we do something else? I don't like maths.'

'But you're good at it.'

Chloe glanced at Charlotte's mobile as it rang. 'Is that *Daddy*?' she asked scathingly.

Not recognising the number, Charlotte said, 'No, but I should probably take it. Sit there, and don't move,' and getting up from the table she clicked on the line. 'Tuki River Wines, how can I help you?'

'Oh, Charlotte, it's Sara Munds here, Olivia's mother. I hope I'm not calling at a bad time, but I was wondering if I might pop over and see you this afternoon?'

'Of course,' Charlotte responded, hoping, praying, this wasn't going to turn into bad news for Chloe. 'Whenever it's convenient for you. I'm at the house. Do you know where it is?'

'I know the cellar door, and I believe I just carry on up the drive from there?'

'That's right. I'll see you when you get here.'

Just in case it turned out to be bad news, and Charlotte couldn't imagine what else it might be, she decided it would be best to end the day's lessons and let Chloe take her fairy outfit to show Rick.

Half an hour later Sara Munds was sitting on the canopied terrace looking as sporty and tanned, and kind, as she always did. She was the sort of woman, Charlotte was thinking, that she'd love to have as a friend if she had the time. She couldn't remember ever seeing her look unhappy, or worried, or as though anything could get her down, although Charlotte was sure it must at times, life was just like that. She imagined Sara would have a way of dealing with issues that would be likely to involve laughing them off, or certainly making sure that things weren't taken too seriously or blown out of proportion.

'I guessed you'd have a spectacular view from here,' Sara smiled, as Charlotte brought lemonade and grapes to the table. 'I can't think you ever get tired of it.'

'No, we never do, but I have to admit we sometimes forget to notice it.'

Seeming to appreciate that, Sara said, 'I always feel there's something mystical, or maybe I mean ethereal, about the vines when they're covered in white nets, don't you? They seem sort of dreamlike.'

Amused, Charlotte said, 'When we were first here Anthony and I used to love the feeling of protecting them, like they were our children, until they were ready to give up their fruit. A harmonious coming together of man and nature was what we decided. I guess we don't think about it so much any more.'

Sara smiled and raised her glass. 'Thanks for seeing me at such short notice,' she said. 'I'm sure you're wondering what it's about, so I should come to the point. But before I do, I want you to know how upset I am about this. I'd give anything for it not to be happening, but unfortunately it is.'

Feeling her mouth turning dry, Charlotte said, 'It's about the party?'

Sara didn't deny it. 'I'm afraid a number of children have pulled out . . . Or I should say their parents called to cancel when they learned Chloe was going to be there.'

Charlotte lowered her eyes as they stung with tears. This was going to break Chloe's heart, and she, fool that she was, should have foreseen it before making the call to Sara.

'I'm so sorry,' Sara said with feeling. 'Olivia is as upset as I am. She even wanted to abandon the party rather than tell Chloe she couldn't come, but the children have put a lot of effort into their costumes, at home and at school.'

'It's OK,' Charlotte said, thinking of the effort Chloe had put into hers. 'I understand.'

'Do you?' Sara replied, 'because I'm damned if I do. She's an eight-year-old child who bears no responsibility whatsoever for what happened in her early years, and the way some people seem to think she's going to influence their kids, corrupt them even, when all children of that age are waking up to their sexuality, is just plain ignorant and bigoted.'

Unused to anyone jumping to Chloe's defence, Charlotte found herself still too emotional to speak.

'I hope you don't mind,' Sara continued, 'but I've spoken with Mike Bain about Chloe's current situation at school. I ought to add that I'm on the Board of Trustees, so I'm a part of the committee that will decide whether or not she should be excluded. Mike and I are all for keeping her at Te Mata, but I'm afraid neither of us is confident of the vote going our way. Mike knows I'm telling you this, by the way. I have his full permission.'

Relieved to know Chloe had champions, even if they were outnumbered, Charlotte said, 'If she is excluded, what will happen then?'

'Mike could probably explain it better than I can,

but essentially it will be the school's responsibility to approach ten other schools in order to find her a place. As a matter of course they will turn her down and you must understand that the reason will have nothing to do with Chloe herself, but everything to do with funding.'

Charlotte frowned, not quite following.

'It's at this point, following the ten refusals,' Sara explained, 'that the Ministry of Education will be forced to step in to decide where she should go. It could be to any one of the ten schools, or they could say she should stay at Te Mata, but crucially they will then provide the necessary resources to put a special care package in place.'

Charlotte was trying to see this from Chloe's point of view, and it really wasn't looking good. 'She's suffered so much rejection in her life already,' she said. 'To be turned down by ten schools . . .'

'Because they have to.'

'But she won't see it like that.'

'Probably not, if you tell her. I don't think there's any reason for her to know.'

'She'll know about the special care package. It'll make her stand out from everyone else . . .'

'They're very sensitively handled, and you know Mike Bain wouldn't allow it to be otherwise.'

'Provided she ends up at Te Mata. And if she does, what are the other parents going to think about that?'

'It's only a small handful and believe me, we're

already doing our best to get them to see reason. I promise you, we're not an intolerant community, most of us believe in helping one another, and I'm very keen to help Chloe. I'm only sorry that it's not going to work out for the party, but we would be very happy to have her over any time after.'

Knowing it was the party that would matter to Chloe, Charlotte said, 'You're being very kind, thank you. And please thank Mike Bain when you see him.'

'Of course.'

'I'm still waiting to hear if a psychologist has been assigned to assess her. I've been told a few times that someone will get back to me, but no one has yet.'

'That's poor, but I know from past experience with kids at the school that these things take time. Has she seen anyone before?'

'Yes, and it didn't go well, on either of the three attempts, so I don't imagine that's working in her favour.'

'It has to be the right person, and they're not always easy to find. Not that we don't have some good people in this area, but what works for one doesn't necessarily work for another. I'll do some asking around, if you like.'

Charlotte smiled gratefully. 'Do you have any idea yet when we have to meet with the Board of Trustees?'

'As soon as we come to a decision, which shouldn't be long now. Mike, or one of his deputies, will be in touch.'

Long after Sara Munds had gone, Charlotte remained on the terrace, staring at the distant horizon, barely even aware of the tears rolling down her cheeks. Polly was on her own with Roxanne now. After Roxanne had sabotaged a family day out – Polly hadn't said how – her husband had declared that he'd had enough. He'd left, taking the younger children with him, and Polly wasn't sure she could forgive him. Maybe she had by now; they could all be reunited with things working out just fine, but it was hard for Charlotte to make herself believe that.

She needed to start reading about other adoptive parents' experiences with traumatised children and stop focusing on this one. It just felt so similar to her own with the ages of the children, the pressure on the marriage, the fear of not being what Roxanne needed, that it was as though her life was playing out in a virtual world, telling her what was going to happen – and a horribly superstitious part of herself was afraid that if she ignored it, it would be at her peril.

It wasn't until she heard Rowan coming up the drive in the Range Rover that she made the effort to pull herself together, ready to face Cooper and Elodie. She couldn't let them see her like this. She'd be fine for the next hour or so, but how on earth was she going to hold it together when she broke the news to Chloe?

Chapter Eight

It was just after six when Anthony came in to find Charlotte curled up on one of the sofas with Cooper and Elodie, while attempting to deal with emails on her phone as Rowan sorted laundry in the kitchen.

Putting a finger to her lips for him to be quiet, Charlotte whispered, 'Cooper's not well. He's been sick and he doesn't want any tea.' For Cooper this was a big deal, given his usual bottomless appetite.

Turning in her arms, Cooper said to his dad in a sorry little voice, 'Chloe can't go to the party.'

Frowning, Anthony looked at Charlotte.

'Sara Munds came this afternoon,' she told him.

His eyes darkened, showing he needed no further explanation. 'Does Chloe know?'

Charlotte nodded and felt herself welling up again. After she'd broken the news to Chloe she'd sobbed with her, holding her close while knowing that nothing she said was ever going to make it better. It was a truly horrible rejection to suffer, and it must be feeling like the end of the world to her eight-year-old heart. The only good part of it was that it hadn't provoked an outburst – at least not yet.

'Where is she now?' Anthony asked.

'In her room. She doesn't want to see or speak to anyone.'

'Ever again,' Cooper finished hoarsely.

Going to fetch a bottle, Anthony poured two glasses of Cabernet Franc and put one down next to Charlotte. 'What are we going to do?' he said, sitting on the opposite sofa.

'I don't know,' Charlotte replied, glad he understood the seriousness of it. 'Sara told me a few other things while she was here, but I'll save them for later.'

After taking a generous sip, he said, 'I guess it's impressive that she came to tell you in person.'

Charlotte nodded. 'She's a lovely woman. I could see how embarrassed and upset she was.'

'Which won't mean much to Chloe. What a day she's had.'

Remembering how she'd hung up on him earlier, Charlotte was about to apologise when Chloe came down the stairs and stood looking at them with red-rimmed eyes and a tragically tear-ravaged face.

Putting his glass down, Anthony held out his arms, and to Charlotte's surprise and relief Chloe went right into them.

'It's OK, it's OK,' he soothed, holding her tight as she sobbed into his shoulder. 'We're going to make everything better, and shall I tell you how?'

Her answer was muffled in his shirt.

'I'm going to take you to Cape Kidnappers for the day on Sunday.'

After a moment Chloe pulled back to look at him. 'Just me?' she asked shakily.

Pressing a kiss to her forehead he said, 'Well, I think we should all go, don't you? You know how Mummy loves riding on the sea tractor . . .'

'And me,' Cooper piped up.

Chloe's eyes went down.

Charlotte said, 'We could go to the growers' market on Saturday morning, just you and me, to get something for a picnic. How would you like that?'

Chloe gave a small nod.

'And tonight,' Anthony declared, 'I think we could do with a trip to Mamacita's so we can have churros for dessert.'

'Chloe likes churros,' Cooper informed them.

Remembering he was unwell, Charlotte said, 'Are you sure you're up to eating something?'

'Yes, I'm all right now,' he assured her, making both her and Anthony smile as he climbed down to go and give Chloe a hug. 'You can come to my party,' he told her generously.

Chloe looked at Charlotte. 'He means well,' Charlotte whispered, and hoisting a still sleeping

Elodie into her arms she said to Rowan, 'You'll come with us to Mamacita's?'

'Love to,' Rowan replied.

Whether Chloe was worried about seeing any of her classmates in the village was hard to tell, for she sat quietly staring out of the car window on the way to the restaurant, not speaking to anyone, nor responding to Rowan when Rowan put an arm around her. She would have noticed, however, as Charlotte did, two small girls breaking away from their mothers and running towards each other outside the library, looking so thrilled and excited to be meeting up it could have been the best thing that had ever happened to them.

That was what it was like to have a best friend.

Chloe said very little throughout the meal and ate almost nothing until the churros arrived, when she managed only one. Charlotte, distracted by the colour blocks on the walls that reminded her of the retreat booking sheets she hadn't checked today, still managed to notice how Chloe kept watching Anthony as he playfully fed Elodie. Every time Elodie laughed, or clapped her hands in delight, Chloe seemed to flinch. Everything was hurting her at the moment, and Charlotte was afraid that it would continue to for a while yet. For her part she started to feel horribly aware of people watching them, and tried her best not to imagine what they might be saying.

That night she slept with Chloe while Cooper and Elodie were allowed in with their daddy. The same happened on Friday night, and on Saturday morning, when Charlotte drove Chloe over to the growers' market, Anthony went to take charge of the cellar door. Apparently it had been his intention to mount the gas gun on the quad bike today, but he'd decided to postpone it until Monday in order for Charlotte to spend time with Chloe. So the dreaded sound of guns going off all over the valley to prevent birds from nesting was about to begin.

Just what her headache needed.

The growers' market was in a natural hollow at the edge of the Black Barn Vineyard and was made up of a circle of food stalls with a drinks stand at the centre, where Charlotte bought herself a coffee and Chloe an apple juice. Chloe was withdrawn, and trailed around after Charlotte taking little or no interest in anything. Usually she was bounding from one vendor to the next, ready to try all sorts of delicacies from homemade harissa paste to a pungent locally produced cheese. As they inspected the freshly baked bread Charlotte began once again to feel as though they were being watched.

Later, she said to Rowan, 'It's like people are thinking "there's the woman with the problem child", or "that's the little girl no one wants at their party, and you know why".'

'Oh I'm sure they're not,' Rowan protested.

'Everyone around here is very friendly and understanding . . .'

'Sadly, not everyone,' Charlotte reminded her.

'Most,' Rowan insisted. 'If they're thinking anything, it's probably how sad it is that things are so hard for Chloe.'

It was certainly how Charlotte felt, and not knowing how to make things better was as frustrating as it was upsetting.

When two o'clock came – the time Chloe should have been going to the party – Rick turned up to take her to the bistro to help set the tables with flowers and napkins. This was something she'd always enjoyed doing, and to Charlotte's relief she didn't refuse to go. However, after bringing her down from her room Rick murmured to Charlotte, 'You need to go and see what she's done.'

Upstairs Charlotte found Chloe's fairy dress and lovely red school hat cut up into shreds, and the word 'hate' was scrawled on the mirror. Imagining Chloe's pain and confusion as she'd set about it all made Charlotte want to cry bitter tears.

After gathering up the dress and hat she lay down on the bed, feeling battered and exhausted, and with her head throbbing painfully again she fell into an uneasy sleep.

That night they ate at the bistro and to Charlotte's relief Chloe seemed a little brighter. She still didn't have much to say, and she was mean to Cooper when he copied what she was having to eat, but at least she agreed she was looking forward to their day at Cape Kidnappers tomorrow.

'It's your favourite, isn't it?' Cooper said, doing his little-boy best to be nice to her.

She nodded and said to Anthony, 'Are we going to Ocean Beach after for our picnic?'

'That's the plan,' he told her. 'I hope you got something nice for us today.'

When she didn't answer, Charlotte said, 'We're going to let it be a surprise.'

Chloe seemed not to be listening. She was staring at Elodie in her high chair, no doubt resenting her as usual, or maybe she was wishing she was that age again when life was so much easier. Except for Chloe it hadn't been.

Smoothing her hair, Charlotte passed Anthony a napkin to wipe the hokey pokey sundae from around Cooper's mouth.

'After I drop you off I'm going over to Black Barn to meet Kim,' Anthony told her, as he called for the bill.

Surprised, since this was the first she'd heard of it, she tried not to sound snappish as she said, 'I was hoping you'd help me put the children to bed.'

'Rowan should be back by now.'

'And if she isn't?'

'I'll help and go after.'

'Why are you going on a Saturday night?'

'Because he asked me to. Apparently there's something he'd like to discuss.'

'That can't wait until Monday?'

'I've no idea, because I don't know what it is.'

Unable to stop herself she said, 'Are you sure that's where you're going?'

Clearly angry, he took out his phone and scrolled to the text he'd received from Kim Thorp earlier in the day. *Something's come up that I'd like to discuss with you. I'll be around this evening, family have gone over to Taupo. Come when convenient for you. KT*

Annoyed with herself, she handed the phone back and mumbled a sorry.

'Why do you have such a hard time trusting me?' he challenged as they drove back to the house.

'Maybe it's not you I don't trust,' she retorted.

He slanted her a look, but said no more, and for a long, raw moment she desperately wished they didn't have any children so she could do what she always used to when they'd had a misunderstanding or falling out.

He's your husband, you can touch him any time you like and wherever you like, she reminded herself.

Her hands remained in her lap and the words she might have spoken were brushed aside by a sudden wail from Elodie.

'What is it?' Charlotte demanded, turning in her seat. Since Elodie couldn't answer she looked at Chloe.

'I don't *know*,' Chloe answered. 'She just started screaming.'

'I think she's got tummyache,' Cooper piped up.

Pulling over, Anthony got out of the car and leaned in to lift Elodie into his arms. 'I'll walk the rest of the way with her,' he said to Charlotte.

Since that often calmed Elodie down, Charlotte got into the driver's seat and by the time he and Elodie arrived home she was upstairs bathing Cooper.

Handing a sleepy Elodie to Rowan, Anthony went to stand in the bathroom doorway. 'Would you like me to take over?' he offered.

'We're done,' she replied, lifting a soapy Cooper into a towel. 'Is Elodie OK?'

'She seems to be.' After a pause, he said, 'I shouldn't be long.'

'It doesn't matter, take as long as you like.' She hadn't meant it to come out snippily, but it had. To try and temper it, she added, 'Send Kim my love.'

'I will,' and after tweaking Cooper's nose he left her to it.

Half an hour later, with the two little ones settled and Rowan on her way into town to meet friends, Charlotte found Chloe sitting on her bed staring at nothing.

'Are you OK?' Charlotte asked, going to sit with her.

Chloe shrugged.

'Uncle Rick said you were very helpful today and the tables were lovely.'

Chloe looked up at her. 'Who don't you trust?' she asked.

Wanting to sigh, Charlotte said, 'No one. It doesn't matter.'

'Is it me?'

Thrown, Charlotte cried, 'No, of course not. Why on earth would you think that?'

'I don't know.'

Remembering that children almost always thought things were about them, Charlotte slipped an arm round her and closed her eyes against a wave of nausea. 'I trust you,' she said softly, only wishing it was true.

Long minutes ticked by and she was almost asleep when Chloe said, 'It'll be nice going to Cape Kidnappers tomorrow. We haven't been there for ages.'

Charlotte gave her a hug and found herself thinking about all the other things she and Anthony hadn't done for ages, such as hold hands and laugh; touch each other's faces in tenderness; stroll through the vines, arms around one another; watch the children sleeping; kiss until the desire they shared became too explosive to suppress . . .

I've been in bed for quite a long time, just lying in the dark and thinking. I heard Anthony come in a while ago, but I pretended to be asleep when he opened my door to check on me. I don't want to talk to him, or to anyone else. I don't want to be here at all, I just don't know how to leave. It's not fair that I don't have a real mummy and daddy to go and live with. Why can't I be like everyone else? Why do I have to be different?

If I was the same I'd have been able to go to the party today, but I don't care about that any more. I hate them all, especially Olivia. I hope they all die of something horrible. It would serve them right.

I'm not sure if I feel like going on Anthony's iPad tonight. The last time was horrible. I found the killing website again, or one like it anyway, but this other one was more about how to kill yourself instead of other people.

Maybe that's what I should do.

That would serve everyone right.

The iPad's in its usual place at the back of the drawer under my bed. I don't think I'll bother with the killing sites again; instead I'm going to see if my creepy daddy's friend is online and chat to him. I've chatted with him twice already and because he says nice things I've decided to instant message with him. He hasn't told me how my creepy parents managed to steal me yet – I'm worried they didn't and that I'm really theirs. That would be totally horrible and disgusting. I'd definitely want to kill myself if that was true.

'Hello Ottilie.'

Being called that makes me feel all strange and like

I want to curl up in a ball to shut out the world; it's the name I had before I was Chloe.

'Hello.'

'How are you this morning?'

'It's night-time here.'

'Where are you?'

'In New Zealand.'

'Of course. I read that you were living there. It's a long way away. Do you like it there?'

'No. Where are you?'

'You asked me about your daddy the last time we spoke, do you want to know any more?'

I'm not sure how to answer that, because I do, but there again I don't. 'How do you know him?'

'We've been friends for a long time. He's very proud of you.'

I wonder what he's proud of.

'You mentioned before that you have a little sister. How old is she?'

'One and a half.'

'I'd really like to see her. Do you know how to upload photographs?'

I think I do, but before I can answer he says,

'Why don't you take some of her with you in the bath?'

'She doesn't like me.'

'I'm sure that's not true.'

'It is.'

'I can tell you how to make her like you.'

'How?'

'I'm going to send you a link that will show you what to do.'

Everyone was up early the following morning, determined not to miss the tide or the trip to Cape Kidnappers would be over before it began. Luckily the forecast rain had drifted off over the mountains already, and the sun was making the moisture on the vines steam and glisten like jewels.

Just after ten Rowan took the Range Rover to go and visit friends in Pourere while Charlotte, ably assisted by Cooper, began loading up the Volvo with swimsuits, beach toys, nappies, towels and of course the picnic. Chloe was trying to take photographs of Anthony feeding Elodie, who seemed set on sending her breakfast flying about the room. Chloe clearly found this funny, whereas Anthony just as clearly didn't. Since it wasn't like Elodie to be naughty, or like Anthony to get cross with his angel, Charlotte decided to take over the feeding, sending Chloe upstairs to brush her hair and teeth, and Anthony into the corner until he could improve his temper.

Cooper gave a shout of laughter. 'Mummy sent you to the corner,' he squealed delightedly. 'That means you've been naughty.'

Managing a smile, Anthony scooped him up and turned him upside down. 'Time you and I went to Dadz and Ladz for a haircut,' he told him. 'You're looking like a caveman.'

'No, you are. Mummy! Did you remember my flippers?' he shouted up at her.

'Yes, they're in the car.'

'And my spade?'

'You put it in yourself.'

'Oh yes. Are we going to do some surfing?' he asked his dad.

'Yes we are,' Anthony replied, setting him down on the floor. 'Have you put my things in?' he asked Charlotte.

'I think so, but you'd better check to make sure I haven't forgotten your Speedos.'

At last he laughed, and she felt such a swell of relief that she laughed too. It might seem childish to be as excited as Chloe and Cooper about a day out by the sea, but why shouldn't she when they hadn't spent time together like this in far too long?

Twenty minutes later Elodie was in her baby seat, Cooper was buckled in next to her and Charlotte was calling out to Chloe to hurry up or they'd miss the tide.

'Where are the car keys?' Anthony asked, checking the dish where he usually left them.

'I don't know,' Charlotte replied, stuffing a pack of baby wipes into her bag. 'You were the last one to use the car.'

'You've been packing it up . . .'

'It wasn't locked. They must be somewhere. Have you tried your pockets?'

'What's wrong?' Chloe asked, coming down the stairs, pretty as a picture in a bright blue beach dress and matching Alice band.

'We can't find the car keys,' Charlotte told her. 'What were you wearing last night?' she asked Anthony. 'You need to check those pockets.'

After doing so he went out to the car in case he'd left the keys in the ignition.

'Where the hell are they?' he growled, coming back into the house.

'They have to be around here somewhere,' Charlotte responded, starting to search. 'Chloe, check the sofas and see if they've fallen down behind the cushions.'

Anthony was opening and closing cupboard doors, and rummaging through drawers. 'Oh, for god's sake,' he cried angrily.

'Do we have a spare set?' Charlotte asked.

'You know we don't. Have you looked in your bag?'

Obediently Charlotte unpacked it, found no keys, so went to unpack everything she and Cooper had bundled into the car.

Still no sign of them.

'I can't believe this is happening,' Anthony shouted furiously.

'All right, calm down,' Charlotte scolded, catching Chloe's worried face.

'Well we can't go anywhere without the keys,' he pointed out, heading into the utility room.

'We'll find them. Chloe, any luck?'

'They're not in the sofas,' Chloe answered.

Turning cold as she remembered Polly's blog about Roxanne sabotaging a family day out, Charlotte said, 'Are you sure you don't know where they are?'

Chloe's eyes flashed with anger. 'Why does it have to be my fault?' she shot back.

'I'm not saying it is. I'm just asking if you've seen them.'

Enraged, Chloe cried, 'No! I haven't. You can go and check in my room if you like.'

Wondering how she could do that without upsetting her any further, Charlotte watched Anthony return from the utility room. The thunderous look on his face was enough to confirm they were still missing.

They continued to search every room, every pocket and every bag, until finally Anthony looked at his watch and said, 'You might as well get the children out of the car, we won't be going anywhere.'

Chloe's eyes were wide as she looked at her mother.

Charlotte was trying to get hold of Rick, but it turned out that he and Hamish were at the Sunday market in Napier, so borrowing their car wasn't an option.

'Go and help Cooper out of the seat belt,' Charlotte told Chloe. 'I'll come in a minute for Elodie.' Once they were alone she said to Anthony, 'Being angry about it isn't helping . . .'

'She's hidden them,' he stated tightly.

'This was supposed to be her special day out, so why would she?'

'I've got no idea,' he retorted.

'I searched her room myself and they weren't there.'

'So she's put them somewhere else.'

Afraid he might be right, she let it go. She didn't want things getting any more heated than they already were or the day would end up completely ruined.

'We're going to have a picnic on the lawn,' she announced when she returned with Elodie.

'I want to see the gannets and go to the beach,' Cooper protested.

'I know, sweetheart, but we can't find the car keys and even if they turned up now, we've missed the tide.'

Cooper thrust out his lower lip.

Charlotte was watching Chloe as she wandered to the stairs and sat on the bottom step with her chin in her hands. Catching her looking, Chloe cried, 'You're still blaming me.'

'No, I'm not . . .'

'Yes you are, I can tell,' and bursting into tears she turned on her heel and stormed up to her room to start throwing things around.

Ignoring the noise, Anthony said, 'If we're not going anywhere I might as well open the cellar door.'

'Which would be much more enjoyable than having a picnic with us,' Charlotte retorted scathingly.

His eyes turned flinty. 'We have a business to run . . .'

'We agreed it could close today.'

'There's no point now,' and grabbing his laptop he started outside.

'Do you know what I think?' Charlotte shouted after him. 'I think *you* hid them because you didn't want to go in the first place.'

He strode on across the lawn and down through the vines, pausing only to straighten a net before he disappeared.

Sighing as she rested her aching head against Elodie's, Charlotte said to a very unhappy-looking Cooper, 'Will you help me to unload the car?'

'Are we still going to have our picnic?' he asked.

'On the lawn, like I said.'

'Is Daddy coming?'

'I don't know.'

'I want Daddy to come.'

Realising he was about to cry, Charlotte turned away before she said something to make matters worse.

'I want Daddy,' Cooper wailed. 'You shouldn't have shouted at him, Mummy. It's all your fault.'

'Yes, of course it is,' Charlotte mumbled, wrapping Elodie more tightly in her arms, while upstairs Chloe continued to rant and thump and kick and smash up whatever she was getting her hands on.

*

Down at the cellar door, Anthony was setting out wines for tasting, thinking of Chloe with fury and frustration. He didn't understand her, had no idea how to control, or appease her, much less how to reach her. She'd hidden the keys all right, he'd been able to tell by the way she'd looked at him – it was as though she was punishing him by spoiling the day out, which was crazy when it was her special treat, not his.

Picking up his mobile he tried calling Charlotte. She didn't answer, probably because she was still too angry, so he left a message saying he was sorry and asking if he was still invited to the picnic.

He'd go, of course, and somehow make himself do a better job of setting aside the stress he'd been under since talking with Kim Thorp last night.

The Australian order was in jeopardy.

After dealing with a group of Indonesian wine buffs who'd wandered in from the road, he connected to Kim at Black Barn. 'Any news?' he asked.

'Not this morning,' Kim replied. 'It could take a while, a couple of weeks or more before we know anything for certain. I just wanted to give you a heads up in case it's true. I'll be in touch the minute I hear anything.'

Ringing off, Anthony abruptly threw the phone into the courtyard as if it might in some way alleviate the frustration building to fever pitch inside him. He didn't want to share what he'd learned with Charlotte until it was certain the rumours were true. If so, they were ruined.

I had the worst, the most horrible dream last night. The man who says he's a friend of my real daddy's reached out of the computer and pulled me inside. Then I was in a big, spooky house, and a very scary woman who everyone said was my real mummy kept banging my head on the floor. She wouldn't stop even though I was crying. Next, my daddy was there and I was so terrified I wet myself. I kept trying to scream for Mummy, but no sound was coming out. Then Mummy was there, but she didn't look at me. She was carrying Cooper and Elodie and walking away. I shouted out to her, but she didn't turn round, so I ran after her and went to get a knife. I was trying to stab myself and pull my hair and scratch my face to pieces.

When I woke up my bed was wet, and Mummy was stroking my face, but I thought she was going to start banging my head so I ran away and tried to find a knife. Anthony caught me and held me so tight I couldn't move.

I don't want to have a dream like that again, but I'm afraid I will, because I can't stop thinking about it. The man who says he's a friend of my real daddy's keeps messaging me. He says he's very sad that I'm not answering him, especially when he knows I'm there. I just look at the screen and try to think of something to say, but nothing comes.

This morning Anthony got someone to repair the window in my bedroom. I don't know how it got broken, I think I might have tried to jump out in my dream, but I can't really remember.

Anyway, it doesn't matter, because it's mended now, but I'm not going to open it, because I don't want anyone to come in and get me.

Chapter Nine

Almost two weeks had passed since the day out that didn't happen, and it was as though they were sliding slowly but inexorably into a whole other dimension of family hell. Anthony had become so stressed he was virtually impossible to talk to, and Chloe was even more erratic in her behaviour, especially towards to the little ones. She'd had several nightmares too, but she'd never say what they were about. Each time she wet the bed and punched and kicked herself, and raged so savagely that she made her mouth bleed. Worse was the way she could be perfectly calm one minute, and the next she'd start threatening to kill them all.

Charlotte hadn't read any more of Polly's blog since the entry about Roxanne sabotaging a family day out and the husband leaving; crazy as it seemed, she was starting to feel that by engaging with it her subconscious was seizing on some ghastly form of mimicry to make the same happen.

If she believed that, she was surely losing her mind.

So was Chloe. She was showing so many signs of going the same way as her birth mother in the peculiar things she said or did, not to mention the random, even terrifying, bursts of aggression, that Charlotte was fearing it more as each day passed.

'Call me Ottilie,' she'd growl out of nowhere, her eyes glittering a malicious challenge. 'It's my name. I want you to call me Ottilie.'

Charlotte ignored it, just like she was ignoring so much else, including the fact that Chloe had hidden the car keys – in Cooper's kindi bag, presumably to get him into trouble – the day they were due to go to Cape Kidnappers. Though it seemed a minor issue when compared to everything else she did, it continued to grate with Charlotte, for she simply didn't understand why Chloe would want to wreck her own day out.

Because somewhere in her tortured psyche she hadn't felt she deserved it? Or was it because Cooper and Elodie were coming too?

She still hadn't tackled Chloe about it because she simply couldn't face the lies or the tantrum that would be bound to follow. She'd told Anthony she'd found them in the fridge, which could only mean that she'd left them there without thinking while putting something away.

'You lied to Daddy,' Chloe accused when they sat down to some social studies later in the day. (At least she'd called him Daddy on that occasion, a rare event these days.) 'You told him the keys were in the fridge, but they weren't.'

Charlotte regarded her coldly. 'Does that mean you know where they were?' she challenged.

Apparently realising she'd walked herself into a trap, Chloe ignored the question and said she was tired so she didn't want to do any lessons today.

Charlotte didn't doubt she was tired, she'd been up in the night and Charlotte wasn't sure for how long. She only knew that something had woken her and when she'd tiptoed out to the landing to investigate who might be out of bed she'd found Chloe, wide awake, in Elodie's room, standing over the cot and staring in.

'What are you doing?' Charlotte asked, an unsteady thump in her heart.

Chloe spun round. 'I'm not doing anything,' she protested.

'So why are you in here?'

'I thought I heard her cry so I came to see if she was all right.'

Charlotte went to check on Elodie, and seeing she was awake and needed her nappy adjusting she lifted her into her arms. 'Go back to bed,' she said to Chloe.

'I don't want to.'

'I'm not arguing . . . Don't do that!' she cried, as Chloe kicked her and tried to thump Elodie. 'Do as you're told or I'll wake Daddy and let him deal with you.'

Invoking the threat of Anthony didn't always work, but fortunately on that occasion it had, although Charlotte probably wouldn't have woken him because he'd started getting up before dawn most mornings.

With the picking of early-season fruit under way he was gone right through the day, not returning home until it was time to read Cooper a story, during which he usually fell asleep himself. Chloe didn't want stories any more, she just wanted to be left alone to read a book or play a game on her iPad. She didn't even want to go to the bistro with Rick, and when Olivia Munds rang to invite her over for tea she told Charlotte to tell Olivia to drop dead. Of course Charlotte didn't, but when Sara Munds came on to the line she did admit that she was finding Chloe very difficult these days.

'Do you have any idea when we might be told what's going to happen at the school?' she asked, sinking into a chair and feeling like she never wanted to get up again.

'It should be any time now,' Sara assured her. 'You sound tired.'

Exhausted was actually how Charlotte felt, but she was afraid if she admitted it it might just swell up and consume her, so all she said was, 'It's been a bit of a trying time lately, but it'll be fine. Thank you for inviting Chloe for tea and sorry she can't make it.'

As she rang off Rowan came in with Elodie.

'Where's Cooper?' Charlotte asked, taking the baby and smoothing a hand over her silky cheek.

'He's at Oliver Crouch's for a sleepover,' Rowan reminded her.

Charlotte felt strangely confused by the answer, as if it wasn't quite connecting. Was Cooper old enough for sleepovers? Had he done it before?

Yes, of course he had, and Oliver had slept here.

'I'm a bit worried about Elodie,' Rowan was saying. 'She seems to be running a fever again and she's hardly stopped crying all day. Poor thing has probably worn herself out.'

Touching a hand to Elodie's warm, damp brow, Charlotte said softly, 'It smells like her nappy needs changing.'

'It does, but I didn't want to wake her, and she kicked up really badly when I changed it earlier. I think she's a bit sore down there.'

Feeling her mouth turning dry, Charlotte said, 'I should have a look. She might need to see a doctor.' This couldn't be what she was thinking. She wouldn't allow it to be. She was tired, she reminded herself, run down, and not able to think straight.

Minutes later, upstairs in Elodie's room, Charlotte was staring at her precious little girl with a hand stuffed in her mouth to stifle the horror erupting all the way through her. She knew what she was looking at for she'd seen it often enough on children who'd been abused, including Chloe.

Realising she was close to panic, she forced herself to breathe and sat down next to Elodie. Her mind was full of the night she'd found Chloe next to the cot, then it was reeling back to the dreadful time that Chloe, aged three, had suffered from a similar inflammation.

Stop, just stop. It might look like vulvovaginitis, it might even be that, but there are other ways of getting it . . .

She tried to think if they'd changed washing powder lately, or used a different cream on Elodie, but she could hardly connect with the thoughts. Her mind was going off in too many directions . . . She should take her to a doctor, but if she did, given Chloe's history, the doctor would immediately be suspicious and the next thing she knew they'd be taking her precious baby away.

As if it were about to happen, she scooped Elodie up and held her tight.

They might take Cooper and Chloe too.

She couldn't let this happen.

She had to deal with it herself. No one must know about her suspicions, especially not Anthony; she was terrified of what he might do if he found out. She'd tell him, and Rowan, that she was taking Elodie to the doctor and when she came back she'd say it was just one of those baby things. While she was in the village she'd get some cream from the pharmacy. She'd look up what kind of cream online. It would treat the burning; they could clear it up in no time . . .

But that wasn't sorting the real problem.

What was she going to say to Chloe? She could already feel herself shrinking from the questions that needed asking, Chloe's heated denials, her fury and the way it was likely to erupt into violence . . .

What was happening? Their lives were turning into an unstoppable nightmare.

That night, for reasons she could barely explain, she went back on to Polly's blog.

This is singularly the worst thing that's ever happened to me. I knew it would happen, but I've been burying my head in the sand, pretending it would go away. I am being forced to choose between Roxanne and the rest of my family. I know where my duty and loyalties lie, but don't they belong to Roxanne too? I'm all she has in the world. If I give her up I can't bear to think of what it might do to her, or what it'll do to me. I'll never stop worrying about her, or feeling that I should have, could have done more. I will never be able to get away from the fact that I've ruined her life, and I'm sure it will be ruined if I hand her into care now at her age.

She's still threatening physical harm to the younger ones if they come to visit, so is it any wonder that my husband refuses to bring them? He keeps asking me if I want her to destroy our marriage, if I'm using her as some sort of excuse to be rid of him, which is hardly fair, but I know how frustrated and helpless he's feeling too. Yesterday he reminded me of what the psychologists believe, that Roxanne would do better as an only child, but what statistics are there to prove this? I must try to find out, but even if it's worked for some, who's to say it will for Roxanne, and who is going to take her in at her age with all her problems? Are they really just going to melt away if she goes into a foster home where there are no other children?

I realise how conceited this sounds, but in spite of everything I truly believe I'm the one she needs, and that no one will love her as much as I do. I want to carry on giving her a chance, but it's killing me to be parted from the other two, and it's not doing them any good either. I love them so much, I wish I could explain things in a way they'd understand, but how can I expect so much of them when they're still so young and we barely understand things ourselves.

If I didn't love Roxanne so much, if I were unable to see the frightened, vulnerable little girl behind the monster's mask, this might be easier. Who am I kidding? Nothing about it will ever be easy.

I'm truly at the end of my tether.

Charlotte was so shaken – and terrified – by the entry that she immediately tried to find the next, only to discover that there were no more. She felt so panicked that it took her a while to remember that Anthony was still with her, that no one was asking her to make the same choice, that in spite of the similarities in their stories she wasn't Polly and Chloe wasn't Roxanne.

She continued to search, feeling a frantic need to contact Polly, but she could find no email address, or phone number, or anything else that could connect her. Polly and her family had turned to ghosts in a cyber world. It was as though they no longer existed, were maybe even a figment of her tortured imagination. It felt like the emotional equivalent of a sudden crash – one minute they were there, the next they'd gone. There was no way to get hold of them, nothing to tell Charlotte what decision Polly had made, or what she and her family were doing now, three years on from that last desperate posting.

Her only hope, she decided, was to email one of the other parents who'd responded to the blog and ask if they knew anything, or if they had a way of passing a message on.

Dear Emily Burrows,

I know I'm very late to Polly Greenborough's blog, but I'm extremely eager to know how Polly and her family are now if you're able to tell me. I am in a similar situation with my own adoptive daughter and I hardly know where to turn. It's probably too much to ask of Polly to give me some advice, but I would find it very helpful to know what she decided to do about Roxanne and how things have turned out.

The following morning Charlotte did as she'd planned. She told Rowan she was going to the doctor with Elodie and instead went to the pharmacy. By the time she got home Elodie seemed brighter, and when Charlotte undressed her to apply the new balm she was sure the inflammation had gone down.

So perhaps it had nothing to do with Chloe.

'Mummy, good girl,' Elodie gurgled, waving her hands and feet in the air like a small baby.

Charlotte's heart flooded with love. This was the first time she'd heard Elodie say anything more than Mummy, Daddy and Wo wo, her name for Rowan. 'Yes, my darling, you're a very good girl,' she told her.

Elodie gave an excited squeal and held out her arms to be picked up.

Since she was seeming so much better Charlotte reluctantly handed her over to Rowan, feeling sure she'd be OK at nursery for a couple of hours, which would give her some time to talk to Chloe.

'She came down for breakfast,' Rowan said on her way out, 'but she went back upstairs when she'd finished and I haven't seen her since.'

Bracing herself, Charlotte got partway up the

stairs when the phone rang. Expecting it to be Rick reminding her that he'd have to leave the cellar door at two, she returned to the kitchen and clicked on.

'Mrs Goodman. It's Pania Brown, from CYFS.'

Thinking of how much she could do without this call right now, Charlotte sank into a chair and said, 'Hi Pania. How are you?' Her head was throbbing so badly it seemed possible Pania could hear it.

'I'm very well thank you. I'm ringing because I'd like to have a talk with you about Chloe. Well, of course about Chloe. I've been having a few thoughts I'd like to share with you if you have the time.'

Not sure how keen she was to hear them, Charlotte said, 'Would you like to come here? Or is it something we can discuss on the phone?'

'Well, perhaps I can start things off on the phone and we can get together after you've had some time to think.'

About what?

Taking a breath, Pania said, 'I'm afraid this might not be easy to hear, but I've talked it over with one of our psychologists and we both wondered if you've been having the same thoughts yourself.'

'What are they?' Charlotte prompted, hearing her voice as though it were a long way away.

As she listened to Pania's answer she felt the room starting to spin. It was as though Polly was coming to life through Pania, speaking the words she'd written, sharing the fate, the devastation and terrifying recommendations . . .

'Are you still there, Mrs Goodman?' Pania asked. 'I realise this . . .'

Catching Chloe trying to sneak out of the door, Charlotte said, 'I'm sorry, I'll have to call you back,' and clicking off the line she tried to steady herself as she barked to Chloe, 'Where are you going?'

'Nowhere,' Chloe scowled.

'What's in the bag?'

Chloe hiked her flowery holdall higher on her shoulder. 'Nothing.'

'It doesn't look like nothing, so come here please.'

'I can't. I'm in a hurry.'

'To go where?' This was happening in another place, a dream, a virtual nightmare . . .

Shouting, Chloe said, 'If you must know, I'm leaving home and *I won't be coming back*.'

As the words assailed her, Charlotte's insides turned to liquid. She felt sick. Chloe's aggression seemed to fill the room; it was suffocating, deafening, overwhelming . . .

'See, you don't care,' Chloe cried, 'so I'm going. *Going, going, going*.'

'I don't know what more I can do to show I care,' Charlotte called after her, feeling dazzled, dizzied by the sun as she followed her on to the terrace. 'Let's sit here on the grass and have a chat,' she suggested, realising she barely had the strength to carry on standing.

'I don't want to chat. I want to leave.'

Pulling up a chair Charlotte sat down at the table. 'OK. So what's your plan?' she asked, feeling as though her voice belonged to somebody else.

Chloe's eyes narrowed. 'What do you mean?'

'Well, when you get to the end of the drive, where are you intending to go?'

Clearly not liking the question, Chloe said, 'I don't know. Anywhere.'

'Do you have money?'

'I've got some.'

'I don't expect it's enough to get a bus . . .'

'I'm catching a *plane*, to England.'

Charlotte said, 'And what are you aiming to do when you get there, presuming you do?'

'If you must know I'm going to find my real mummy and daddy.'

The throb in her head was explosive. 'Chloe, you know very well you won't find them, so please stop doing this.'

'It's only *you* who says I won't,' Chloe raged, 'but you're lying, I know you are, because I've found one of my real daddy's friends.'

Charlotte turned to ice. Had she heard that right? She couldn't have. 'Stop!' she shouted as Chloe turned away. 'Stop right there.'

Chloe turned round, hands on hips.

'What do you mean you've found one of his friends?' Charlotte demanded.

'It was a joke,' Chloe cried. 'Don't you know a joke when you hear one?'

Charlotte tried to take a breath, but it wasn't easy. Her vision was blurring in the sunshine, and strange colours, lights were flashing in her eyes. She could hear Pania's voice like a distant echo, feel Polly's despair . . .

'Chloe if you've done something . . .' she mumbled. Her hands were starting to shake so badly that her whole body was reacting.

'I haven't done anything,' Chloe shouted. 'You always think I have and that's why . . .' Her eyes began to dilate, and her face turned white as Charlotte slumped forward. 'Mummy? What are you doing?' she gasped, running to her. 'Don't do that! Get up . . . *Mummy! Get up.*'

Anthony was in the winery with Will. Both men's expressions were grim as they read the email Kim Thorp had rung to let them know was on its way. It was the news Anthony had been dreading; the rumours Kim had heard were true, the Australian company who'd bought their outstanding stock of Pinot Gris had gone bust.

'Did we ever receive a deposit?' Will asked.

'I've been chasing it,' Anthony replied, turning at

the sound of a car pulling up outside. It was Zoe, back from Auckland.

'Hi guys,' she said cheerily. 'I hope you've missed me.'

Will glanced at Anthony.

Directing her to his laptop, Anthony said, 'Read the email on the screen and tell me what you know about this.'

Frowning, and clearly surprised by his tone, she went to the desk and tilted forward to read.

Anthony's eyes went to Will. It appeared his focus had switched to the wine press, where the early fruit was on its first path to fermentation.

'Oh my god,' Zoe murmured, pressing a hand to her mouth. She turned to Anthony, wide-eyed with shock. 'I don't know what to say,' she told him. 'Are you sure this is true?'

'If you look at the sender's address you'll know it is.'

Apparently she already had, for she didn't look again. 'I'm truly sorry,' she cried, making to touch his arm and withdrawing again. 'If I'd known they were in trouble . . . I swear I didn't. I'd never have put you together if I had.'

'Where's the wine now?' Will asked Anthony.

'That's what we need to find out,' Anthony replied, checking his phone as it rang. Seeing it was Charlotte he was tempted to let it go to messages, but thinking of the children he clicked on.

'Daddy! Daddy!' Chloe screamed down the phone. 'It's Mummy. She's on the ground and she won't get up.'

Stunned, Anthony tried to make himself think. 'What do you mean, she's on the ground?'

'She fell there. She was shaking, but she's stopped now, but she won't open her eyes.'

Grabbing his keys, he said, 'Where are you?'

'At home. Daddy, you have to come. I'm scared.'

'Don't worry, I'm on my way,' and running to the car he shouted to Will, 'Find that damned wine and let's hope to god it hasn't already left the country.'

Chapter Ten

Anthony was slumped in an armchair next to his and Charlotte's bed with his eyes closed. The blinds were partly down, preventing too much sunlight from flooding in as he fought off the exhaustion of waiting and worrying and tearing himself apart with guilt and dread. Charlotte was going to be fine, the doctor had assured him of that when he'd discharged her from hospital; she just needed to take things easy for a while.

'Stress can manifest itself in all sorts of ways,' the doctor had continued kindly, 'and I'm pretty sure from what I've heard and seen that that's what we're dealing with here.'

Given what Anthony knew of the pressure Charlotte had been under, he was prepared to believe him. However, what he wasn't prepared to do was forgive himself for having pushed her this far.

It wasn't working out for them here.

As hard as that was to admit, and as goddamned clueless as he felt about the future, he had to face the fact that they'd given it their best shot, and it simply hadn't been good enough. They were out of money – worse, they were actually in debt – and even if they managed to get back the wine that was on its way to Australia, it would only return them to the position they'd been in before. They were unable to afford any more storage, or to employ the staff they needed to help run Charlotte's side of the business, or to pay the pickers for this year's vintage. Whichever way he looked at it, they simply couldn't continue.

How the hell was he supposed to break that to her? When was it ever going to be a right time? Certainly not now, when she was only waking long enough to ask for Elodie, or to use the bathroom. Just Elodie, never Cooper or Chloe. It was as though she'd forgotten they existed.

'I'm fine, I'm fine,' she'd insisted when she'd woken earlier and tried to climb out of bed. 'I need to see Elodie . . .'

'I'll bring her to you,' he'd soothed, easing her back to the pillows. 'You need to rest. The doctor said at least a week.'

'No, not that long. Where's Elodie? Is she all right?'

'She's fine. So are Cooper and Chloe. Your mother's taking care of them.'

'My mother? Are the children in Kerikeri?'

'No, your mother and Bob arrived yesterday.' It had alarmed him to know that she'd seen and spoken to them, but apparently didn't remember they were there.

She was sleeping again now, with Elodie dozing beside her. Anthony didn't want to leave her side in spite of his mother-in-law's insistence that he also needed some rest.

'Will is perfectly capable of taking care of things at the winery,' Bob had pointed out earlier, 'and don't forget I have a vineyard myself. I'll grant you not as big a deal as this one, but I understand the business so I can give Will as much backup as he needs.'

'With a broken foot?'

'That's well on the mend. You just concentrate on your wife and family and leave the business to me.'

Bob must surely know by now what a mess things were in, but he hadn't mentioned it and Anthony wasn't ready to bring it up either. He needed to think things through, decide what their next steps should be, if they should even stay in New Zealand. At least in England he could return to practising law, but Charlotte wouldn't want to go back. The schools were better here, her mother was a short flight away and the quality of life all round was far superior to that in the overcrowded and overstressed UK.

Nothing could happen, one way or another, until he'd sold the vineyard, and god only knew how much of a hit he was going to take there.

Not once had it crossed his mind that it wouldn't work out for them here; even now he was having a hard time making himself accept it – until he looked at Charlotte and thought about how much she must have been suffering without him knowing, or even wanting to know.

What a selfish, egotistical bastard he was.

'Hey you,' Charlotte whispered croakily.

Immediately coming to, Anthony reached for her hand. If he'd ever been in any doubt during these stressful times about how much he loved her, these past few days had put him completely straight. She and the children meant everything in the world to him, and always would. 'Hey,' he whispered back.

Her eyes seemed clearer than earlier, her skin slightly less pale.

'How are you feeling?' he ventured.

She frowned as she thought, and glanced around the bedroom. 'A bit strange, but OK I think.' She turned to Elodie and touched a kiss to her cheek. 'How long's she been asleep?'

'A few minutes. Your mother fed and changed her just now and brought her back again.' Having Elodie with her had seemed to calm her, so Elodie had been here for most of the time these past two days.

'*Mum* fed and changed . . . Oh yes, you told me she was here. She didn't need to come. She has Bob and Shelley to take care of.'

'Bob came too. He's still limping but doing OK, and apparently Shelley's had her last treatment.'

Charlotte was still gazing at Elodie. 'That's good,' she said. 'How is she?'

'Doing fine, I think, but Anna will be able to tell you more.'

Charlotte turned to look at him and as their eyes met he brought her hand to his lips. 'I'm sorry,' he murmured. 'I should never have let this happen . . .'

'Ssh, it's not your fault. Anyway, what did happen?'

'You had some kind of a blackout they're saying was caused by stress.' He wouldn't bother telling her that they'd suspected a seizure at first as they'd ruled it out now, thank goodness. 'You've had too much to cope with,' he told her, 'the business, this house, the children, Chloe in particular . . . We can't allow things to go on like this.'

Using her fingers to wipe the tears from his cheeks, she said, 'I've never seen you cry before.'

He smiled. 'I guess I've never been so worried about you before – or realised how much I love you.'

Her eyes softened as she stroked his face. 'I was afraid you might have stopped.'

Kissing her hand again, he said, 'That's never going to happen.'

She smiled and looked past him as someone knocked on the door.

'I thought I heard voices,' Anna said, putting her head round. She was blonde and slim and looked very like the older version of Charlotte that she was. 'Can I come in?'

Anthony rose to his feet, feeling the stiffness in his legs from having sat for so long.

'How's the patient?' Anna asked, coming to sit on the edge of the bed.

'I'm fine,' Charlotte assured her. 'You didn't need to come all this way, honestly.'

'Well there's a nice greeting,' Anna commented wryly. 'And was I really going to pass up a chance to spend some time with my only daughter and three wonderful grandchildren?'

'I didn't come into it?' Anthony enquired.

Laughing, Charlotte said, 'Where are Chloe and Cooper?'

Anna glanced at Anthony. 'Bob's just taken Cooper to the village, and Chloe's in her room.'

'Is she all right?'

Anthony said, 'You gave her a bit of a scare. She's been pretty quiet since.'

Charlotte struggled to sit up. 'I should talk to her.'

Again Anna looked at Anthony. 'I'll go and get her,' she said, 'but tell me first that you're ready for something to eat.'

'Are you kidding? Whatever you're offering, please double the helping.'

After her mother had gone, Charlotte said to

Anthony, 'Would you mind if I have a few minutes alone with Chloe?'

'Of course not. Shall I take Elodie?'

'Yes, you probably should.'

As he lifted the baby on to his shoulder, he said, 'You don't have to give me an answer now, but your mother and Bob have agreed to stay with the children if you'll let me take you to Lake Taupo for a couple of days. I think we need some time for the two of us.'

Charlotte's eyes were suffused with feeling. Lake Taupo was where they'd spent their honeymoon.

'Of course we won't go until you feel up to it,' he continued, 'but I thought it might be a good place to carry on getting some rest.'

With a mischievous twinkle she said, 'Rest?'

'It was a euphemism,' he assured her.

As the door closed behind him Charlotte's smile faded. A predatory dark cloud was closing in on her. She'd been awake for longer than she'd let on, watching him doze, loving him and feeling for his concern, but shutting her eyes each time he started to wake. Though she'd wanted him to lie with her and hold her, she'd remained still and silent as she thought about Chloe and the suggestion Pania had made, and how deeply it had resonated with Polly's experience.

'Have you ever considered that Chloe might be

better off with a parent, or parents, who have no other children to distract them?' Pania had said.

It was what had tipped her over the edge, she was in no doubt of it, and realising she was starting to feel panicky again, she took several breaths and reminded herself over and over that it was only a suggestion that she didn't have to agree with, much less go along with.

'Mummy,' Chloe whispered, putting her head around the door.

Seeing her sweet, frightened face, Charlotte held out her arms and Chloe ran straight into them.

'I'm sorry,' Chloe sobbed. 'I didn't mean to make you ill. I wasn't really going to run away. I promise.'

'I know, I know,' Charlotte murmured, tears starting in her own eyes as she stroked Chloe's hair. 'Don't upset yourself now. Everything's going to be all right. I promise. Everything's going to turn out just fine.'

With her mother and Rick helping Rowan to take care of the children and cellar door, and Bob overseeing everything at the winery, it was easy for Charlotte and Anthony to escape for two days, even to put everything out of their minds for a while. They really were in sore need of spending some time together, of rediscovering the importance of having fun, feeling close and making love, which was why Charlotte had yet to mention anything about her decision to take Chloe to England. She didn't want to spoil this special time at Lake Taupo, and she knew that once they got on to the subject of the future everything would change. They'd talk about nothing else; there might even be no more lovemaking, and she really didn't want that to happen any time soon.

It wasn't that she'd forgotten how powerfully he could make her want him, or how aroused she became simply to watch his hands on her body, or to see his beloved eyes darkening with desire, she simply hadn't allowed herself the time these past months to connect with it. Now, she felt that they had returned to being a part of the same world, the same marriage, and even during the moments they weren't making love they were together in a way they hadn't been in too long.

It was early evening now, and they were lying on the same bed they had shared during their honeymoon here at Tauhara Sunrise Lodge. It might not be as grand as some places around Taupo, but it was certainly as luxurious, and with its spectacular view of the lake through the vast picture window of their private cottage, it was infinitely more romantic.

Charlotte was resting against Anthony's shoulder, a sheet barely covering her as she gazed across the water to the mountain beyond known as the pregnant lady. She was remembering how Anthony had run his hands over her pregnant belly the last time they were here, how close they'd felt then with Cooper on the way, and how they'd even discussed naming the baby after the mountain.

'Tauhara,' Anthony murmured.

Charlotte turned to him.

'Isn't that the name of the mountain?' he asked.

'Yes,' she smiled, 'the same as the lodge. I was just trying to remember it and here you are answering my questions without me even asking.'

'Let that be a warning,' he teased. 'I can read your mind.'

Thankful that he couldn't while she was hiding so much, she sat up and reached for a robe. This was their last night; they were driving home tomorrow, so she needed to talk to him now.

After pouring them both a Scotch, she watched him slip into his own robe and went to join him on the sofa.

'You're looking worried,' he told her as she touched her glass to his.

She attempted a smile. 'I have something to tell you that isn't going to be easy.'

Though his eyes narrowed, his tone was light as he said, 'Whatever it is, I'm on your side.'

Knowing there was a chance he might not be once she'd revealed her plans, she bolstered her courage with a sip of Scotch.

To her relief the first words came easily enough. 'I've decided to take Chloe to England.'

Clearly surprised, he said, 'When?'

'Soon. I think she needs to go.'

'You mean so you can prove her birth mother's dead and her father's in prison?'

'Partly, but she doesn't really need proof of that; she knows it's true. I just think going there, or getting away from here for a while, might do us both some good.'

He remained silent, waiting for her to continue.

Taking a breath she said, 'The day I collapsed I had received a call from the young woman at CYFS. She said that she'd discussed Chloe with a psychologist collcague and they wanted to bring me in on a theory – did she call it a theory? She might not have used that word . . . Anyway, what they were wondering was whether Chloe might benefit from being an only child.'

Anthony frowned. 'But she's already got a brother and sister, so . . .' He stopped as suspicion sharpened his eyes. 'Please don't tell me you're planning to leave us and be a mother to her in England.'

It had crossed her mind, but how could she give up her own children and the man she loved to go and live a life she didn't want? 'No, that's not what I'm saying.'

'Then you need to spell it out.'

Taking another fortifying sip of her drink, she said, 'It didn't really come as a shock to me when the woman from CYFS said what she did . . . Well, it did, I hated it, I wanted to scream at her that she was a fool and they had no right to be making such a terrible suggestion for a girl who was a very important part of our family . . .' She put a hand to her head as the horror of those moments unsteadied her.

'Charlotte . . .'

'No, you have to listen, please. I'm not saying I think they're right, but I need to talk to someone I know and trust, someone who knows all about Chloe and her history, and that person is in England.'

'You're talking about Wendy, your old boss?'

Charlotte nodded.

After mulling this over for a while, he said, 'And what if she agrees with the suggestion?'

Charlotte's eyes closed as her heart wrenched. 'I don't know. I guess I'll have to deal with that when, if, it happens, but if you think about it you'll see that it does make a certain sense for Chloe to be an only child. She's different to other children. She shouldn't be, and wouldn't be if she hadn't been born to such terrible parents. We can't erase that, any more than we can wipe out the damage that's been done. It haunts her, it drives her and as time goes on it's getting worse.' She took a breath. 'We both know she hasn't been happy since the others came along, especially since Elodie . . . I guess it's because of having another girl in the family. My attention's split three ways now instead of one, actually more ways if we include you and the business. However we look at it, she's a child with far greater needs than most, and this past year has shown us that we're not dealing with them. We're doing our best, but . . .' Her hand went up as he seemed about to interrupt. 'I know you're going to say I'm jumping ahead, that we need to hear from the school, to explore all the possible backup we could get here, but I need to do something now and this feels right.'

'OK, I can see that, but you're her world, Charlotte. You've got to know that whatever anyone says you can't possibly give her to somebody else, somebody you don't even know. It'll break her heart and it'll break yours.'

Knowing he was right, Charlotte wanted to howl and cry with despair as she said, 'It might not come to that. I'm hoping, praying it won't, but you have to ask yourself, what if it *is* best for her? What if it's best for our family?'

'How can it be? Charlotte, have you forgotten how hard you fought for her? Yes, she's a handful . . .'

'She's more than that and you know it, and I've no idea how much worse it might get. But what I do know, or what I'm afraid of, is that she's already done things to Elodie . . .'

He became very still. His eyes were at their fiercest as he regarded her, taking in the enormity of what she'd just said. 'What sort of things?' he growled. 'Jesus Christ. How long have you kept this from me?'

'A few days, no more. I needed to be sure before I told you because I knew you wouldn't want her to stay if it was happening . . .'

'And is it?'

'The only way I can be certain is to take Elodie to a doctor . . .'

'So you did. And?'

'I didn't, I couldn't, because I was afraid that they'd end up taking her away.'

Clearly stunned by the answer, he said, 'So you let it carry on? Christ, Charlotte . . .'

'No, of course I didn't. As soon as I suspected I made sure never to let them be alone together.'

'We need some proper answers to this,' he told her darkly. 'We have to take Elodie to a doctor . . .'

'Don't you think I want to, but you and I both know what powers the authorities have when it comes to child protection. If they thought Elodie was in any danger they could take her . . .' She broke off as he got to his feet and started to pace, afraid of what he must be thinking, of what he was going to say next.

After pouring himself another drink he came back to the window and stood staring at the darkening sky. Only he knew what terrible emotions were raging away inside him, but Charlotte could imagine.

After a while, she said, 'I thought I'd ask your sister, Maggie, if Chloe and I could stay there for a while. I'd ask my own sister, but . . .'

Turning around, he said, 'Maggie's the right choice, she'll help you . . .' Suddenly realising how close she was to the edge, he went to her quickly and pulled her into his arms. 'It'll be OK,' he assured her. 'You're doing the right thing, getting advice from someone you know, someone who did everything in her power to make it possible for you to adopt Chloe. She'll know what to do for the best.'

Though Anthony felt sick to his stomach about what might have been happening to Elodie, it was the thought of Chloe going to England and never returning that was really tearing him apart by the time they drove home the following day. He simply couldn't see how they'd be able to live with themselves if they ended up letting her go. But allowing her to stay if she was harming Elodie . . . They couldn't permit even the slightest possibility of Elodie becoming a victim of abuse – any more than they could run the risk of her being taken into care.

Reaching for Charlotte's hand, he gave it a comforting squeeze. There was absolutely no question of him telling her about the trouble they were in at the vineyard; she didn't need any more to be coping with, and since there was nothing she could do anyway the problems had to remain entirely his.

'Have you discussed any of this with your mother yet?' he asked, as they approached Havelock North.

Charlotte was staring blindly out of the window as she shook her head. 'She'll be upset when I tell her, obviously, but she'll understand when I explain about Elodie, and what some experts think about the benefits of a traumatised child being an only child. I'm hoping she might stay on to take care of you all while I'm gone.'

Feeling certain that Anna would, he said, 'How long do you think that'll be?'

'I'm not sure. A few weeks. I don't want to be away from the little ones for any longer than that, or you, but in this instance deciding what's best for Chloe has to come first.'

He didn't argue, because he agreed, but thinking of the ordeal that lay ahead for Charlotte was bothering him a lot.

'You know what I'm finding really hard right now?' Charlotte said, gazing out at the familiar shops and cafes of the village as they drove through. 'It's how thrilled she's going to be when I tell her we're going to England, just her and me.'

It's very late, but I'm too excited to go to sleep. Mummy and I are flying to England tomorrow, just us, no one else, not even Anthony or Cooper or Elodie. We're going to stay with Auntie Maggie and Uncle Ron in their new house by the seaside, and we'll be doing all sorts of things while we're there. I've already thought up lots of ideas, but I'm keeping them a secret from Mummy so they'll be a surprise.

My real daddy's friend wants to know when I'm going to get there so we can meet, but I can't give him Auntie Maggie's address because I don't know it yet. I'm not sure I want to see him anyway. He's been asking me to do all sorts of bad things lately, like sending him pictures of Elodie with no clothes on, or showing her how to feel nice between the legs. It's wrong to do that, even though it really does feel nice. Elodie's too little, and he should know better.

I'm beginning to think he's the kind of man who'd do the same to her as my real daddy did to me, but I don't ever think about that because it was horrible and wrong and I was really, really scared of him.

I think I might leave Boots behind to show that I'm growing up now. He'll be sad without me, but I'll be coming back so he doesn't need to worry.

I wish I could go to sleep, because when I wake up it'll be time to leave and I'll be the happiest, most excitedest girl in the whole wide world.

Chapter Eleven

Almost five years had passed since Charlotte had left Kesterly-on-Sea, but for how alien it felt with its dreary Victorian town houses and tired old promenade, not to mention the dismal weather and oppressively low skies, it could have been twenty-five years. Here the sea was grey, the surf muddied and tame, while the trees rose nakedly between empty flower beds and the beach was littered and sad. To be fair she'd come straight from a New Zealand summer into the middle of an English winter, so the town clearly wouldn't be at its best. In the height of the season it came alive with tourists, novelty stalls, fish-and-chip shops, donkeys, weird and wonderful street acts, and sunshine if they were lucky.

She'd obviously become so integrated into New Zealand that she was finding it hard to connect with the fact that this had been her home for the best part of thirty years. True, she'd lived in a village about half an hour inland, but Kesterly was where she'd gone to school, attended college and to where she'd returned after uni to start her career in child protection for the local authority. She used to love it here, had never imagined leaving – now she couldn't imagine ever coming back.

'Almost there,' Ron said, casting a smile her way. He was Anthony's brother-in-law and couldn't have resembled a slimline Santa more if he'd tried. Like his wife, Maggie, who was waiting for them at home, he was almost fifteen years older than Anthony, but that didn't mean they weren't close as a family, for Maggie adored her brother. She and Ron had come to visit every Christmas since Anthony had left, and they were in regular contact by email or Skype.

There hadn't been too many Skype calls recently, which Charlotte felt bad about, even though she knew Maggie and Ron understood what a busy time of year this was in Hawkes Bay.

'Is she still asleep?' Ron asked as a red light brought them to a stop at the junction of the promenade and North Road.

Glancing over her shoulder to check on Chloe, Charlotte felt a rush of emotion tightening her throat. What memories did Chloe have of this place, most particularly the road to their left that Charlotte knew Ron would be careful to avoid? It was where Chloe had spent the first three torturous years of her life until Charlotte had found and rescued her. The house didn't exist any more; it had been pulled down soon after the discovery of the paedophile ring Chloe's father had operated from a studio shed in the back garden. Apparently the flats built to replace it had recently been converted into a nursing home, but Charlotte had no idea if that were true; nor did she have any inclination to find out.

'Yes, she's still sleeping,' she said, turning back as they drove on. 'She's been very excited about coming.' It was heart-wrenchingly true, and now they were here Charlotte was wishing with all her soul that the visit was about something else. But if she didn't talk to Wendy and at least get some advice there was every chance the authorities in New Zealand would take Chloe in order to keep Elodie safe, and Charlotte simply couldn't allow that to happen.

Yet she was considering allowing them to take her here in England?

'Don't think about it now,' Anthony had advised when she'd called from the airport while Ron took Chloe to get a drink. 'You need time to get over the jet lag, it won't be possible to think straight about anything until you do.'

How she wished Anthony was with her now, yet at the same time it was a great comfort to know that he was with Cooper and Elodie. She could hardly bear to think of Cooper's tears when she and Chloe had left; he'd been desperate to come too, had clung to her begging her to forgive him for being naughty – he'd thought he was being punished – until Anthony had taken him away with a reminder that he needed help to run the vineyard. Chloe's smugness that she was the only one Mummy wanted to take with her hadn't helped at all. Had it not been for the truth of why they were going, and how harrowingly it might end, Charlotte might have given her a sharp telling-off; as it was she'd had to leave it to Anthony to warn Chloe that there would be no trip for her either if she didn't behave more kindly.

'Of course, you haven't been to the new house yet, have you?' Ron said chattily as they headed along the coast road towards the lower rises of Westleigh Park Mount. 'Maggie can't wait to show you.'

'And I can't wait to see it,' Charlotte replied truthfully. She knew it was one of the smart Georgian villas on exclusive Trefford Avenue overlooking the estuary, but neither her past lifestyle, nor journey home to Mulgrove village had given her cause to go that way often.

'Ah, here she is,' Ron declared as his mobile rang, and clicking on to the hands-free he said to Maggie, 'We're about five minutes away.'

'How are you feeling, Charlotte?' Maggie asked. 'Did you manage to nap in the car?'

'A little,' Charlotte replied. 'Chloe's still out for the count, so it looks like she'll be up half the night.'

'Not to worry about that, we'll soon have her

straightened out. Anthony just rang wanting to know if you'd arrived yet. He said he'll call again when he gets to the winery.'

Imagining him in the dawn hours, driving through the vines in their trusty Volvo, probably on the phone to Will, or catching up on the day's radio news, she closed her eyes. Maybe by now he was already out organising the pickers . . . Wherever he was, she ached to be with him. In past years she'd always helped with the harvest; everyone did, it was a joyous, strenuous undertaking that connected them to the very essence of winemaking in a way that nothing else could. She wouldn't be a part of it this year, but at least all the signs were for a good vintage.

Ron and Maggie's home turned out to be every bit as elegant and welcoming as Charlotte had felt certain it would be, for Maggie had a way of making a place feel loved and lived in just by being there herself. With her merry eyes, infectious smile and enveloping warmth she was as natural a homemaker as she was a mother. She had an extraordinary knack for making people feel safe, especially children, which was why she and Ron had taken up fostering when their own two had flown the nest. It was how she and Charlotte had met, when Charlotte had been forced to remove a troubled and troublesome young boy from his home on the notorious Temple Fields estate. She'd brought him to Maggie and Ron, and in just a few short days this remarkable couple had introduced the boy to talents and interests he didn't even know he had. Tragically for him his mother had been allowed to have him back, and Charlotte had no idea where he was now, though it was likely to be in a young offenders' unit along with several members of his extended family.

It had been a great loss to the community, not to mention disadvantaged children, when Maggie had decided she couldn't continue as a carer. She got too involved with her charges, and the emotional wear and tear had begun to affect her health.

'This place is wonderful,' Charlotte told her, looking around the large pale blue and white kitchen with its towering sash windows, hanging-rack pans and fireplace niche for the Aga. Past the deep sills full of herbs and candles there was a captivating view of the garden, and no doubt when the fog lifted the outlook down to the estuary would be one of the best in the area.

'It's lovely, Auntie Maggie,' Chloe informed her. 'Just like the photos you sent, but better.'

Embracing her, Maggie said, 'Oh, it's good to see you, my angel. Did you bring that rascal Boots the bear with you?'

Chloe twinkled as she glanced at Charlotte. 'Mummy thinks I don't know he's in the suitcase,' she confided. 'I said I was too old for him now, but I saw her sneak him in anyway.'

Charlotte was rigid with guilt. Once Chloe realised what was happening – if it did happen – she'd be as desperate for Boots as she'd been when she was her father's victim and the bear was her only friend.

'So did the flight seem *very* long?' Maggie asked, putting a glass of juice and a cookie in front of Chloe.

'It was OK, but I'm glad it's over. Mummy is too, aren't you Mummy?'

'Absolutely,' Charlotte confirmed, remarking how Chloe's best behaviour had taken no time at all to assert itself. It was the Maggie effect, of course, but it was also a part of getting her own way over coming here.

What on earth did she think was going to happen? Was she seeing this as a holiday? How long did she imagine they were staying? She hadn't asked, and Charlotte hadn't tried to explain anything; there would be plenty of time for that when it could no longer be avoided.

As a hearty meal was a staple in Maggie's kitchen, the one she had bubbling away on the Aga was ready to be served the instant Charlotte and Chloe returned from their rooms after freshening up. It was a delicious home-made lamb tagine, followed by upside-down pudding and lashings of cream. A hard feast for Charlotte to cope with at what was only seven in the morning for her and Chloe, but Chloe had no problem at all.

'Your sister's coming tomorrow,' Maggie announced over coffee and cocoa.

Charlotte's eyes widened with surprise as Chloe clapped her hands.

'Is she bringing the twins?' Chloe asked, referring to her ten-year-old cousins.

'I wouldn't expect so,' Maggie replied. 'They don't break up for Easter until the end of the week, but Auntie Gabby is very keen to see you.'

Since Anthony had rung both Gabby and Maggie while Charlotte was on the plane to let them know why she and Chloe were coming, Charlotte shouldn't have been surprised that her adoptive sister was making such an early visit. Though she loved Gabby dearly, she wasn't looking forward to what she might have to say about the reason Charlotte was here, and she could only feel thankful that Maggie and Ron were hiding their own feelings so well for now.

'I've made a list of all the places we want to see,' Chloe informed them, a moustache of frothy cream crowning her upper lip. 'Well, I want to see them and I think Mummy will too, because one of them is the village where she grew up, and the house where she hid me after rescuing me from my wicked first mummy and daddy.'

Noting the change of language – rescuing instead of stealing, wicked first parents – Charlotte said to Maggie, 'I should probably rent a car . . .'

'Oh, you can use one of ours,' Maggie insisted. 'Mine is smaller, so easier to park if you're going into town.'

She'd forgotten about the stress of trying to park, and traffic jams, and road rage, it never seemed to happen in Havelock North.

'Would you like to know what else is on my list?' Chloe asked chattily.

'Of course,' Maggie encouraged.

Intrigued, Charlotte listened as Chloe said, 'I want to ride on the carousel that Mummy used to take me to after nursery when I was three, and please can we go to the cafe where they have great big brownies that I ate all up even though I was only little. Oh yes, I thought Mummy would like to visit the cemetery where her grandparents, auntie and brother are buried, you know, the ones who were killed by the evil man who was really after Mummy and Nana, but they managed to escape.'

Since Charlotte herself had told Chloe about the carousel and brownies and even the tragedy that had robbed her and her mother of most of their family, it wasn't the listing of these things that surprised and touched her, it was how thrilled Chloe seemed to be at the prospect of doing something for her mother.

'Mummy and I both had evil daddies,' Chloe informed Maggie and Ron.

'Actually,' Charlotte said gently, 'if you remember,

the evil man who killed my family wasn't my daddy. He was Nana's husband at the time, and the reason he went berserk the way he did was because he found out that I wasn't his child.'

'Oh yes, that's right. Your real daddy was called Nigel and everyone thought he was Auntie Yvonne's boyfriend, but really he was Nana's. The evil man killed him too, and Auntie Yvonne. She was Nana's sister,' she told Maggie and Ron, in case they didn't know, which of course they did.

It had been dubbed the Temple Fields massacre, and was probably still known as that, though Charlotte doubted it came up often considering how long ago it had happened. Her mother's injuries had kept her hospitalised for a year after the frenzied attack, and she'd been so afraid that the monstrous Gavril Albescu wouldn't ever give up trying to find the innocent child that wasn't his, that she'd agreed to let the rector who'd discovered Charlotte hidden in an attic room adopt her to keep her safe. Anna, whose name had been Angela then, had eventually gone to join her best friend in New Zealand and had been there ever since.

It was during the months that Charlotte had been involved in Chloe's case, here in Kesterly, that her mother had come to find her, and together they'd ended up hiding Chloe while a nationwide search had been under way for her. Eventually, miraculously, they'd managed to smuggle her out of the country.

It felt like a dream now, or part of a story that someone had once told her, rather than something so deeply involving her. Of course she hadn't thought anything through, she'd acted out of instinct and love. Knowing that Chloe was too fragile for care, that she wouldn't even speak to anyone apart from her and Anna, she simply hadn't been able to hand her over to strangers.

So she'd kept her, and had ended up being arrested, repatriated to England and had even spent some time in prison before Maggie Fenn's brother, Anthony, had taken the case and got her out. Chloe had also been brought back to Kesterly, but not at the same time as Charlotte. A social worker had travelled to New Zealand to collect her from the authorities there, and as soon as she'd returned she'd been put into care. She'd stopped speaking, Charlotte had been told later, and because that was how she'd been when Charlotte had first found her, afraid to utter a word to anyone, it had broken Charlotte's heart to think of the tiny creature she loved so much feeling so lonely and afraid again.

She and Chloe had become the nation's love story during Charlotte's trial for child abduction; in spite of knowing she was guilty almost everyone had been rooting for her, wanting her to get off so she and Chloe could be together again.

Anthony, and the jury, had made it happen.

It turned her hot and cold all over to imagine

what that jury, or the public would think of what she was considering now. They'd all believed in the happy ending, that Charlotte and Anthony were taking the tragic, deserving little girl to a new country to start a new life where she'd be properly nurtured and loved and safe. And why shouldn't they have believed that, when Charlotte and Anthony had been in no doubt of it at the time? It had never occurred to anyone that Chloe's tragic past would rise up to torment her at such an early age; that having a brother and particularly a sister would antagonise the demons to such a horrifying degree. Nor would anyone ever have imagined that Charlotte would end up trying to protect her birth daughter by what she could only think of as casting out the cuckoo in the nest.

If it happened there was no reason for anyone ever to find out. She hoped to god they didn't, for the shame and guilt were already building to a horrible pitch; being on the receiving end of press condemnation and universal contempt would be beyond intolerable.

But it wasn't about her, it was about Chloe and what was best for her. Although Charlotte was already hating herself far more than anyone else ever could, seeing how differently Chloe was behaving now she had her mother's attention all to herself was starting to convince Charlotte that she really might fare better as an only child.

What had happened to Roxanne, she wondered. Had Polly ended up letting her go? She felt desperate to know, but there had been no reply to the message she'd sent, not even to say that it wasn't possible to forward her email as Polly's whereabouts were unknown.

The following afternoon while Ron took Chloe into town to watch *Kung Fu Panda 3*, Charlotte, Maggie and Gabby stayed behind to talk things through in front of the sitting-room fire.

'I just don't know how you're going to make yourself do it,' Gabby protested, her beautiful, tear-ravaged face starting to crumple again. 'I mean, I understand about Elodie, of course I do, and Martin and I have thought for a long time that things were coming apart for you and Chloe . . . I'm sorry, I'm sorry,' she gasped as Charlotte winced. 'You know what I'm trying to say, but that you'd give up on her . . .'

'You don't have to see it like that,' Charlotte snapped angrily. She hadn't managed much sleep through the night, so was on a short fuse already without having knives twisted in her guilt. 'What I'm trying to do is the right thing for her.'

'You mean for *you*. You took her, adopted her, gave her a lovely life until things started to go a bit wrong . . .'

'They're more than a bit wrong . . .'

'But she's not the first child to interfere with a baby. It happens. Talk to Martin, he's a GP so he knows.'

'They don't all have the kind of background Chloe does. And if you don't see it as such a problem, why don't you offer to take her? She loves you and the twins, you have plenty of room and the wherewithal to give her a great life, so maybe you'd be better at dealing with her than I am.'

Gabby baulked. This clearly wasn't the kind of challenge she'd expected to come up against. 'I thought you said she needed to be an only child,' she pointed out lamely.

Charlotte looked at Maggie who'd said nothing yet, had simply sat quietly listening to the sisters trying to thrash things out.

'There's a couple used to live in the next village to us,' Gabby blurted, 'they gave their adopted child back . . .'

'It's not a case of giving a child back,' Charlotte interrupted tightly. 'Chloe didn't come from care in the first place, and anyway, they're not items bought in department stores with open-ended return dates stamped on their bottoms. Once an adoption is made legal the child's yours. It doesn't belong to the state or social services, or anyone apart from *you*.'

Gabby was confused. 'So what are you saying?'

'That you don't give a child *back*. You give it up, hand it over . . .' She really didn't want to be doing this; she could hardly believe what she was saying.

'It all amounts to the same thing, I guess,' she admitted weakly, 'because what you're really saying is you don't want the child any more.'

'Exactly,' Gabby stated, 'and this couple, no one ever spoke to them again, not even their own family. I swear, people actually ignored them in the street, and someone sprayed graffiti on the woman's car calling her a child-hater. In the end they had to move away. I don't know where they are now, but it was hell for them, and I couldn't bear to think of you being treated the same way.'

Having witnessed for herself just how maligned and shunned failed adopters could be, Charlotte said, 'We used to hate those cases when they came up. No one ever wanted to take them, because it was next to impossible to know how to deal with someone who'd led a child to believe they were part of a family, that they were loved and wanted, only then to turn around and say, "actually, you're not the little cutie I was expecting you to be so you have to go back to where you came from". Of course it's always a lot more complicated than that, but believe me, I'm fully aware of the prejudice against people who give up on a child. I guess this is showing me how wrong it is to pass judgement without knowing all the facts.'

'But you must have known them if the child was being given to social services,' Gabby pointed out.

'Not always, because people don't always tell the truth.'

Maggie said, 'Well, we do know what's going on here, and neither Gabby nor I are going to turn our backs on you. We only want you to be sure you're doing what's best for your family, and of course for Chloe.'

'I think it's best for Chloe to stay with you,' Gabby declared forcefully.

Realising she already couldn't bear the thought of her world without Chloe in it, Charlotte fought hard with her emotions as she said, brokenly, 'I'd agree, if we weren't living on a knife-edge all the time. If the tempers weren't getting worse, if I felt I could cope better than I've managed . . .'

Taking her hand, Gabby squeezed it tight. 'I don't want to make things any more difficult than they already are,' she promised, 'I'm just trying to make sure you've really thought this through.'

After an awkward pause, Maggie tried injecting a more practical note. 'Have you contacted your old boss yet?' she asked.

Charlotte shook her head. 'She's still there though, and apparently she's been promoted.'

'So she could be in a stronger position to help you?'

'If she wants to. I think she'll be quite upset when I tell her what's in my mind; after all, she moved heaven and earth to make it possible for me to adopt Chloe. Now I'm going to be one of those hateful people who come back and say sorry, but it's not working out so I want you to take responsibility for this child from now on.'

'But they're not hateful,' Maggie objected. 'Like you they've probably done their best . . .'

'Some will have, others won't . . .'

'But we know you have.'

'What I did,' Charlotte cried, pressing her hands to her head, 'was take a child that wasn't mine, because I thought I knew best. If I'd brought her here that night, to you, they'd have let her stay with you until the right parents could be found.'

'You don't know that for certain,' Maggie protested. 'True, the law says you should have put her into the system, but you didn't, and in the end it was the law that made it possible for you to keep her. No one could have known then that she wouldn't thrive in a family with more than one child. And look at it this way, if you hadn't taken her you wouldn't have met Anthony and if you hadn't met him you wouldn't have any children at all.'

'So you see, it all worked out for the best,' Gabby chipped in cheerily.

Used to her sister sometimes not quite getting it, or hitting the wrong note, Charlotte said, 'It's true what you say, Maggie, and obviously I wouldn't be without Anthony and the children, but this is tearing me apart. I keep saying it's the right thing for Chloe, but is it, really?'

'Think about what's happening at school as well

as at home,' Maggie advised gently. 'She's not settled. She's struggling, and it's up to you to do whatever you can to help her.'

'By casting her off like she means nothing, has no feelings?'

'You don't have to phrase it that way, but however you put it, it's not a decision you have to take until you've had some expert advice. Wendy, your old boss, will have plenty to say, I'm sure, and you'll remember Julia Minor who was Chloe's guardian for the court during the adoption?'

Charlotte nodded.

'Well, Julia could be very helpful to us too. She's now a fully-fledged child psychologist – or do I mean psychiatrist? Whichever, Chloe responded very well to her, as you no doubt recall, so maybe she'll be more willing to talk to her than she's proved with anyone else.'

Charlotte could only hope. 'Are you still in touch with her?' she asked.

'Not exactly, but I have her number, and even if you do end up deciding that Chloe would be better with different parents, she'll need someone like Julia to help with the transition.'

A spectacular sunrise was taking place over Hawkes Bay, blood-red streaks of light shooting through swathes of purplish-grey cloud turning the sea to a shadowy molten mass and casting the mountains with an almost mystical glow. Anthony was finding it strange to think of Charlotte in yesterday while he was here in her tomorrow, part of another day, another world, it felt. Yesterday he'd made Chloe laugh on the phone about the time difference between them, teasing her that he knew what was going to happen, because he was already there. Afterwards, knowing what he did, it had seemed almost cruel to have made such a joke and he'd been regretting it ever since.

It was just after five in the morning and he was in the kitchen on the phone to Charlotte, listening quietly as she told him about her call to Julia Minor, who'd apparently qualified as a child psychologist since their last dealings with her.

Should he tell Charlotte now about the iPad her mother had found in Chloe's room, or wait until she'd met with Julia before dropping the bombshell? A psychologist would have been able to advise on the best way to handle it.

'I'm seeing Julia on Thursday at eleven in town,' Charlotte was saying. 'She still does a lot of work for the courts, apparently, but she's more than happy to talk to Chloe.'

'So you'll take Chloe with you?'

'No, she wants to see me on my own first to get a clearer picture of what's been happening and the reasons we think Chloe needs help. The trouble is, it'll be a drawn-out process and if we end up deciding to let her go I want it to be over as quickly as possible. Does that sound cruel? Oh god, it does, doesn't it.'

Having lost sight of what was and wasn't cruel, he simply said, 'I'm sure you're right that it'll take some time to help straighten her out, months, maybe even years, and you can't stay over there for that long.'

'No, of course not. I'm missing you all so much already. How are the children? Are they still asleep?'

'I hope so, at this hour, and they're both fine. Cooper's been helping with the picking, supervised by Uncle Rick to make sure he doesn't mash, or eat the grapes.'

'And Elodie?'

'She's great. No more inflammations or rashes.' He let the unspoken words lie; they both knew what they were – that everything had calmed down since Chloe's departure – so they didn't need to be voiced. 'I think she misses you.'

'With her daddy and Nana spoiling her to bits, I doubt it.'

Aware of the picking crew starting to congregate around the vines in front of the house, Anthony went out on to the terrace. They were only just visible through the fiery dawn mist, but their excitement and urge to get going was palpable in the air. 'Have you arranged to see Wendy Fraser yet?' he asked, spotting Will turning up in the vineyard truck.

'Tomorrow at four. She's coming here, to Maggie's. We thought it was better than meeting at the office.

I expect most people would think I was there to visit old friends, but there could be some who'd draw the wrong conclusion.'

'Or the right one.'

Charlotte fell silent and he immediately regretted his insensitivity.

'You sound low,' she told him. 'How are things there?'

Where could he begin?

Better not to begin at all when the only news he could give her was bad – apart from the fact that the wine destined for Australia had been located at the docks in Auckland, so was now on its way back to Hawkes Bay. What the hell they were going to do with it when it got here he had no idea. There were definitely no funds for storage, but at least having charge of it was going to make it a whole lot easier to sell than if it had been seized by an Australian bankruptcy court.

Making a note to go over to Wineworks later in the day, he said, 'Everything's pretty normal here. The harvest is going well. Will reckons we've got a good vintage all round. Oh, and Zoe's photographer has turned up. He's been shooting just about everything that moves, and Zoe's organised some models to stand in for you and me.'

'You mean to pose as the owners of Tuki River? How would that work?'

'I don't think they're going to claim to be us, they're

just here to make the location and the wines look glamorous.' He didn't add, because he couldn't, that Zoe – or her conscience more like – had assured him there would be no extra charge for the models, nor did he go into any details about Zoe's flat-out efforts to find a new buyer for the wine. He was spending almost as much time on that as she was, had even reduced the price to a level where there would be no profit, but no one, as yet, had committed.

'Please don't tell me you're thinking about Zoe in anything but a professional way, with me not there to distract you,' Charlotte teased.

Almost groaning aloud he said, 'You are so up the wrong tree with that one. I have no interest in the woman other than what she can bring to the vineyard.'

'But we know she's interested in you.'

'Don't let's go there, Charlotte, please. We have enough to be worrying about without adding problems that don't exist.'

'OK, I'm sorry. I guess being away from you and with all that's going on I'm feeling stupidly insecure.'

'Are you taking the medication the doctor prescribed?'

'Yes. I think it's taking the edge off things, although it's hard to imagine feeling any worse when I think about Chloe. Tell me, how are Mum and Bob?'

'They're great. I'm not sure how Rowan and I would be managing on our own. Your mother's got everything under control, and Bob's throwing himself into the harvest.'

'Ask Mum to call me later, will you? I'm guessing you're about to head off into the vineyard.'

'That's the plan. Where's Chloe right now?'

'Asleep. We still haven't got ourselves on to UK time. She wants me to take her to the village where I grew up on Friday. Actually what she really wants to see is the house where I kept her hidden while the police were looking for her.'

Able to understand why that might have a fascination for Chloe, he said, 'Has she asked about her birth parents since you've been there?'

'No. She's hardly mentioned them, and the one time she did it wasn't in fond terms.'

'So she doesn't want to see her father, or anyone who might be connected to him?'

'No. Did you think she would?'

Knowing what he did now, he wasn't sure. 'What about Cooper and Elodie?' he asked. 'Has she mentioned them?'

With a sigh Charlotte said, 'Apart from when she spoke to you this morning – last night your time – she's behaving as though it's just me and her.'

Unsurprised by that, he said, 'I should go. Call me after you've spoken to Wendy.'

After ringing off he turned back into the kitchen and found his mother-in-law making coffee.

'Did you tell her about the iPad?' Anna asked.

He shook his head as the blackness of Anna's discovery descended like a storm cloud. He didn't even want to think about the damned iPad. *His* damned iPad.

Coming to put a hand on his shoulder, she said, 'From what I hear about the headmaster at Te Mata Primary, he might be the one to speak to first.'

'He'll want to go to the police. It's what we should do, but I'm afraid of how it might play out. We haven't monitored her properly, that much is evident, and you've read what's in some of those messages.'

Anna's expression was bleak. 'Do you think it could be her father pretending to be someone else?' she asked.

His eyes went to hers. 'It can't be him,' he stated. 'He'd be too closely monitored to get that sort of access to the Internet.'

'Whoever it is, we know from the things he said that he has knowledge of Chloe's past.'

Feeling suddenly furious, he said, 'I can tell you this, Anna, I don't want my children being sullied, contaminated even, by the daughter of a paedophile.'

Looking as shocked as he felt by the outburst, Anna cried, 'She's a victim, Anthony . . .'

'I get that, but what's going on, that disgusting set of messages on *my* iPad telling her what to do to Elodie . . . It wouldn't be anywhere near us if it weren't for her. I'm sorry, but it's true,' and snatching up his phone he left the house.

Chapter Twelve

Another outing had been arranged for Chloe, this time to the shops in town where Maggie and Ron would help her to choose some winter boots. Though she'd wanted Charlotte to go too, she'd been sweetly ready to understand that Charlotte was still a little jet-lagged so was going to stay behind and catch up on some sleep.

Lies, deceit and the most complicated and tortured love; a heavy and harrowing combination that was proving as hard for Charlotte to understand as it was to support.

She'd received a text a few minutes ago informing her that Wendy had been held up, but was on her way. Since Charlotte had no idea how long that was going to delay the start of their meeting she'd begun pacing up and down the elegant sitting room, wringing her hands as she tried to prepare herself for the emotional haranguing to come, not to mention condemnation. She'd deserve it, of course, but that would make it no easier to cope with. Perversely, she'd felt calmer while Chloe was here, probably because she had to; now she was alone with her fears and her conscience she wasn't holding it together very well at all.

If it weren't four in the morning with Anthony she'd ring to talk things through again, but she didn't want to wake him. He was so busy with the harvest now that he needed whatever sleep he was managing to get. Besides, what was there to say that hadn't already been said?

Remembering the ridiculous question she'd asked about Zoe when they'd last spoken, she felt her insides sink. She couldn't even think where it had come from, other than a deep-rooted paranoia that she was going to be punished for what she was planning to do to Chloe. But why should she be punished when Chloe's best interests were at the heart of her decision?

Was she fooling herself about that? What if Gabby was right and this was really all about her? There was no doubt her life would be easier, calmer without Chloe's hysteria and aggression. Elodie would be safe, Cooper too, and the strain on her marriage, not to mention the worry about schooling, socialising and early sexualisation that seemed to be getting worse by the day, would be over. Looking at it objectively (if that were even possible), she had made a terrible mistake when she'd taken Chloe almost five years ago, and now she was trying to put it right by doing what she should have done then.

Why was she trying to rationalise this in her mind, defend herself even, when her conscience knew the truth and would never let it go? The rejection she'd force on Chloe would very probably prove as traumatising for her as the abuse she'd experienced at the hands of her father. Thanks to Charlotte she would have trust issues for the rest of her life, and trust was only the beginning. The damage was almost beyond imagining, while she, Charlotte, would be a prisoner, a *victim*, of her conscience, possibly even afraid to love her own children for fear of the reprisals fate might visit on her for what she'd done.

Round and round, back and forth, nothing felt right, and she could hardly remember a time when it did.

Hearing a car pulling up outside, her heart gave such a sickening twist that she couldn't make herself move. She didn't want to go through with it. She couldn't speak to anyone or even think about it any more. Yet here she was walking to the door, letting Wendy in while knowing that she was going to move things ahead in spite of the crushing guilt and misgivings.

'Charlotte, it's good to see you,' Wendy smiled, looking almost exactly as she had the last time Charlotte had seen her, pale with dark-rimmed glasses that lent an owlish look to her hazel eyes, and not a trace of make-up on her wide, thin mouth.

Her mousy hair was styled in the same flat bob, and her navy padded coat was either a replica of the one she'd had before, or was a durable original.

Remembering Wendy was uncomfortable with any physical displays of warmth, Charlotte greeted her in as friendly a way as she could while she ushered her in. 'Seeing you is making me feel that almost no time at all has gone by,' she commented, directing her along the hall. Did that sound rude? She certainly hadn't meant it to.

'Not far short of five years,' Wendy murmured. 'It's hard to believe, isn't it?'

Charlotte was trying to remember how they'd lost touch, for they'd emailed regularly when Charlotte was first in New Zealand. She used to send photographs of Chloe and Cooper at the beach or in the vineyard, and Wendy would reply with ironic shots of Kesterly at its gloomiest. Feeling certain she'd been the one to let the contact drop, she felt a burn of guilt for how thoughtless that was, when it had probably meant quite a lot to Wendy to have news of the little girl for whom she'd broken so many rules.

And now, here was Charlotte, on the verge of asking Wendy to break even more, or at least to help smooth a way for Chloe that Charlotte couldn't even bear to think of her undertaking.

For a while, as Charlotte poured tea and offered her old boss some of Maggie's home-made madeleines, they made small talk about the weather and how different life was in Hawkes Bay to Kesterly-on-Sea.

'I've always wanted to visit Australia and New Zealand,' Wendy confided, 'but it's such a long way and I'm not sure I'd ever be able to afford it.'

Was she angling for an invite? Under any other circumstances Charlotte might have jumped right in, under these she simply couldn't.

'How's Anthony?' Wendy ventured. 'Are you loving being the owners of a vineyard? It sounds so romantic, like something you'd see in a film.'

Grimacing, Charlotte said, 'It doesn't come without its pressures, and I can promise you it's definitely not as glamorous as it might sound, but we love being there and I can't ever see us coming back.'

Seeming to think that quite reasonable, Wendy said, 'And how about our little star? How's she getting along these days? Her life is so very different to the one she started with, bless her. If a child ever deserved a decent, loving home it was her.'

Swallowing dryly, Charlotte managed to say, 'She's here with me, actually. Maggie and Ron have taken her into town.'

Wendy nodded, as though unsurprised. Then changing the subject she said, 'I can't help wondering why you didn't want to come to the office? There are lots of people who'd love to see you, and I don't think you ever visited the new hub, did you?

It's working out very well, everyone being under the same roof.'

'I'll have to drop by before I leave,' Charlotte replied, knowing she almost certainly wouldn't – unless she had to.

Wendy smiled benignly and took a sip of her tea. After a lengthy pause she closed both hands around her mug and said, 'So really, why didn't you want to come to the office?'

Though Charlotte took a breath she could make no words come out.

'I see,' Wendy said as though Charlotte had answered the question. 'I was hoping my suspicions weren't correct, but it would appear that they are.'

'What – what did you suspect?' Charlotte asked.

Bluntly, Wendy said, 'It's not working out, is it?'

Charlotte's throat tightened as her face flooded with colour.

Wendy's eyes were showing neither censure nor understanding as she said, 'I can't say I'm surprised, this sort of thing happens, but of course I'm very sorry and sad, especially in this case.'

Charlotte watched her, unable to gauge what more she was thinking.

'So what do you want me to do?' Wendy asked as though they were discussing an everyday issue, though Charlotte knew very well that she would be viewing this as anything but everyday.

It was several moments before Charlotte could

make herself say, 'I've heard that some traumatised children do better in a family where there are no other children and aren't likely to be in the future. They can be the focus of attention, their needs will be fully met and understood . . . I – I think Chloe requires more attention, more care than I can give her.'

Wendy was watching her closely. 'And you think this because you've consulted a psychologist who's confirmed it?' She spoke in a manner that suggested she already knew the answer.

Almost squirming, Charlotte said, 'It was put to me by a social worker in New Zealand. She and a psychologist colleague are of the opinion that . . .'

'Has Chloe had any therapy or counselling since her adoption?' Wendy cut in.

Charlotte had to admit that she hadn't. 'She won't speak to anyone, but I'm seeing Julia Minor tomorrow. I expect you know that Julia is now a qualified child psychologist. I'm hoping Chloe will feel relaxed enough with her to start receiving the help she needs.'

'I see. And when, exactly, would you expect Chloe's treatment to begin?'

'I guess as soon as Julia can fit her in.'

'Which could be months considering Julia's workload for the courts, and even when she can fit it in I'm sure you're aware that it's likely to be a lengthy and potentially traumatic process. Are you prepared to see it through with Chloe? You are her mother, after all.'

Charlotte flinched at the reminder, knowing Wendy had intended her to. 'It's impossible to put an end date on the treatment,' she said, 'but I was hoping Julia might do private appointments that she could fit her into so I can at least be there as it gets under way.'

Wendy frowned. 'That would be between you and Julia; what interests me is how you see your own overall involvement in Chloe's life, going forward. If I'm understanding this correctly, just so we're clear, it's your intention to relinquish her into care?'

Charlotte could hardly breathe. 'It's not my *intention*, it's a con—'

'How carefully have you thought this through?'

Swallowing, Charlotte said, 'I hardly think about anything else.'

'And you've obviously discussed it with Anthony?'

'Of course. There have been issues with our younger daughter . . .' She looked away, embarrassed, ashamed, knowing Wendy would be holding her responsible for anything that might have gone wrong.

'Could you expand on that?' Wendy pressed.

'I think you know what I'm saying.'

'Are we talking about a repeat of what happened to her?'

'It's along those lines, yes, but not as severe.'

'And you believe this is the right way to deal with it?'

Turning crimson again, Charlotte said, 'We're exploring the possibility. For Chloe's sake. We know she needs more than we can give, than we even know how to give, and obviously we have to think of our other children.'

Wendy nodded slowly. 'Have you asked your sister-in-law if she'll take her in?'

Wishing that were an option, while knowing that she couldn't commit Maggie to something that had the potential of driving her to a breakdown, Charlotte said, 'I think it would be asking too much of Maggie and Ron. They're not getting any younger, and given their relationship to me and Anthony . . .'

Seeming to have expected this response, Wendy said, 'So let's put all our cards on the table, shall we? I can see you're finding it difficult, but we won't get anywhere until you do.'

Knowing how naïve she was going to sound even before she uttered the next words, Charlotte forced herself to say, 'I was hoping, if we do decide that she should go to someone else, that you could find a new family before I leave, and that it could be a couple, or a single person, who don't already have children and would be willing to go through the counselling with her.'

Wendy's eyes widened in surprise. 'It's starting to sound as though your mind is made up.'

Charlotte simply stared at her.

'You know very well that the system doesn't work like that,' Wendy continued.

Yes, Charlotte did know.

'Getting her established in a new home could take years. Long-term placements have to be worked at – I'm imagining that ultimately you're hoping someone will take her under the special guardianship scheme, or are you actually considering revoking the adoption?'

'No! I—'

'Haven't thought that through either? You'd need a court order, and as you know they're almost never granted. Have you spoken to a lawyer?'

'Wendy, please . . .'

Apparently unmoved, Wendy said, 'So what we're looking at is you relinquishing her into care and letting us do the rest while you return to New Zealand and get on with your life without her?'

Charlotte could hardly bear it; this was proving even worse than she'd feared. 'Is it so bad to want to give her a better chance with somebody else?' she asked shakily.

'No, if we knew we could give her that chance, but we don't. Finding homes for traumatised children, especially of her age . . .' She broke off as Charlotte shot awkwardly to her feet.

'I know how difficult it is,' Charlotte cried, 'but it's not working out for her with us. Would you rather she stayed and got worse than she already is?'

'You don't know that would happen. If you found her the right help . . .'

'We've tried.'

'How hard have you tried?'

'Whatever I say, you're going to say it wasn't hard enough.'

'Perhaps because it wasn't. It's not unheard of for adoptive parents to regret taking on someone else's child once they start having children of their own . . .'

Furious, Charlotte shouted, 'It's not about her being *someone else's child*, it's about her history, her needs . . .'

Wendy's hand came up. 'I realise it's too late for this now, but you should have thought of all this before you took her. You'd had enough experience by then to know how hard it is for children as traumatised as she is to fit into a normal family.'

'I didn't know when I took her that I was going to have a family of my own.'

'But you knew it when you adopted her.'

Unable to deny that, Charlotte's rage died. 'By then she was a huge part of my life,' she said quietly, 'as I was of hers. You surely aren't saying I should have turned my back on her?'

'It might have been easier if you had, at least you'd have saved her from going through it now she's older and more able to understand. Or were you afraid of what the press would say if you abandoned her right after you'd been cleared of child abduction?'

Charlotte gasped. 'That never even entered my head,' she protested furiously. 'All I wanted then was to make her legally mine and take her back to New Zealand.'

'But that's not what you want now?'

'Wendy, for heaven's sake, you surely can't think I'm considering this just because it doesn't suit me any more. It's because I *know* she needs special care and I can't give it. But I could, with your help, try to find someone who's prepared to make her the centre of their world.'

Wendy eyed her harshly. 'We've already been through how long that could take, and you're making it sound as though you're expecting to be involved in finding these miracle people. Do you think you have the right to vet them first? Is that it?'

'I'm not saying that . . .'

'I think you are, and so I should remind you that if you decide to relinquish her she will go into the system and it will be up to fostering services to place her with a family *they* feel to be right. Of course, as her legal mother, you'll retain the right to take her back again should you so wish, but having given her up once I'm not sure the courts would look favourably on such an application.'

Charlotte felt so sick with shame and self-loathing that she couldn't think what to say. It was hard to believe this was happening, that she'd actually put herself and Chloe in this position when all she'd ever wanted was to be a good mother to a little girl who'd been so badly in need of one.

After several tense moments, Wendy sat back in her chair. 'OK, I've been hard on you,' she stated in a slightly gentler tone, 'but I felt it was necessary to spell things out in a way that leaves you no room for doubt or self-deception. What you're considering is enormous, not only for Chloe, but for you too. I'm not saying I won't help, but nor am I saying I'll do anything for you that is likely to have a negative impact on Chloe.'

Charlotte's eyes felt raw and wide as she looked at her.

'I'll need to give it a lot more thought before we go forward,' Wendy declared, getting to her feet, 'and I think you do too, because make no mistake, this will be one of the most painful things you'll ever do.'

Already in no doubt of it, Charlotte walked her to the door.

'With your permission,' Wendy said, before stepping outside, 'I'd like to speak to Julia before you see her.'

'Of course,' Charlotte mumbled. And because it seemed right to say so, she added, 'Thanks for coming, and thanks for being so honest.'

'I was brutal,' Wendy corrected, 'but you know I needed to be,' and with no perfunctory goodbye she returned to her car.

Minutes later Charlotte was upstairs, still reeling from her meeting with Wendy as she spoke to Anthony on the phone. 'It was awful,' she confided, 'I've never felt so . . . despicable in my life. She didn't pull any punches, and I can tell she's utterly disgusted with me.'

'But she's going to help?'

'I think so. In the end, if we go that route, she has to . . .' Hearing the others arriving home she went to the window to check, and seeing Chloe's excitement as she pulled a handful of bags from the car she closed her eyes against the inner torment. 'If you could see her now,' she said to Anthony, 'she's been such an angel since we got here . . . There are moments when I feel as though I'm making it all up, that it was a bad dream – and I'm starting to wonder if your sister feels the same.'

'You have to remember that Chloe's in a good place at the moment,' he cautioned. 'She doesn't have any rivals for your attention, or Maggie and Ron's, and look at it this way, it's showing you how well she'd do if she could be the main focus for someone all of the time.'

'It's the "someone" that's bothering me,' Charlotte sighed past the taut heaviness in her heart. 'How equipped will they be to deal with her problems? They can say or promise anything they like to social services, but how can we be sure they're not fostering for the money, or won't end up feeling unable to cope further down the line? Placing her in care now, after she's been with us for so long, is bound to have a catastrophic effect on the rest of her life . . .'

'I realise that, I can hardly think about anything

else myself, but I'm also thinking about Cooper and Elodie, and what happened to you only a couple of weeks ago. We can't go on like that, Charlotte. The way things are she's destroying our home, and there's something you should know before going to see Julia. Your mother found my missing iPad while going through Chloe's room . . .'

Charlotte snapped, 'Why was my mother going through her room? Has she been clearing things out, throwing them away? Anthony, you have to stop her . . .'

'Listen,' he came in firmly. 'You need to know what we found on the iPad, because it's important. She's been exchanging messages with someone who claims to know her father, and . . .'

Charlotte reeled. 'What! How the hell . . .'

'Please, just listen. I've been in touch with the prison and I'm assured that there is no way Brian Wade could get unsupervised access to the Internet, much less cover up the kind of messaging we found. So it would seem that some creep claiming to be a friend of Brian Wade's has got to her. He's been asking about Elodie, telling her to take photos of herself and Elodie in the bath. He's also given her instructions on how to masturbate, as if she doesn't know that already.'

Charlotte's hand was pressed to her mouth in horror. All this had been happening under their roof, presumably while they were there, and they'd had no idea. What the hell kind of parents did that make them? 'Please tell me there aren't any photos,' she said hoarsely.

'None that I've found, but it's lucky you took her to England when you did, because there's no knowing how far it might have gone if you hadn't.'

'Oh my god this is . . . *evil*. Have you told the police?'

'I have now. Mike Bain came with me. I went to him first to alert him, in case this lowlife had managed to get access to any of the children at school. It's unlikely, because I think he was targeting Chloe. Heaven only knows how long he's been waiting to make contact.'

Horrified by the very thought of someone closing in on an innocent little girl like a silent, deadly poison, Charlotte suddenly started to panic about what the authorities might do in response to this. Were they going to end up having all their children taken away, due to neglect? 'What did the police say?' she demanded shakily.

'They're examining the iPad and will get back to me. Incidentally, this bloke calls himself Tiger Tim.'

Charlotte's eyes closed as bile rose to her throat. Tiger was what Chloe's father used to say while raping her, *be a good girl now and ride the tiger*.

'. . . so we need to make sure she has no more access to the Internet,' Anthony was saying. 'Has she been online since you arrived?'

'Not that I'm aware of, but obviously I'll check her iPad.'

'This is showing us,' he said, 'that she needs to be closely monitored the entire time to make sure no one gets to her this way again. Someone who has no other children to distract them, or to cause her to feel jealous or insecure, will surely be far better placed to do that than we are.'

Wishing he was fighting Chloe's corner, while knowing he couldn't, Charlotte turned as she heard Chloe calling her. 'I have to go, but I'm sorry about the iPad. I should have found it . . .'

'It's not your fault. It was hidden at the back of a drawer full of old clothes that you probably never bother to open.'

'Thank goodness Mum did, but I'm hardly daring to think about where this might take us. I guess we'll find out. Before you go, it's probable we'll have to see Julia privately. Is that going to be OK?'

There was only a moment's hesitation before he said, 'It's fine. Do you have enough in your account?'

'I have some, but I'm going to need more.'

'OK. I'll make sure you get it.'

As he rang off at his end Anthony stood staring at the computer screen where an email from Wineworks was displayed, warning him that if outstanding accounts weren't settled within the next seven days all bottles and bottling services for Tuki River Wines would be suspended. In other words, everything, including the 2015 vintage recently collected from the winery, was to be frozen until they got their money.

This amounted to more than twenty-five thousand bottles of wine.

'Smile!' Zoe sang out from the doorway.

Anthony's scowl deepened as he closed his laptop and looked round. Frank, the photographer, was with her; a nice enough chap, obviously dedicated to his art, but Anthony really wasn't in the mood to be photographed right now.

'Everything OK?' Zoe asked, skirting a couple of interns who were busy at the press.

'It's fine,' he told her shortly. 'I need to be going . . .'

'Before you do, I have some good news. If you check your website I think you'll find an order has come in for five thousand bottles of the 2014 Pinot Gris.'

Anthony hardly knew what to say. Yes, it was a welcome order, but it wouldn't even come close to covering the outstanding bills; and Wineworks wouldn't release the wine anyway until they had their money.

'OK, it's not huge,' Zoe conceded, 'and I realise it doesn't solve all the problems, but they want the Tuki River label and they have outlets all over New Zealand.'

Anthony was still staring at her, trying to work

out what he could do to convince Wineworks to let him fulfil the order.

'Something's wrong,' Zoe said worriedly.

Anthony shook his head. 'Just a lot on my mind,' he responded, and standing aside for the photographer to get a better angle on the interns, he clicked on his phone to answer.

'Mr Goodman, Thomas Reilly here,' the caller announced.

The broker he'd contacted to handle the sale of the vineyard.

'I've had a cancellation this afternoon,' Reilly told him, 'and I've also got a potential buyer in from Marlborough who'd like to come with me, if it's convenient. Shall we say two o'clock at the cellar door?'

Anthony assured Reilly he'd be there, and ringing off he said to Zoe, "Have you seen Will this morning?'

'Not yet,' she replied, 'but we've only just come out.'

Guessing his winemaker was supervising the pickers at the Cab Franc vines, Anthony was about to call him when his mobile rang again.

'Mr Goodman, it's Pania Brown here, from Child Youth and Family Services. Do you have a moment?'

He didn't, but he said, 'Yes, of course,' and signalling to Zoe that he needed to speak in private, he took the phone outside. 'What can I do for you?' he asked, kicking aside a pile of pallets and hoses, and wandering in amongst the closest vines.

'Actually, there are a couple of things,' Pania answered. 'Mr Bain at the school tells me that your wife has taken Chloe to England with the intention of relinquishing her into care.'

Hating the words as much as the wretchedness they inflamed, he said, 'We're looking into it.'

'I see, well I think that's a shame. I'm sure we could help Chloe . . .'

'I'm not doubting you,' Anthony interrupted, 'but things have happened since your visit . . .'

'Are you talking about the iPad?'

He hadn't been, but it would certainly do. 'I take it the police informed you?'

'Yes, they did. They were obliged to. Would it be possible to come and see you so we can have a chat about this?'

How on earth could he put her off without seeming uncaring, or rude, or overly defensive? 'Uh, yes, of course,' he said, glancing at his phone screen as the line beeped. 'I've got another call coming in,' he told her, 'but I'll ring you back to work out a time,' and clicking to take the call he said, 'Anthony Goodman speaking.'

'Mr Goodman, it's Jessica Peach. We met yesterday when you came to see us with Mr Bain.'

The local police. 'Yes, I remember,' he assured her. 'Do you have any news?'

'Not as such, but we have been in touch with Puawaitahi, which is the child protection division of the New Zealand Police. They're based in Auckland, but a member of the team is flying in today. He'd like to interview you at two thirty if you can make it.'

Anthony's eyes closed as the hideousness of it all crowded in on him. Were they going to start seeing him as a suspect, given it was his iPad? He had nothing to hide, but he sure as hell didn't want anyone thinking, even for a minute, that he did.

'I can make it,' he told Jessica Peach, and ringing off he scrolled to Thomas Reilly's number to rearrange the viewing for a potential buyer.

I'm lying on the bed with Mummy and Boots, staring at the lavender-blue patterns on the wallpaper and thinking all sorts of things. I like being here, mainly because Mummy hasn't wanted me to come into her room before today. She keeps saying she's tired, or needs to think, or that I should go to sleep and stop frowning, because if the wind changes I might stay like it.

I definitely don't want to be saddled with a bad expression, so I'm doing my best to keep smiling, but it isn't very easy. I really thought coming to England would make everything better, but Mummy's obviously missing Cooper and Elodie, which isn't how it's supposed to be at all. I wish Mummy could forget all about them and be happy that it's just me and her the way it used to be when we had lots of fun together and Mummy loved me enough to rescue me from my wicked parents.

I keep feeling afraid that Mummy doesn't love me any more. I wish I was still three, I think she would then.

I want to run away to a place no one will ever find me.

I think it's tomorrow that Mummy's going to see someone called Julia who I'm supposed to remember, but I don't think I do. I can't go with her, she said, because she and Julia are going to catch up on old times and for some reason they can't do it while I'm there.

They're not the only ones who have a secret they're keeping from me, because everyone does. All the children at school, and the teachers, even people walking down the street. They all look at me as though they know something I don't. It's like being an alien, all alone in the world where no one else is the same as me. I'm not sure if they're laughing at me, or feeling sorry for me, but I can tell they hate me. I don't care, because I hate them even more.

I know Daddy doesn't like me because I'm not his the same as Cooper and Elodie, but that's all right, because he's not my real daddy anyway. My creepy daddy's still in prison, and Tiger Tim who says he knows him has promised to take me to see him if I want to. I don't know if I do or I don't, but I can't think of another way to ask about the rich people I got stolen from. If they exist. I hope they do, but I suppose they might not.

Anyway, I can't get in touch with Tiger Tim, because there's a password on Uncle Ron's Wi-Fi that I can't make work.

It doesn't matter, because I'd much rather be with Mummy like this, even though we're just lying here doing nothing.

I'm glad Mummy remembered to pack Boots. It would have been mean to leave him behind. When I run away to the place no one can find me I'll be sure to take him with me.

'Chloe? Are you crying?' Mummy whispers.

I shake my head.

Turning so she can see me, Mummy looks into my eyes and smooths my hair. 'What is it?' she asks. 'Why are you upset?'

'I don't know,' I sob. 'I just am.'

She gives me a hug and gets up from the bed. 'Shall we go and see how Auntie Maggie's getting on with dinner?' she asks.

As I follow her down the stairs I'm thinking that she didn't try very hard to find out what was wrong with me. She always used to, but she's different now. I think this proves that she doesn't love me any more.

I'd like to keep on going out of the front door along the drive and then I'd run and run and run to the place where no one can find me. The trouble is, I don't know where it is.

Chapter Thirteen

Charlotte wanted to shout at Gabby to shut up and go back home to Devon; to stop moralising and prophesying and telling Charlotte things she already knew about adopted children being handed over to social services. What the hell did Gabby know about anything anyway, with her ideal upbringing, perfect marriage and untraumatised children? She'd never done anything remotely risky, or controversial, or criminal (it had to be said) in her life, so she had no idea how it felt to be Charlotte, much less to be Chloe. (To be fair, she wasn't trying to put herself into Chloe's shoes, whereas Charlotte could hardly take herself out of them.)

It was all imagined, of course, for she had no idea how Chloe really felt about anything, although she did know the loneliness and bewilderment of being an adopted child. She'd experienced it often enough while growing up. She hadn't felt as loved or valued as she could see her sister was. She'd been a cuckoo in the nest as far as Gabby's mother was concerned – she never thought of Myra as her mother now – although she knew Myra had tried to hide it. It hadn't worked very well, for Charlotte had never felt like a real member of the family, hadn't ever believed that Myra wanted her even when Myra was trying to be nice. The rector, her adoptive father, had been a true Christian, kind and sensitive and as generous with his time as he'd been with his affection. She'd always known she wasn't his though, any more than he was hers.

Was that how Chloe felt about her and Anthony? That she didn't belong, that she was in the wrong place with the wrong people and all she really wanted was her rightful mummy and daddy – the king and queen of a faraway land – to come and rescue her from the wicked people who'd stolen her and told her nothing but lies.

Charlotte knew how the fantasies went because she'd had them all herself.

She also knew, because Anthony had told her earlier, that it was Chloe's Google search for information about her father that had brought the depraved individual into her world. How desperate and lonely she must have felt to do this, when she knew the man had tormented and abused her. Surely she hadn't been so unhappy that even a life with him had seemed better than the one she was living now?

Shooting to her feet as though to escape the distressing thoughts, Charlotte headed for the door.

'Are you all right, dear?' Maggie asked worriedly.

Realising the abruptness of her movements must have startled them, Charlotte said, 'Sorry. I just want to make sure Chloe's asleep. We wouldn't want her hearing what's being said.'

'I've been careful to keep my voice down,' Gabby assured her in a whisper.

Had she? Since Charlotte hadn't been paying attention, she couldn't say for sure.

'I've upset you,' Gabby said anxiously.

Charlotte couldn't help wondering why Gabby was so insecure when she'd always been so cosseted and loved, the privileged one, with a charity case for a sister. 'No you haven't,' she insisted. 'I'll be right back.'

Upstairs in Chloe's room Charlotte sat at the end of the bed in the soft glow of the nightlight, gazing at the sweetly sleeping face next to the beloved bear. Just the hint of a scowl betrayed how troubled Chloe was inside. The way she was holding on to Boots was another indication that she was worried, or afraid, or sensing something out there, beyond her understanding. The fact that she'd been ready to leave her bear in New Zealand, clearly not dreaming that she might need him once she was in England and had her mummy to herself, was clawing at the terrible ache in Charlotte's heart.

What a hard and complicated world fate had created for Chloe.

She'd seemed to have had no idea that by using Anthony's iPad the way she had she could have put herself in terrible danger, or she could have turned Anthony into a suspected paedophile, someone who was pretending to be her. He still wasn't sure whether he was in the clear or not, but at least no accusations had been made during his interview with the Puawaitahi investigator. However, they could expect no conclusion any time soon, because he'd been informed that the case was being referred to the Child Exploitation and Online Protection Service in London, which could mean that someone there was already running background checks on both Charlotte and Anthony.

In a normal, sane world they'd have had nothing to worry about, but they both knew, from cases they'd been involved in themselves, that where child protection was concerned there were no guarantees. Many innocent people had had their children removed from the home, and just as many had found themselves in prison with their reputations, future and family in ruins.

She and Anthony were no more immune to miscarriages of justice than anyone else.

Chloe murmured in her sleep and turned closer to Boots. One little girl, one bruised and tender human being who, through no fault of her own, was causing untold stress and heartache to those who loved her. Looking at her now it was hard to believe that she wasn't like most other girls her age, although in many ways she was. It was the differences, the invisible, irreversible damage, that was tearing her blameless life apart, and Charlotte's heart to pieces.

Feeling a painful rush of love engulfing her, Charlotte clasped her hands to her face. How could she give this child up who needed her so much, who'd been showing her day after day since they'd been here that she couldn't love her more if she were her own?

And yet, knowing what Charlotte did, and fearing for how much worse things could get if she didn't give Chloe a chance with somebody else, somebody more able to deal with the trauma, would it be right to allow her to stay?

Word had obviously got out that Tuki River Winery was in trouble, for the price Thomas Reilly had put on the vineyard didn't even come close to what Anthony had paid for it. Considering all the work that had gone into the estate, the improved quality of the vines, the complete makeover of the cellar door and retreats, not to mention the luxurious family home he and Charlotte had built, Anthony felt almost physically violent towards the broker when he'd had the nerve to suggest such a risible sum.

He couldn't accept it, and wasn't going to, and yet he couldn't refuse it either, for time wasn't on his side. Already he was having to go back to the bank to borrow more funds against the sale, and that was the kind of loan only a madman would allow to run. He wasn't even sure if they'd lend him enough to cover the outstanding debts; if they didn't then god only knew what kind of financial chaos would ensue by the end of next week.

'Have you spoken to Charlotte this morning?' his mother-in-law asked, carrying a freshly changed Elodie into the kitchen.

'About an hour ago,' he replied, and taking the baby from her he inhaled her sweet, talc scent and felt the responding flood of adoration sweeping through him.

'Is she all right?' Anna asked, going to get Cooper's latest favourite cereal from the cupboard.

'He told me last night he wants Cheerios this morning,' Anthony informed her.

With a typical roll of her eyes, Anna swapped the boxes and filled a jug with milk. 'Charlotte?' she prompted.

The honest answer to Anna's question was, no Charlotte wasn't all right. How could she be when she was in the process of doing something that had the potential to destroy the rest of a little girl's life, possibly her own too?

Realising Anna was still waiting, he said, 'She's seeing Julia Minor today, the psychologist.'

Anna nodded thoughtfully, and gave a laugh as Elodie grabbed her daddy's face with her jammy fingers.

'Mm, delicious,' Anthony twinkled, licking her hand.

'D-shush,' she cried delightedly. 'Nana, nana, dad, dad, dad.'

'Dad! Dad! I'm taking my scooter to kindi today,' Cooper shouted, banging the scooter down the stairs.

'Careful you don't fall,' Anna cautioned.

'Cooper!' Elodie exclaimed, pointing at her brother.

Anthony planted a kiss on her cheek. He hadn't told Charlotte yet how much better Elodie was doing with her words; he'd leave it until the time felt right.

'Nana, I want Cheerios today,' Cooper instructed, as he whizzed and wobbled through the kitchen on to the terrace.

'Please,' Anthony scolded, 'and you need to come and sit at the table.'

'Coming,' Cooper called back.

'I'm getting together with Sarah Munds again today,' Anna told him, setting more toast and a boiled egg on the table.

'Egg!' Elodie declared, and before anyone could stop her she'd banged her hand into the shell, crushing it. Because it was hot she cried until Anthony kissed it better, and Anna sorted it out ready to eat.

'Me,' Elodie protested when Anna tried to feed her.

'You?' Anna laughed. 'OK, off you go,' and she handed Elodie the spoon.

'Asking for trouble,' Anthony warned as Elodie began trying to dig at the egg.

'She's an interesting woman, Sarah Munds,' Anna continued, glancing up as Bob came in looking hot and dishevelled from his early morning power limp. 'Ah, here's Ben Kingsley in all his manly glory,' she quipped.

'I don't know who you mean,' Bob retorted, resting his hands on his bony knees, 'but Ben Kingsley's an actor.'

'Really? Yes, of course he is. I guess I don't know who I mean either, then. Did you go far?'

'Only up to Craggy Range and back. Fancy partnering me in a game of doubles later?' he asked Anthony. 'Me and you versus Kim and Andy at Black Barn. Of course you'll have to do most of the work, but being a younger man and all that . . .'

Thinking of how much he'd love to lose himself in a game of tennis, Anthony was sorely tempted to accept. However, picking was still under way, the winery was working at full tilt, and he needed to focus on persuading Wineworks to fulfil the new order. Added to that was getting the vineyard broker to up his price, Zoe and Will to accept delayed payments on their contracts, and at least a thousand other things that weren't going to sit calmly on the sidelines while he thundered about a court waving a racquet.

'How about you, Anna?' Bob asked. 'Fancy it?'

'Even with that foot you're too strong for me. Anyway, as soon as Rowan's back from her mother's I'm going into town to meet Sarah.'

'Again? You were with her half the day yesterday.'

'Is there something wrong with that?'

'No, I'm just saying, that's all. Cooper, fancy making up a four at tennis?'

'Yes!' Cooper cried, punching his hands in the air and letting his scooter thud to the ground.

'OK, well you get a couple of friends together from kindi and we'll thrash 'em when you get home.'

When he'd finished steering Elodie's egg in the direction of her mouth, Anthony kissed her again and planted her in the high chair.

'Dad, dad, dad,' she gurgled. 'Coo-ooper.'

'Elodie,' Cooper growled back, pretending to be a monster and making her squeal with laughter.

Unable to remember when he and Charlotte had last been this relaxed with the children, Anthony picked up his phone and laptop and headed out to the car.

'Got a minute?' Bob called, coming after him.

Anthony checked his watch. 'As long as it's only a minute.'

'Then I'll catch you later. Any more news from the police?'

'It's still early in the day, but given the time difference something might have come in from London overnight.'

'Are they saying they think this scumbag is in Britain?'

'I'm not sure, but given it's where Brian Wade committed his crimes against Chloe I guess it makes sense to contact the police there.'

Bob nodded thoughtfully, then clapping Anthony on the shoulder, he said, 'Go to it, and if you change your mind about the tennis you know where I am.'

Charlotte had been with Julia Minor for fifteen minutes or more by now, sitting in the room Julia used for therapy in a double-fronted Victorian town house two streets back from the marina. It was a large, shambolic space full of toys and blackboards, colouring books, child-size furniture, building blocks and a low-hanging punchbag draped in front of the old-fashioned hearth.

The two women were seated at each end of a sumptuous corduroy sofa with a tray of coffee on the table between them, and Julia's notebook computer beside it. Every now and again she picked it up to type something into it, but for the most part, her round, sunny face was focused on Charlotte as they went back and forth along memory lane.

However, it didn't take long for Charlotte's light-heartedness to fade; laughter was so alien to her these days that more than a moment of it inflamed her guilt with thoughts of Chloe, and how helpless and wretched she felt about failing her.

'Do you really think you have failed her?' Julia probed, her plump features taking on an expression of surprise.

'I know I have,' Charlotte confessed. 'She needs so much more than I can give her, which is something I didn't stop to consider when I took her. If I had, I'd have realised that I wasn't in any way qualified to deal with a child who'd suffered the way she had, at least not on a permanent basis. It takes a very special kind of person to be able to handle those sorts of issues.'

'Yes, it does,' Julia agreed, 'and it's true, not everyone can cope, but there were no indications back then of how the trauma might manifest itself at a later date. You just saw a child in need and gave her all the love and reassurance she needed. Apart from anything else, it was your job to rescue her from her father.'

'But we both know what should have happened next. I should have put her into the system.'

'Should have, could have, it's irrelevant now. We can't change the past. All we can do is try to work on the future. You told me on the phone that to date she's refused to participate in any form of therapy?'

'We were advised, after the adoption, not to try

and force it,' Charlotte replied, 'and she really didn't seem to need it back then.'

'How many times have you tried since?'

'I guess four or five, all in the past year. The problem is, the minute anyone starts asking her questions she doesn't want to answer she just clams up, or throws the kind of tantrum you really don't want to see.'

'When was the most recent attempt?'

'About a month before Christmas. I had the backing of the school, someone was brought in specially, but on that occasion she turned violent.'

After making some notes, Julia put the computer down again and said, 'After the adoption I believe you and your husband took her straight back to New Zealand?'

'That's right.'

'And your son . . .'

'Cooper.'

' . . . came along about six months after that?'

'That's right, and she seemed to love having a baby brother. She wanted to help with everything, she read him stories, tried to change his nappies, fed him, always wanted to buy him things when we went out.'

'So she never behaved in a negative way towards him?'

'Not as far as we were aware. Of course they squabbled and fought the way most kids do, but there was never anything to cause us any concern.'

'So the problems really began after your daughter was born, which was . . .'

'Eighteen months ago. They weren't too bad at first, just the normal sort of jealousy kids can feel when a baby comes along.'

'Give me some examples.'

'Pinching or punching, not very hard, although sometimes enough to leave a bruise. Hiding or breaking toys; shouting at the baby to shut up when she cried.'

'Did you speak to her about it?'

'Of course, and we'd send her to her room and tell her she couldn't come out until she learned to behave properly. Then one or other of us would go and have a chat with her to make sure she understood that the way she treated Elodie was wrong.'

'Did it ever occur to you that being sent to her room might have been something her birth father used to do?'

Charlotte stiffened with surprise. No, it hadn't occurred to her, but it was almost certain that Brian Wade would have done that. Most parents did. But most parents weren't like him.

'I'm not trying to make anything of it,' Julia assured her. 'Remember, this is just a preliminary chat so I can get a general picture of things. Go on telling me about the ways she acts up.'

Charlotte glanced down at her hands. 'It started to get really bad around Elodie's first birthday.

I think Chloe resented all the attention Elodie was getting, and she became so angry with me at the little party we gave that she started kicking and punching me with all her might. It took most of Anthony's strength to wrestle her upstairs to bed. She was screaming the whole time, mostly gibberish, we had no idea what she was saying, but there was no mistaking her fury. He shut her in her room and she smashed the place up, even toys she liked were broken; some were even destroyed. It was awful, horrifying . . . We'd seen her angry before, but not as bad as that.'

'How long did it take her to calm down?'

Charlotte shook her head. 'It's hard to remember; there have been so many eruptions since. I guess it usually takes a couple of hours, sometimes until the next morning. Then she carries on as though nothing has happened.'

'So she never refers to the outbursts?'

'Not really. I've tried talking to her about them, mainly to find out if she understands how . . . unusual and frightening they can be, but it runs the risk of tipping her over the edge again so I tend not to press it.'

'How often do they happen?'

'Sometimes two or three times in a week, then she might go for a fortnight before something sets her off again.'

'And in your mind the triggers are . . . ?'

'I think not getting my undivided attention bothers her a lot.'

'Is she the same with Anthony?'

'She's less likely to turn violent with him, but yes, I think she resents not having his attention too.'

'What sort of things does she say to try and communicate her frustration?'

'She'll accuse me of not being her real mummy, or that I lied when I told her her real mummy was dead. She reminds Anthony that he's not her father, she's even started calling him Anthony instead of Daddy.'

'But she used to call him Daddy?'

'All the time.'

'And this stopped around the time Elodie was born?'

'A few months after.'

Apparently finding this interesting, Julia made more notes before indicating for Charlotte to continue.

'There have been times,' Charlotte said, 'when I've found myself thinking of her mother's mental health problems, and worrying that she might have inherited them.'

'Her mother was a paranoid schizophrenic?'

Charlotte nodded, and waited as Julia noted that down too. 'Do you think it's likely?' she ventured, her nails biting into her palms.

'I really wouldn't like to say at this point,'

Julia replied. 'So tell me about school. She's been excluded, is that right?'

'We were waiting to hear before we left, but it's pretty certain it'll happen. She's been incredibly disruptive in class, bossy, spiteful with others, and then there's the . . . inappropriate behaviour.'

'Of a sexual nature?'

Charlotte didn't deny it.

'Does she masturbate regularly?'

Charlotte's dismay showed. 'She's been teaching the other children how to do it. Boys and girls. So you can understand why a lot of parents have complained. I guess I would if I were in their shoes. These kids are only eight, after all.'

'I've come across it in children a lot younger,' Julia commented, 'and I'm talking about children who haven't been abused in the same way Chloe has.'

Accepting this, Charlotte said, 'I'm not sure how far she went with Elodie, or Cooper, but I know things happened, and something's come to light in the last few days. Apparently, my mother found Anthony's iPad in Chloe's bedroom. She's been using it to correspond with someone claiming to be a friend of her father's. The police are looking into it, but I don't think there are any leads so far.'

'I presume her father's still in prison.'

Charlotte nodded.

'Have you spoken to her about this communication?'

'Not yet. I wanted to talk to you first, to ask for some guidance on the best way to handle it. She's been so good since we arrived, and I'm afraid bringing this up might send her off the deep end again.'

Nodding her understanding, Julia made another note and was about to speak when Charlotte said, 'I don't know if this is connected to the online activity, but I found her one night standing next to Elodie's cot, staring in at her. When I got closer I saw that Elodie's nappy was awry, and Chloe got very angry when I asked what she was doing.'

'Did she have an explanation?'

'She said she hadn't been doing anything, and that I was always picking on her and blaming her for things she hadn't done.'

'Was Elodie all right?'

'Not really. By the next day her vagina was swollen and inflamed . . .' She swallowed hard. 'I've seen vulvovaginitus enough times to recognise it. Of course I realise it's not necessarily caused by an interference of the kind we're talking about, but the coincidence . . .'

'So what did you do?'

Ashamed, Charlotte said, 'I panicked. I was afraid to take Elodie to the doctor in case he realised she was Chloe's sister – well, he would, he knows us as a family, and everyone's heard Chloe's story. It was all over the papers four years ago, not just here, but in New Zealand as well.'

'So you thought, based on her history, that the doctor might involve social services?'

Charlotte nodded. 'And if that happened, I was afraid they'd end up taking one or both of them away. I wasn't even sure Cooper would be safe. If they decided I was an unfit mother . . .'

'Why would they decide that?'

'It happens, you know it does. Social workers, doctors, child protection officers, they can make mistakes, jump to the wrong conclusions. They're very capable of acting before asking, I know because I've seen it, I might even have done it.'

Frowning at that, Julia let a moment pass.

Charlotte said, 'You're thinking I could have jumped to the wrong conclusion about Elodie?'

'Actually, I wasn't thinking that, but do you?'

Charlotte shook her head. 'I was very stressed at the time. Everything was getting on top of me . . . But I know what I saw and . . . I think I've managed to get Chloe away before she did something that we'd all regret.'

The natural kindness in Julia's eyes was troubled as she raised them from her notebook. After a while she said, 'Going back to Anthony, has Chloe ever tried to behave inappropriately with him?'

Shocked by the question, Charlotte said, 'No, never.'

'Do you think he'd tell you if she had?'

'Yes, of course. Or, I don't know, maybe he

wouldn't want to upset me, and he can be very protective of her at times.'

'In what way exactly?'

Charlotte tried to think, but found it hard to come up with a scenario that wasn't from over a year ago. 'He used to be that way before things started going wrong,' she said. 'She was the apple of his eye, he couldn't do enough for her, and she completely adored him. Then Elodie came along and we started having problems with the business . . . We were both very distracted . . .'

'And stressed, if you were under pressure outside the home as well.'

Charlotte nodded, realising it had been too long since she and Anthony had felt relaxed anywhere, apart from the short time at Lake Taupo.

Coming back from her notebook again, Julia said, 'Does Chloe ever show any signs of being jealous of you?'

'Of *me*?'

'If she loves Anthony – and we have to remember that her perception of love might be different to other children's – she could feel jealous of the closeness you share. Are you affectionate with one another in front of her?'

Thinking of how uncomfortable she'd come to feel with any sort of intimacy between them when Chloe was in the house, Charlotte said, 'We used to be, but I don't think it stopped because I sensed some kind of jealousy . . . I think it was more to do with being afraid she might be watching, or listening. It got so it didn't feel right to engage in anything that might be construed as sexual when she was around.'

Apparently intrigued by that, Julia asked, 'Did Anthony feel the same?'

'Not that he's ever said.'

'So this could perhaps be your problem rather than Chloe's?'

Not having considered that, Charlotte was thrown. 'Yes, I suppose so,' she had to admit.

'I'm not saying it is,' Julia assured her, 'we won't know until I've spoken to Chloe, if she'll speak to me, but even if she does it's unlikely we'll get many answers straight away. Eight, going into nine, can be a troublesome age. She probably thinks of herself as very grown up, whereas she's still way too young to be able to articulate anything she's feeling on a deeper level.'

'But you think you can help her?'

'I'm willing to try, but until I've had the chance to talk to her I can't tell you anything for certain.'

Having expected this answer, Charlotte said, 'I realise it might be difficult to fit her in at this short notice, and obviously we're not a part of the NHS any more, so if you're able to see her privately we're happy to pay. Do you think twice a week is too often?'

Julia's smile was sardonic. 'I understand you're

keen to know that she's getting the care and support she needs to go forward with her life, but I'm afraid this kind of therapy doesn't work to a timetable. How many times per week, or month, or even six months, will depend very much on Chloe, and I'm afraid achieving positive results will take as long as it takes.'

Which could be years, Charlotte knew that, and felt as crushed by it as she did by the shame of seeming to want to rush it to suit herself.

Reaching into her bag, Julia pulled out a small book and handed it over. 'I expect you've seen this before,' she said, 'you've probably even recommended it to parents yourself, but have you ever actually read it?'

Loving and Living with Traumatised Children. Yes, Charlotte recognised it, and yes she'd read it – and it was making her feel more inadequate than ever to be reminded that she wasn't as noble or courageous as many other parents in her position.

Was this Julia's way of suggesting she wasn't trying hard enough?

'Wendy would like you to give her a call,' Julia said, as they walked to the door. 'My understanding is that she wants to be sure that you've exhausted all possibilities within the family.'

'She mentioned my sister-in-law when I saw her,' Charlotte said. 'Maggie used to be a foster carer.'

'Indeed, but you also have a sister, I believe?'

'Gabby has two children and I can't see Chloe behaving any better with them than she does with me – even if Gabby would take her, and I'm sure she wouldn't. Besides, that wouldn't make her an only child, which I think is what she needs. Do you agree with that? Would it be best for her to be an only child?'

'I really can't answer that at this stage. For some it works, for others . . . We're all different, even traumatised children.'

Accepting that, Charlotte said, 'Have you ever recommended it?'

'No, but I haven't been doing this job for long. Tell me this, if you do go through with it, how do you see the future panning out with Chloe? You'd still be her mother, after all. Nothing but the law can change that, and these circumstances don't qualify for an adoption reversal.'

Charlotte's mouth turned dry. Being reminded for a second time that she would always be Chloe's mother, no matter where she was or who she was with, was making it all feel harder and more unforgivably selfish than ever.

Opening the door, Julia said, 'I know this can't be easy. Deciding whether to relinquish a child never is, but I'll help in any way I can.'

Charlotte attempted a smile, but it didn't come.

'Before you bring her here,' Julia continued, 'you should tell her that I need some help with a four-year-old girl who's had some similar experiences to those she had when she was little. It might make it easier for us to get started if she thinks she's helping me, rather than the other way round.'

As Charlotte drove back to Maggie's, tears were rolling silently down her cheeks. She was no closer to making a decision now than when she'd arrived, but what she did know was how afraid she was that the authorities in New Zealand were going to carry out physical checks on Cooper and Elodie. It hadn't been mentioned yet, and she kept trying to comfort herself with the fact that it might not happen, but if it did . . . She knew only too well how traumatic those examinations could be for a child, and if her own had to go through it she needed to be there.

'It's all such a mess,' she wept to Maggie when she got home, 'but I can't help thinking that if I do let her go the authorities in Hawkes Bay will have no reason to take the other two away.'

'You don't know that's what they're intending,' Maggie reminded her.

'But if there's even the slightest chance . . .' Clasping her hands to her head, she cried, 'It'll be like sacrificing Chloe to keep the others safe. How on earth can I make myself do that?'

Maggie shook her head helplessly.

'I have to make a decision soon,' Charlotte told her, 'or I'm going to end up losing my mind.'

Chapter Fourteen

I'm in Auntie Maggie's conservatory watching the gardener's children playing outside by the greenhouse. There's a boy who's probably about six and a girl who might be the same age as me. I wish I could go and play with them; it's boring being stuck in here all the time, but I'm afraid to ask in case I'm told no I can't. I always manage to upset other children, or their parents, or my own parents, so it's probably best for me to play video games on the TV, or on colourful boards with Uncle Ron. I can't even connect to other children online to take part in building a Lego village, or join in composing a song, or share some jokes, because no one will explain the Wi-Fi code to me.

I think it's probably because they've found out I stole Daddy's iPad and I've been using it to be in touch with my creepy daddy's friend, but no one's said anything yet, so I haven't either.

My cousins, Auntie Gabby's children, are breaking up for the Easter holidays tomorrow. I was really looking forward to seeing them, but Mummy told me earlier that they've already arranged to go to their grandma's in Kent, wherever that is. It's a long way from here anyway, and I know that everyone's trying to keep my cousins away from me, because I'm not as special as they are.

Anyway, I don't care. Everyone can drop dead as far as I'm concerned, including Mummy who's not being as kind as she usually is, and she keeps going off places without me.

They think I don't know what's going on, but I do. I've worked it out. Mummy's planning to give me away. I don't know who to, and I don't want to go, but I'm too afraid to ask her about it in case she tells me it's true. She doesn't want to put up with me any more. Well good; I don't want to put up with her either. I don't want to put up with anyone in the whole wide world ever again, because everyone's stupid and mean and they don't understand anything, and I won't bother speaking to them again because they don't deserve it.

'Are you all right, sweetie?' Auntie Maggie's just come in from the kitchen. 'Aren't you cold in here?'

I'm freezing, but I say, in a voice that tells her I'd rather be on my own, 'There's nothing wrong with me.'

She tries to put an arm around me, but I shrug her away.

'I can tell something's on your mind,' she says softly, 'but I'm not going to make you . . .'

'You're not going to make me do anything,' I tell her crossly.

She sits on the flowery sofa and I can feel her watching me. I don't mind too much, because I like Auntie Maggie, and in a way I'm glad she's come to talk to me, because I was fed up of being on my own.

'You're a very brave girl, Chloe Goodman,' Auntie Maggie tells me kindly.

I've got no idea why she would say that and I'm not going to ask, or wipe away the tears that have just stung my eyes. I'm only going to carry on being brave, because it's the best way to be so no one will ever think I'm scared, because I'm not.

Lots of minutes tick by without either of us saying anything. I'm staring at a photo of Daddy with Auntie Maggie. It looks like they're at a wedding and they're laughing their heads off at something.

I don't think I've ever seen Daddy laughing like that, or not that I can remember.

In the end, because my legs are aching, I go to sit next to Auntie Maggie, not right next to her, but close, on the edge of the seat. Then, in a couldn't-care-less voice, I say, 'Is Mummy going to send me away?'

Auntie Maggie smooths a hand over my back, but instead of saying, 'Of course not,' which is what I expected, she says, 'What makes you think that?'

I turn to her quickly. 'Please don't let her send me away,' I beg. 'I promise I won't be naughty any more, or do anything to upset anyone. I don't want to live with anyone else, I want to go back to New Zealand with Mummy and Daddy.'

'Sssh, sssh,' Auntie Maggie soothes, pulling me into her arms, 'all anyone wants to do is make you happy.'

I want to believe her, I really do, so I think I will.

It was three in the morning New Zealand time when Anthony took a call from Maggie. 'I'm sorry to wake you at such an unearthly hour,' she apologised, 'and I promise there's no emergency. I just need to speak to you about something while I'm in the house on my own.'

Giving himself a moment to come round, Anthony said, 'Where are Charlotte and Chloe?'

'Gone for their first joint visit to the psychologist. Chloe thinks she's going to help solve another little girl's problems, and you should have seen how pumped up she was about that.'

Relieved to think of Chloe feeling good about something, Anthony asked, 'So what's the problem?'

'Well, I'm afraid Chloe's got it into her head that she's being sent away. I don't know where she's picked it up from, but she's clearly frightened to death and the fact that she's sensing something . . . I haven't mentioned it to Charlotte yet. She's under so much strain already, poor thing, and having to explain to Chloe what's going on . . .'

Anthony turned on a bedside light as someone knocked on the door.

'Is everything all right?' Anna called. 'I thought I heard the phone.'

Telling her to come in, Anthony said, 'It's Maggie. Don't worry, Charlotte and Chloe are fine, but Maggie has a bit of a dilemma.'

'Is it anything I can help with?' Anna offered.

'Can you put her on?' Maggie asked.

Handing over the phone, Anthony went to check on the children, and returned in time to hear Anna saying, '. . . of course we want to be truthful with Chloe, but I'm not sure how helpful it will be, for her or for Charlotte, if Chloe were to know in advance that she's not going to be a part of our family any more.' She glanced awkwardly at Anthony as Maggie spoke and then said, 'Actually, I've been doing a lot of thinking since Charlotte left, and I've started to wonder about some things that I'd really like to run past Julia. Do you think it would be OK for me to ring her?' Maggie apparently did, because Anna began rummaging for a pen.

Handing her one, Anthony waited for the call to end and watched his mother-in-law walk out of the room apparently so deep in thought she'd forgotten he was there.

Deciding if he was still awake in an hour, and he suspected he would be, he'd ring Charlotte, not to pass on what Maggie had told him about Chloe's fears – his sister and mother-in-law apparently had that in hand – but to find out how Chloe had got on with Julia Minor.

It would be a distraction, albeit a harrowing one, from what was going on in his part of the world.

Dear Charlotte, I want you to know that I passed your message to Polly Greenborough and she's asked me to forward her reply.

With best wishes
Emily Burrows

As she stared at the screen Charlotte was aware of so much apprehension, hope and dread building inside her that she was finding it hard to move.

This is only Polly's story, she reminded herself forcefully. It won't be a voice from the future telling me what's in store; it'll simply be another mother's experience of a traumatised child who she had to let go . . . or whom she found a way to keep without losing her family.

Unless she read the message she wouldn't find out.

Dear Charlotte,

First of all let me express how deeply sorry I am that you are facing the same agonising decision with your daughter as I faced with Roxanne. Since being in that position I have discovered that it happens to far more people than we realise, but not everyone makes the mistake of going public the way I did. I stopped when I did because I hadn't realised until then just how judgemental people could be, especially about things they don't understand or have never experienced. It's astonished and torn me apart to discover just how unforgiving some of my blog followers were, and how ready to damn me and tell me what I should have done.

Coming to a decision about Roxanne's future was, as I'm sure you can imagine, the hardest thing I've ever had to face. Even if I'd decided to let her stay, I don't think it would have been any easier, because I know now that it would only have been delaying the inevitable. You see, in my heart I already knew I had to let her go, it was making myself accept it, and do it, that caused me so many problems. I should never have let it drag on for as long as it did; spending six months or more talking to social services, psychologists, the parents of other traumatised children, was only prolonging the agony, not only for me, but for the rest of the family, including Roxanne. She didn't know what was happening, but of course she sensed something, and I never found the courage to explain it. I couldn't when I still hadn't accepted that I was really going to let her go.

In the end the decision was taken out of my hands when she stabbed my son in the face with a kitchen knife. The injury was quite serious, he came close to losing an eye, but it could have been so much worse, and to be honest I think she meant it to be. It's my belief that fear and frustration got the better of her, and she lashed out without thinking about what she was doing. Of course, once they knew about it, social services took her away, and the investigation that followed was brutal, accusatory, as if the police believed that we were in some way to blame for what she'd done.

Maybe on some level we were. All the secrets, the uncertainty, the sensing of something being wrong was very likely what tipped her over the edge – and what might have resulted in us losing our son.

I haven't seen Roxanne since the day they took her. Please know this isn't my choice, because I've tried on many occasions, but she refuses to see me. She won't engage in emails or texts either, or the letter-box communication that social services set up.

It's only through the social workers that I know she has finally, after two years of being passed from one foster carer to another and yet another, settled into a home with a single woman of around my age. Apparently she's doing well at school and her new guardian seems to have no problems with her at all. So I guess this leads me to conclude that the psychologist was right and Roxanne really is benefiting from being an only child.

As for me, I can't help feeling a failure. I think about her every day and I long to see her, and to meet the woman who's taking care of her now, but I realise that can't happen unless she wants it too. There's no doubt that our family life is calmer; we laugh a lot, have successful days out, and my birth children are blossoming in confidence now they no longer have anything to be afraid of. So you could say that letting her go – or having her taken away – seems to have worked out for everyone, but I still have nightmares about her and it can take me some time when I wake up to remind myself they aren't real.

I truly believe if I hadn't taken so long trying to make that painful decision she would never have attacked my son, so my advice to you, Charlotte, is if you really believe your daughter is in need of more attention, more support and care than you can give, if you are concerned at all for your other children, please don't make the mistake I made. Let her go sooner rather than later, don't drag it out and frighten her into doing something you'll all end up regretting. It'll be very hard for you, but in the long run it will be much kinder to her.

Charlotte didn't sleep that night. She read Polly's message over and over, went into Chloe's room to lie down with her but had to leave before panic and tears overwhelmed her.

By morning she was calmer, at least she thought she was. She rang Wendy several times, but she was in meetings and in the end Charlotte had to accept that she wasn't going to get back to her until the following day.

It wouldn't be too late. The situation would still be the same, but now that Charlotte had made up her mind, she was anxious to the point of frantic to carry it through.

She was going to hand Chloe over on Friday. Exactly why she'd decided on that day she couldn't say, and since then she'd hardly stopped shaking or thinking the worst in every possible way. It wasn't helped by today's news being full of the rapists from Rotherham who'd been sentenced for the insidious grooming of young girls in care. Chloe was going to be a young girl in care; she'd be as vulnerable and alone as it was possible for a child to be, and predators like that were all over. They prowled the streets and Internet meaning real harm to defenceless children who'd already suffered too much.

It was some small comfort for Charlotte to think of how well Chloe had connected with Julia Minor during their initial session. 'I'm sure we'll hit some hurdles from time to time,' Julia had said on the phone later, 'they're inevitable, I'm afraid, but based on our first meeting I believe that behind all the angst and delusions she genuinely cares about others. Certainly that's what's coming through where our fictitious little girl is concerned. She doesn't realise yet that I'm painting a picture of her at that age. Hopefully, by the time she does we'll have moved on far enough for her to start caring about herself in the same way.'

Those sorts of miracles did happen, and there was no reason to think they wouldn't for Chloe. In spite of being in care, she would receive the best possible support from Julia, and Wendy would definitely keep a close eye on her too. It would be Wendy's aim, Charlotte was certain of it, to make sure Chloe was placed with the best of all foster carers with the hope of securing a special guardianship for her as soon as the system allowed. If there was someone who loved Chloe as much as Charlotte did, and felt able to cope in a way Charlotte couldn't, she would know beyond doubt that she'd done the right thing.

Getting up too fast from the bed she staggered, and became aware of how wildly her heart was beating. Her breathing was ragged and so many thoughts were colliding in her head that she hardly even knew what they were. She needed to pull herself together before going downstairs or Chloe would sense something was wrong, and so would Maggie.

At last her mobile rang, and seeing it was Wendy she almost dropped it in her haste to click on.

'Wendy,' she gasped, 'I need to . . .'

'Listen to me,' Wendy interrupted. 'I swear I've no idea how this happened, but it seems someone has tipped off your old nemesis from the *Kesterly Gazette.*'

Charlotte froze.

'If you haven't already seen the online edition you need to,' Wendy told her. 'I've been trying to find out who leaked the information. I feel sure it must have come from this end, unless you can think of anyone who'd want to do it.'

'What does it say?' Charlotte asked hoarsely.

'Go read it, then ring me back. I'll be on my mobile.'

Running down the stairs, Charlotte found Maggie in the kitchen. 'Where's Chloe?' she asked, looking around.

'She went with Ron to pick up some things at the supermarket,' Maggie replied. 'What is it? Charlotte, you're shaking.'

Explaining that they needed to turn on the computer, Charlotte followed Maggie into Ron's study, waited impatiently for her to put in the password, then linked straight to the KG Online website.

The story was on the home page.

Charlotte and Chloe – No Happy Ending, by Heather Hancock

As regular readers of the KG will know, Charlotte and Chloe Goodman shot to fame almost five years ago when Charlotte, a social worker from the area, stood trial for the abduction of three-year-old Chloe (aka Ottilie Wade). Charlotte was dramatically cleared of the charge and allowed to adopt the child. A remarkable story in itself (link), and one that warmed the hearts of the nation. Who couldn't be moved by the way Anthony Goodman QC (now Charlotte's husband) managed to pull off a verdict that owed far more to sentiment than it did to justice? We all rejoiced; little Chloe was getting the mummy – and daddy – she deserved after the horrendous abuse she'd suffered at the hands of her birth father, now serving a life sentence for his crimes at HMP Long Lartin (link).

When this reporter heard that Charlotte and Chloe were visiting Kesterly for the first time since they emigrated to New Zealand, I was keen to find out how life was treating them down under. Apparently there are more children now, and it seems Anthony has stayed behind to take care of them and the family vineyard (link) while Charlotte and Chloe are away.

All sounds good so far. Chloe is now almost nine years old and Charlotte, who is lucky to be alive after most of her family was slain in the infamous Temple Fields Massacre some thirty years ago (link), is also the mother of Cooper aged four and Elodie not yet two.

Wanting to learn more about their idyllic-sounding lives on the other side of the world, I was about to embark upon some background research when a rumour reached me that all was not well in paradise.

'Oh god,' Charlotte groaned, not wanting to go on. Maggie was still reading.

In fact, according to my source, Charlotte has brought Chloe back to England with the intention of relinquishing her into the care of social services. If true then I'm sure, like me, you will be shocked and deeply troubled by this. There we all were thinking that Chloe was living happily with the mummy she'd chosen, and who had chosen her, but it turns out we could be wrong.

Could it be that now Charlotte has children of her own she doesn't want her perfect world upset by the problematic offspring of a paedophile?

'What the . . .' Maggie muttered incredulously. 'Didn't it occur to her that Chloe is old enough to read this and understand it?'

'People have already started to comment,' Charlotte pointed out.

Kylie from Exmouth: It's disgusting thinking you can do this to a child. If you ask me Chloe will be better off without her.

Nigel from Taunton: If it was her birth child she wouldn't be able to hand it back just like that.

Sandra from Minehead: Actually Nigel, you can hand your own children into care if you can't cope. Not that I'm saying it's right, or that anyone should do it. In this instance it's a disgrace. Think how much more traumatised that poor little girl is going to be.

Mattie from Mulgrove: We don't even know if the rumours are true, or who Heather Hancock's source is. As she's got things wrong in the past

I don't think it reflects well on anyone to start passing judgement on something they know nothing about.

'Do you know Mattie from Mulgrove?' Maggie asked.

Charlotte's hands were pressed to her face. 'I've known her for most of my life. We went to school together, and she was my co-producer in the am-dram group we ran in the village.'

'Well at least she's able to see through bloody Heather Hancock. Thank goodness she reminded people of how wrong that wretched reporter has been in the past.'

'Indeed,' Charlotte mumbled, 'but she isn't wrong this time.'

'What are you going to do?' Maggie asked.

Charlotte said, 'Wendy thinks the leak came from her end.'

Maggie nodded. 'I meant about Chloe,' she said gently.

Feeling as though she was on a runaway train that just wouldn't stop, Charlotte said, 'I need to call Wendy back,' and running upstairs she found her mobile and connected to Wendy.

'I want to bring her in on Friday,' she said brokenly. 'I've thought of a way to do it, I just need you to help me make it happen.'

*

Having finished reading the article Charlotte had sent him, Anthony stood staring at the computer screen, incensed and racked with every bit as much guilt as she was. Though he was aware of his father-in-law watching him, and knew that Bob had read the piece too, neither of them spoke.

Unusually they were alone in the winery; with an easterly tropical low heading their way Will had gone to speed up the final stages of picking, and it seemed the cellar rats were busy elsewhere for the moment.

'So,' Bob finally broke the silence, 'when are you going to wrestle that beast to the ground?'

Knowing how his father-in-law loved to speak in metaphors, or riddles, or whatever the heck was going on right now, Anthony turned to him, obligingly responding, 'Beast? I guess that's one way of describing Heather Hancock.'

'I'm not talking about the article,' Bob explained, 'we can deal with that later. What I'm talking about now is that pride of yours. When the hell are you going to knock it out, step over it and start doing what's necessary around here?'

Bristling, Anthony said, 'And what exactly would that be?'

'You know as well as I do that it's time you asked for help. OK, I get that might be a problem for a guy like you, you want to make a go of this place on your own, sole owner, self-made man and all that, but it isn't happening, Anthony. And it won't if you can't strike some sort of deal with Wineworks, or pay the workers, or meet all the other commitments you've got piling up around you.'

Admiring the frankness, if not the words, Anthony said, 'I'm on it.'

Bob looked sceptical. 'Is that so? Then tell me exactly what you're doing to get yourself out of this mess, because from where I'm standing it really isn't looking good.'

Tightly, Anthony said, 'You're right, it isn't, but I've got a broker handling the sale who happens to have an interested buyer.'

Bob's eyebrows arched. 'So that's your answer? To sell?'

'It's the only answer that makes sense. We can't go on like this, Charlotte's health has already suffered thanks to all the pressure we're under, and it sure as hell won't be improved by what she's going through now.'

'She's getting it sorted . . .'

'But how? And at what cost?'

Both men's faces were pale as they failed to come up with any answers.

'What I need to do now,' Anthony said eventually, 'is put my family first, and the best way I can do that is to sell up here and return to being a barrister.'

Bob frowned. 'In London?'

'In London.'

'You want to bring your children up *in London*?'

'It's not what I want, and it won't be what Charlotte wants either, but it's what I have to do.'

Bob shook his head in amazement. 'So you're going to quit, and take your family back to England where none of you want to be, rather than ask for my help?'

Anthony started to answer, but Bob raised a hand to stop him. 'Listen, son,' he said firmly, 'I get that you're all over the place with priorities right now. All that's going on with Chloe, how it's affecting her and Charlotte, you too, the problems here at the vineyard, it's a bloody nightmare, that's for sure, but if we work together I'm telling you we can turn it around.'

Anthony shook his head. 'That's good of you Bob, but . . .'

'Stop! I don't want to hear about why you can't accept me as a partner. Whatever your reasons they'll be to do with pride, and I've got no time for it. You've put body and soul into this place for the past four years, Charlotte has too, and I'm not going to let you walk away when I know damned well it's not what either of you want. We're going to go through the books together, you and me, and after I've transferred sufficient funds to get you out of the mire and back on track we're going to talk to a lawyer to make our partnership official. After that, we'll get together with the guys at Black Barn. They have plenty of ideas as well as contacts they're willing to share – I know because I've already asked – and then we're going to draw up a proper business plan for how to run things going forward. I don't want you taking this as criticism of how you've managed this far, you haven't done badly, but you've run into some lousy luck. We're going to kick that into touch, and one of the ways we're going to start is by looking at what should stay and what should go.'

Sensing that Bob already had some suggestions for that, Anthony waited for him to continue.

'Tell me about this Zoe person,' Bob prompted. 'I know she's good to look at, and she's a damned hard worker if all the tastings she's got set up for the winter are anything to go by. But can we really afford her, and do we need this brochure she's pulling together?'

'We can discuss her position,' Anthony responded, 'but as you say, she's got a lot of potential business lined up . . .'

'Which you could be doing yourself if you make use of the Black Barn experience and learn to take your hands off the wheel now and again. Will is more than capable of running this place, and that Zoe girl's got the hots for you. I guess you know that.'

'It's hardly relevant.'

'I hope it isn't, because she's a distraction you can definitely do without.'

Resenting the morality lecture that didn't say much for trust, Anthony bit back with, 'What she has, which is relevant, is a conscience about the

Australian deal going south. She's desperate to make up for it, and I think we should exploit that, at least to the end of her contract. It won't do any harm, and it could do a lot of good.'

'OK. What about the brochure? That must be costing a bit with a top-flight photographer . . .'

'Not as much as you might think, and given that it's already under way we might as well let it happen.'

Bob nodded thoughtfully, and glanced at his phone as a text arrived. After sending a brief message back, he said, 'Do you have time now to look at the accounts?'

Although Anthony didn't, he said, 'Let's do it, and if you decide when you see the full picture that you don't want to take it on . . .'

'I've already decided that I do.' Turning as Anna came to join them, he slipped an arm round her as he told her that he'd said his piece. 'He listened,' he added, looking at Anthony. 'Now let's hope he does the same for you.'

Anna's eyes were gentle as she fixed them on Anthony. 'Did you know,' she asked, 'that Charlotte's made arrangements to hand Chloe over tomorrow?'

Stunned that neither Charlotte nor Maggie had said anything to him, Anthony waited for Anna to continue.

'Charlotte didn't tell me either,' Anna confessed, 'I learned it from Julia, the psychologist, when I rang about an hour ago.'

Anthony glanced at Bob, but he was staring at the ground.

'The process of giving Chloe up is going to be traumatic enough,' Anna continued, 'but have you thought about how Charlotte's going to live with herself after?'

Anthony was turning cold, for it was that, as much as anything, that was keeping him awake at night.

'Have you thought about how *you're* going to live with *your*self?' Anna added. 'That little girl thinks of you as her father. Oh, I know she calls you Anthony now, but have you ever taken a moment to ask yourself why?'

He hadn't, or not in a meaningful way. He'd had too much else on his mind.

Nodding, as though he'd spoken, Anna said, 'Rick's at the cellar door and Rowan has the children. The car's outside and I'd like you to come with me.'

Frowning, Anthony looked at Bob again.

'I've got it covered here,' Bob assured him.

Realising he needed to give this some time, Anthony followed Anna out of the winery. 'Where are we going?' he asked, as she opened the Range Rover's passenger door for him to get in.

'First we're going to stop by the house,' she replied, glancing at her watch as she went round to the driver's side.

'And then?'

'You'll see.'

Chapter Fifteen

I don't want to go to Julia's today. I was looking forward to it before, but now me and Mummy are on our way I'm not feeling very well. It's like everything's going strange and dark and scary inside my head and stomach, and making me feel sick.

'You'll be fine when you get there,' Mummy said when I complained as we got in the car. 'Come on, we don't want to be late.'

Mummy doesn't look like herself. She keeps talking too fast, and she's white and kind of grey round the mouth; and her eyes are all bloodshot like she's been crying.

'What have I got to cry about?' she laughed when I asked, but it wasn't a normal kind of laugh.

I don't know what she has to cry about, but there must be something and whatever it is I know it's my fault. I've upset Mummy without knowing it, because I always do, but it's hard to say sorry for something if you don't know what you've done wrong. The way I screamed and shouted last night because everyone was ignoring me doesn't count, because they were the ones doing the ignoring, not me. And I didn't mean to knock over a chair or smash some ornaments, that was an accident, just like the way I fell up the stairs and bumped my head on the banister.

No one cares about that. I know, because no one came to make sure I was all right. I heard Mummy saying to Auntie Maggie, 'Leave her to calm down. It's the only way.'

'But are you all right?' Auntie Maggie asked her. 'You're shaking like a leaf and you haven't eaten anything all day.'

'I'm fine, honestly. Or I will be when it's over.'

'Oh Charlotte, are you sure . . .'

'Please don't say any more. I can't discuss it, it'll only make things worse.'

I'm not stupid. I know what they were talking about: as soon as the Easter holidays finish I'm going to be sent away and then it will be over.

I realise now it's why Mummy sneaked Boots into the suitcase and put in so many of my clothes, because she knew all along that I wouldn't be going home with her.

I'm feeling sick again. It's rising up in my throat and making my head grow bigger and bigger like it's going to explode. I don't know what to do or say, so I just sit looking out of the car window, banging my feet on the floor and scratching my hands, while Mummy drives and doesn't say anything either.

When we get to Julia's I walk in first, keeping my head up, and holding Mummy's hand.

'You're squeezing my hand very tight,' Mummy whispers. 'Are you . . . Are you OK?'

I don't know how to answer. If I say no it might get on her nerves, so I say sorry instead and let her hand go.

Julia comes out to meet us and I feel quite glad to see her, because she's nice and friendly and she listens when I tell her things as though they're really interesting and clever.

'Are you all right?' Julia asks Mummy.

I look up as Mummy nods, even though she doesn't look all right at all.

Julia smiles at me and Mummy kneels down to give me a hug.

'You be a good girl now, won't you?' she whispers in a voice that sounds like somebody else's.

I look at her, feeling frightened and panicky. 'Are you coming back for me?' I ask. Am I being given away today?

Mummy tries to speak, but instead she sobs.

I start to cry too. 'Mummy,' I wail.

'Ssh, ssh, it'll be fine,' Mummy says. 'You're going to . . . help Julia . . .'

'I don't want you to go. Mummy please . . .'

'I'll just be outside,' Mummy promises, clasping my face in her hands. 'You go on with Julia now.'

I put my hands over Mummy's to try and keep her there.

Mummy's head drops on to mine. 'It'll be all right,' she murmurs. 'I promise, it'll be all right,' and after hugging me really hard, she stands up again.

Not wanting to make a fuss in case it makes everything go wrong, I let Julia take my hand and walk me across the big hallway. When we reach the door I turn back to look at Mummy again.

Tears are streaking down her face. 'I love you,' she whispers.

I snatch my hand from Julia's and run back to give Mummy a hug. 'I love you too,' I say, 'always and forever.'

Mummy tries to repeat it, but the words won't seem to come out.

'You said forever,' I remind her, wanting her to say it.

'I know,' she gasps brokenly. 'Oh Chloe, Chloe. I'm so sorry.'

I take a big swallow. 'It's all right,' I tell her, remembering how Auntie Maggie said I was brave, and even though I don't feel at all brave I let Mummy go and follow Julia into the room where we're going to talk about the little girl who doesn't have a mummy and daddy or anyone in the whole wide world to love her.

I know how she feels.

'She's gone!' Charlotte sobbed into the phone. 'Oh god, Anthony, I've handed her over and I can't bear it. Please call me as soon as you get this.'

Charlotte was still in the car outside Maggie and Ron's, unable to go in, or drive on, or do anything apart from tear herself apart with so much grief and guilt it might destroy her. She kept hearing Chloe saying 'always and forever', and knowing she'd meant it the words ripped through her in a tide of longing and despair.

'Chloe, Chloe, Chloe,' she cried desperately.

She could picture her sitting with Julia now, innocently trying to help a little girl she didn't yet know was her, believing her mother was outside, and that she would be going home in an hour.

Was that what she believed? It was always hard to tell with Chloe, but she surely wouldn't have any idea yet that her mother had abandoned her.

There was no other way to put it; it was what she'd done and in such a cowardly way that she knew already she had no hope of ever forgiving herself. But would explaining it and saying goodbye have been any easier, any better even? The mere thought of it made her cry out again – she could never have said goodbye to her precious girl, any more than she could have tried to explain that someone out there would give her a better, a happier life. How would she have been able to promise that, when she had no idea if it was ever going to come true? More likely she'd condemned Chloe to years in care that would not end well.

As her head fell back against the seat she was seeing Chloe as she'd been the day they'd first met, at a park right here in Kesterly. She'd found her, aged three, sitting in a box swing, all alone. 'Hello, and who are you?' she'd said, and Chloe, beautiful and waiflike, had been too afraid to answer.

She remembered the first time Chloe had spoken to her. 'Boots,' she'd said, telling Charlotte the name of her bear. Then there was the day Chloe had hidden in the back of her car because she hadn't wanted to go home to her terrible parents. The way she'd cried when Charlotte had returned her to that awful house had broken Charlotte's heart, and had made her more determined than ever to do whatever it took to rescue her from the abuse Charlotte had *known* was happening. She could see Chloe, small and baffled, quietly waiting in an upstairs room of the rectory while the police had questioned Charlotte downstairs about the missing little girl's whereabouts. She recalled Chloe's excitement when she'd got on a plane for the first time to go to New Zealand, how proud she'd been of her lighting-up trainers. There were endless memories of her playing on the beach at Te Puna, her mother and Bob's home on the Bay of Islands. They'd lived an idyllic life for four whole months before the police had caught up with them. She would never forget Chloe's tears of shock and joy the day she'd been brought back to Charlotte, after being put into care during the time of the trial. She must have thought Charlotte had stopped loving her; then suddenly one day, like magic, Charlotte was there again.

It wasn't going to happen that way this time. After leaving Julia's just now Charlotte had driven to the car park outside Wendy's office, where she'd transferred Chloe's belongings from her boot to Wendy's. In just over half an hour Wendy would go to Julia's to collect her. By five o'clock Chloe would be in a home she'd never seen before with strangers, people who'd been told about her background and behaviour, and who, Wendy had promised, had a good track record where introducing problem children into care was concerned.

It didn't matter how kind and patient they were, Charlotte simply couldn't bear to think of anyone but her taking care of Chloe, even though she'd done such a bad job of it. They were bonded in a way that went beyond words, that was embedded in their very souls. They'd been brought together by fate, and fate had gone on, against all odds, to make them mother and daughter. Their connection might not be through blood, but Charlotte knew for certain that she couldn't love Chloe more if it were. Giving her up was like ripping out her own heart.

'Oh god, oh god,' she sobbed, banging her hands on the wheel. 'I can't do this, I can't, I can't.' How was she ever going to live with the empty space that Chloe should be occupying, thinking about her day after day, tormenting herself with what might be happening to her and how lonely, angry and afraid she might feel. Wherever she was, whomever she was with, she'd know she hadn't been loved enough by the only mummy she'd ever really had, and whom she loved with all her innocent and troubled little heart.

'But I do love you, Chloe,' she cried wretchedly. 'Please don't ever think I don't. Always and forever.'

Realising her mobile was ringing, she reached for it and clicked on.

'Charlotte? Are you there?' Anthony barked down the line.

'Yes, I'm here,' she managed to gasp. 'Oh Anthony. I don't know what to do. I've just left her . . .'

'Get her back! Go now and get her back.' He was almost shouting.

Not sure she'd heard right, Charlotte tried to steady herself.

'Do whatever you have to do,' he told her, 'just *get her back*.'

'I – I don't understand . . .' Was this really happening?

'Just do as I say, please,' he implored. 'I have to go now . . .'

'Where are you?'

'In Singapore, about to board a plane for London. Get Chloe, then call your mother. She'll explain – or maybe she won't, I don't know, but I'll be there as soon as I can.'

Afraid she was in a dream, while suddenly aware of how urgent this was, Charlotte turned the car around and sped back towards town.

'I'm coming, Chloe, I'm coming,' she called, as though Chloe could hear. Fumbling for her phone to call Wendy, she realised the battery had died and panic engulfed her. 'No! No!' she cried, looking at the time, and jamming her foot harder on the accelerator she pulled out to overtake a lorry, narrowly missing an oncoming car. 'Please don't have taken her yet,' she mentally begged Wendy while shooting through red lights on to Marina Drive. 'She mustn't know, must never find out.'

She arrived at Julia's with minutes to spare. Wendy was already there, and seeing Charlotte pulling in she got out of her car.

'I can't do it,' Charlotte gasped as she reached her. 'I just can't. Anthony's on his way . . .'

Wendy nodded, and in a rare display of tenderness she squeezed Charlotte's hand. 'My car's open. If you transfer everything back again, I'll go inside to make sure she doesn't come out until it's done.'

Loving her for understanding, Charlotte grabbed Chloe's bags, books and the beloved Boots, and had just closed the lid of Maggie's Punto when Julia's front door opened.

'Mummy!' Chloe cried, and Charlotte could tell by the surprise and relief in her tone that on some level, deep inside her young psyche, she'd been afraid that her mummy wasn't going to be there when she came out. She sensed so much, even if she didn't understand it, and Charlotte knew she must never forget that.

'Come on,' Charlotte smiled through her tears as she hugged her precious girl hard, 'let's get you home before the rain starts.'

*

It was after eight by the time Anthony arrived the following evening. Ron had gone to collect him from the airport, while Charlotte and Maggie took Chloe to the Seafront Cafe for tea. Chloe had talked so much, about the times she and Charlotte had been there when she was little (all repeats of the stories Charlotte had told her), about the things she'd helped Julia with, and about all the special treats they could have with Daddy when he got here, that she'd worn herself out completely. As a result she was fast asleep in bed by the time Anthony came through the door.

The instant Charlotte saw him, looking as though he'd been travelling for days, she ran straight into his arms. The feel of him holding her, the strength of his embrace and the way he drew back to look at her with his familiar tenderness and irony was so overwhelming that she could only laugh and cry and wish they were alone. She'd missed him so much, and the urgency of her need to be closer was pulsing through her shamelessly.

Apparently sensing it, he murmured something that fortunately only she caught, for it would have been sure to make his sister and brother-in-law blush.

Since they'd already spoken on the phone during his journey from Heathrow he knew that Chloe was safely home. Nevertheless, they went upstairs to check on her and stood looking over her for a long time, feeling stunned, *chilled* to the very core by what they'd almost done. It was going to take a long time for them to come to terms with how blind and prejudiced by the early trauma they'd been, but no matter how many heart-stopping nightmares their mistake might give them, how racked their consciences would inevitably be, what mattered was that Chloe should never know.

'Did you speak to your mother?' Anthony asked as they went back downstairs.

'Only briefly,' Charlotte replied. 'She said she wanted you to tell me yourself about the decision you've come to.'

Anthony glanced at his sister, and from the way she raised her eyebrows Charlotte suspected Maggie might already know what was going on.

Covering Charlotte's hand with his own as they sat down at the kitchen table, Anthony said, 'Your mother and I had a long chat before I left, and she made me see things that I should have seen a lot sooner. Now it's staring right at me, I can only wonder where our heads were that we didn't realise it ourselves, but maybe you did?'

Confused, Charlotte shook her head.

'Your mother thinks, and apparently Julia Minor agreed during a discussion they had when Anna rang her, that at least some of Chloe's problems, most specifically the attachment issues, could be down to me. They think she felt secure enough when you and I were first together, and seemed to deal with it pretty well when Cooper came along. It was after Elodie was born, another girl in the home, that the insecurity kicked in and she began to feel less than special, rejected even. The little ones were definitely mine, whereas she knew that she wasn't, and the hurt and frustration she feels is at least partly what drives her to behave the way she does.'

Sensing how terrible he felt, Charlotte said, 'I understand what they're saying, and I think you're right, we should have realised it ourselves, but I hope you're not blaming yourself . . .'

'Of course I am. How can I not when she was practically telling us what the problem was? She was always going on about her real daddy, and calling me Anthony. If that wasn't some kind of challenge I don't know what was. And to think that we kept blaming her, and her parents . . .'

'Her birth parents bear all of the responsibility for her problems,' Maggie reminded him. 'If it weren't for the way they treated her . . .'

'She wouldn't actually be with us,' he cut in. 'Charlotte and I might never have met. I think we can all agree that fate has a peculiar way of bringing people together. It happened this way for us, and I should have recognised as soon as Charlotte and I got married that Chloe needed to feel as secure in our relationship as Cooper and Elodie do now. She has to know that she's as much mine as she is yours,' he said to Charlotte.

Unable to stop the tears, she grabbed his hands and brought them to her face.

'I realise there are no guarantees that adopting her will fix everything,' he said earnestly, 'but we absolutely have to give it a try, for her sake as well as ours.'

Loving him with all her heart, Charlotte went to slide on to his lap and put her arms around him.

'Julia would like to see you tomorrow if you can make it,' Maggie informed them. 'I said I'd call in the morning to work out a time.'

Very much wanting to talk to Julia, Charlotte said, 'I'm sure she'll think Anthony adopting Chloe is the right way to go.'

'Oh, she does,' Maggie confirmed. 'It was mainly what your mother discussed with her; she wanted Julia's professional opinion before putting it to Anthony.'

Intrigued, Charlotte said, 'Just how much has been going on behind the scenes that we – or I – don't know about?'

'You'll have to talk to your mother about that,' Maggie smiled, 'but I will tell you that while you were putting Chloe to bed Anna rang to find out what I thought about it.'

'And we can assume you were in agreement,' Anthony stated.

'Of course,' she nodded. 'Anything to save your

family, and before you get the hair shirt out again, we're all feeling bad that we didn't see this sooner.'

Charlotte's head fell against Anthony's. 'To think of how close I came to letting her go,' she murmured, the horror of it rising up to torment her with what could have been happening to Chloe right now if Anthony, for whatever reason, hadn't agreed with her mother's theory. 'Thank you,' she whispered, pressing her lips to his forehead. 'Thank you so much.'

Sardonically, he said, 'Only you could thank me for getting something so spectacularly wrong. My meagre defence is that I've been too focused on the vineyard.'

'We're both guilty of that,' she told him.

'But it's going to change,' he promised. 'Bob and I have had a chat, I'll tell you more about that tomorrow, but from now on, family comes first and you might not be surprised to hear that your mother has a theory on that too.'

'It's a good one,' Maggie assured her, 'and Ron and I will be playing our parts, which is lovely.'

Interested to know more about that, Charlotte and Anthony looked at her expectantly.

With a glowing smile, Maggie declared, 'We've decided to start splitting our time between here and New Zealand. I didn't say anything before, because all this obviously took precedence, but as soon as we find the right place we'll be six months here and six months there.'

Amazed and completely thrilled, Charlotte and Anthony immediately threw their arms around her and Ron. 'This is the best news imaginable,' Anthony told his sister. 'Will you be looking in Hawkes Bay?'

'Of course. Maybe even in Havelock North, we'll see. But that's enough about us. What I want to know is when you're going to discuss your decision with Chloe.'

'Ah,' he said, stifling a yawn as Charlotte turned to look at him, 'I have a plan for that, but like a lot of things, I'm afraid it'll have to wait until I've caught up on some sleep.'

Chapter Sixteen

Anthony had been awake for several hours by the time Chloe peeped round the door in the morning, possibly to check he was really there, or maybe she was hoping he hadn't come. Although Charlotte had insisted Chloe was excited to see him, he was mindful of how her moods could change in a heart-beat, and what she might say when something was a prospect could easily bear no relation at all to what she did when it became a reality.

'Is that you?' he whispered into the semi-darkness.

'Yes,' she whispered back.

He opened up his arms, and to his relief she raced across the room straight into them – as she almost always did, he realised, when invited. She'd just lost the confidence to throw herself at him the way she used to, or the way Cooper always did.

'How are you?' he asked, snuggling her on top of the duvet.

'I'm fine,' she answered. 'How are you?'

'Jet-lagged. Did you suffer when you got here?'

'Yes, but I'm OK now. Did Mummy tell you I've been helping a lady called Julia with a little girl who thinks no one loves her, but it isn't true.'

'That's sad. Why does she think no one loves her?'

'Well, her first mummy and daddy were mean to her. They did all sorts of things to her that were cruel and against the law. Julia doesn't know whether to ask her what sort of things, but I said she shouldn't because the little girl might want to forget it.'

'That's wise of you,' he said, genuinely impressed, even if it wasn't the answer Julia had been looking for.

'Anyway, the little girl got another mummy and daddy, but now she says they're being mean to her too.'

'And are they?'

'I think so, sometimes, but she isn't always a good girl, so she has to be told off and she doesn't like it.'

'I see. Well, no one likes being told off.'

'That's what I said, but she shouldn't be naughty.'

'Perhaps she's just trying to get their attention.'

Chloe frowned as she thought about that. 'You might be right,' she conceded. Then abruptly changing the subject, 'We're going to do lots of things while you're here. Me and Auntie Maggie made a list last night before I fell asleep. I tried to stay awake, but I couldn't.'

'You're awake now,' Charlotte said, turning drowsily towards them.

'Daddy and I are having a chat,' Chloe told her proudly.

'No kidding.'

'We've got a lot to catch up on,' Anthony added. 'Everyone's missed you at Tuki River. The place is very quiet without you.'

Apparently not sure how to take that, Chloe said, 'Cooper and Elodie make a lot of noise too.'

'Oh they certainly do,' Anthony agreed, 'but they're not quite as good at it as you are.'

Apparently finding that funny, Chloe rolled on to her back and straight off the bed. She found this so hilarious that she couldn't stop laughing, and when she really couldn't stop Anthony realised she was in her own little state of euphoria. What was driving it was anyone's guess, but he hoped that being pleased to see him was at least a part of it.

'Is Auntie Maggie up yet?' Charlotte asked, when Chloe finally calmed down and went to sit in front of the dressing table.

'Yes, she's downstairs making breakfast,' Chloe replied, watching herself in the mirror.

'Why don't you go and give her a hand while Daddy and I get dressed?' Charlotte suggested, her right hand making it clear to Anthony that they might take a little longer to arrive downstairs than a mere few minutes.

After Chloe had gone, Anthony went to close the door, and slipping back under the duvet he covered

Charlotte's body with his own. Not until their desire was spent did either of them realise that they hadn't even considered Chloe's presence in the house.

'She's obviously very happy having you to herself,' he commented, as Charlotte reached for a robe. 'I wonder how she's going to like having me here, taking some of your attention?'

'I think she's going to like it just fine, especially when you tell her why you came.'

Watching her as she turned to him, he reached for her hand and pulled her back on to the bed. 'It's amazing how different things already feel just from taking that one decision.'

'It was a pretty big one.'

'Very late in coming. What we don't know yet is how she'll react to it. It's going to be quite a blow if she says she doesn't want me.'

'I honestly don't think that'll happen,' Charlotte reassured him, adding with a teasing smile, 'I do believe you're nervous.'

Laughing, he gathered her into an enveloping embrace, and loving the feminine scent of her he found it very hard to make himself let her go.

It was much later in the morning, with the breakfast dishes cleared away and a feisty storm battering the windows, that Anthony called everyone to the sitting room to hear an important announcement.

'Do you know what it is?' Chloe whispered to Charlotte as she climbed on to the sofa beside her.

'I've got an idea,' Charlotte whispered back, 'and you don't need to look so worried. I'm sure it's not bad.'

Chloe's dark eyes remained troubled as she hugged Boots close to her chest.

Realising she thought she'd done something wrong, Anthony went to stand with his back to the fire and gave her a reassuring smile. Apparently it didn't do the trick, because her face turned pale and her fingers tightened around Boots.

'I wonder what it's all about,' Maggie said conspiratorially to Chloe.

Chloe's eyes darted to her and straight back to Anthony.

Dismayed by how alarmed he could make her feel without even trying, Anthony said, 'Actually, it's not exactly an announcement that I have to make, it's more of a question. In fact, it's a very big question for a very important person in my life.'

Chloe glanced up at Charlotte, clearly thinking he was talking about her.

'I've given a lot of thought to how I might ask this,' Anthony continued, 'and I've decided that I should do it this way,' and coming forward he dropped to one knee in front of Chloe and took her hand.

She was still looking wary; her fingers were stiff.

'Chloe Goodman,' he said gently, 'would you do me the great honour of allowing me to adopt you so I can be your real daddy?'

As Charlotte stifled a sob, Chloe's eyes widened in shock. She turned to Charlotte and suddenly broke into an enormous grin.

'Can I take that as a yes?' Anthony asked.

Chloe nodded, and Boots was abruptly abandoned as she flung her arms round Anthony's neck.

Choked with emotion, he held her tight, and rested his head against Charlotte's as she hugged them both.

Were Chloe any older, Charlotte was reflecting as Maggie said she must call Anna, this might not have gone as well as it had, but fortunately she was too young to engage in artifice or to hide a flood of happiness as a means of self-protection or punishment.

'When can we do it?' Chloe asked Anthony, gazing earnestly into his eyes.

'Well now you've said yes, we're going to find out the answer to that just as soon as we can.'

'I'll call Wendy,' Charlotte said, getting up from the sofa. 'Or should we do it in New Zealand?'

'Call Wendy,' he replied. 'You never know, she might be able to fast-track it through the courts so it's done before we get home.'

'Am I coming back to New Zealand with you?' Chloe asked, looking hopefully from Charlotte to Anthony.

'Of course you are,' Charlotte cried, hugging her. 'You didn't think we were going to leave you here, did you?'

Though Chloe didn't admit it Charlotte could see that it was exactly what she'd been afraid of, and her heart ached with guilt, and relief that it wasn't going to happen.

'Nana wants to speak to you,' Maggie declared, holding the phone out to Chloe.

Seizing it, Chloe hardly said hello before launching into what had happened over the last few minutes. 'So Daddy's going to try and make me adopted before we come back,' she finished, 'but we don't know if we can yet. Mummy's going to call someone to find out.' Her eyes went to Charlotte as she listened to Anna's response, and the way she laughed at whatever Anna said made everyone in the room smile and laugh too. 'Yes, OK, I will,' she promised, 'love you too,' and bringing the phone to Charlotte, she said, 'Nana wants to speak to you.'

'Hi Mum,' Charlotte said. 'I hope you don't mind being woken up, but we had to tell you.'

'We were only just going to bed,' Anna assured her. 'She sounded so thrilled it brought tears to my eyes.'

'It's all thanks to you.'

'You mean to Anthony, he's the one who's adopting her.'

'You know what I'm saying. You saw what we were too busy, or self-involved, or misguided to see.'

'It's often easier to see things from the outside.

Now I have some other news, which is also good, although I wouldn't normally have described it that way.'

Puzzled, Charlotte glanced at Anthony, who was in the process of agreeing to adopt Boots as well.

'Elodie has another genital inflammation,' Anna told her. 'I've taken her to the doctor and he's quite sure it's an allergy of some sort, so we're trying to get to the bottom of it. Sorry about the pun.'

Charlotte sank on to the sofa, hardly knowing what to say. It was awful for Elodie, but such a profound relief to know it was happening while Chloe was on the other side of the world that she felt almost faint with it. On the other hand, how completely wretched she felt for blaming Chloe the first time around.

'I thought you'd want to know,' Anna said. 'Now it's time for my bed so I'm going to ring off.'

Charlotte waited until she and Anthony were on their way to see Julia to tell him the news about Elodie. Luckily they were stopped at a red light, for his eyes closed in the same profound relief Charlotte had experienced.

'Can we assume this means Chloe wasn't responsible for bringing it on in the first instance?' he asked.

'I think so,' she replied, and reaching for his hand she brought it to her lips and kissed it hard. She had so much to make up for with Chloe she hardly knew where or how she was going to begin, but begin she certainly would.

'I wish I could promise you that it'll all be plain sailing from here,' Julia was telling them over tea and biscuits later, 'but I doubt very much that it will. She's a child, after all, and they're nothing if not unpredictable, and of course her past hasn't gone away. The important thing is the response you got, Anthony, to your willingness to adopt her. This tells us that it was a pretty major issue for her, though whether she fully recognised it is hard to say. I'm guessing not, or she'd have been more straightforward in telling you.'

'She was telling us,' Charlotte confessed, 'we just weren't listening, or taking the time to understand.'

With a smile, Julia said, 'Don't be too hard on yourselves. Most parents lead crazy busy lives these days, and the way children communicate can often be perplexing at best, that's if they communicate at all and plenty don't. This is partly because they don't recognise what's going on in their minds themselves, or sometimes because they're afraid to speak out. I've only spent a couple of hours with Chloe, so it's not possible to give an informed view of where she's at in her mind. However, I will say that on some levels she appears quite sophisticated for her age. She has excellent cognitive skills, she's obviously bright in a learning sense and she's a good listener, which isn't something I say often about eight-year-olds, especially those with difficult pasts. Of course we know she's more advanced than she should be in her sexual behaviour, but she's also very immature in other ways. That could be because she's wishing herself back to the time she was an only child, a precious little person who got fussed over and probably spoiled rotten to try and make up for what she'd been through. She was happy then, her world was safe and perfect, and she's trying to make it like that again, but obviously she can't. Not only because she's eight, so no longer a baby, but because she has a brother and sister she has to share your attention with and that's not working quite so well for her.'

'So what do we do about that?' Anthony asked, feeling Charlotte tightening her hold on his hand.

'As a start I'd suggest spending special time with her. This is where she gets one or both of you to herself for an entire day, or half a day if that's too much. The point is to make her the focus of your attention and do all the things she wants to do. The same goes for the other two – it'll be important for her to realise that they matter just as much as she does, and it might be a good thing for her to have some special time with each of them too. Fifteen or twenty minutes could be enough to begin, and you can increase it if you find it's helping to create the kind of bond we're looking for. What's really important is that you get some support locally, for Chloe of course, but also for yourselves. I can't tell you how often I find that it isn't the child who's the problem, it's the parents, and it happens a lot with the parents of an adopted child who's experienced such a horrific early trauma as Chloe did.'

Charlotte and Anthony were taking in every word.

'You need to try and stop attributing everything she does of an aberrant nature to what went before. If you don't, then you're the ones who aren't letting it go, and if you don't she won't be able to either.'

Charlotte turned to Anthony. It hadn't occurred to her that they were the ones hanging on to the past, but she could see now that it was true. They used it as an excuse or a reason for practically everything Chloe said or did, when not everything needed to be as deep or complicated as that.

'Just let her be herself,' Julia continued, 'accept that there will be difficult days, periods even, deal with them and move on. And remember, she's of an age where many children are discovering their sexuality – usually for the first time – so try not to overreact when something of that nature happens. If she's instigating it you'll need to talk to her, but I'm guessing two things. One is that other children have found out about her past and are encouraging her to do what she does; the other is that things will calm down on that front once she starts feeling more secure at home.'

Taking a breath, Anthony let it go slowly as he digested it all. 'I wish you were coming with us when we go back,' he commented. 'Apart from all the great advice you're giving us now, we know she'll talk to you.'

Julia smiled. 'There are plenty of good therapists in New Zealand. You just have to find the right one, and I have a feeling Anna's already on the case about that.'

'Of course,' Charlotte murmured, 'what isn't she fixing, is what I'm starting to wonder.'

'Well, that's what mothers do,' Julia reminded her with twinkling eyes, 'they fix things.' Turning to Anthony, 'And so do dads.'

Although fast-tracking an adoption was possible in certain circumstances, even Wendy couldn't bypass all the assessments that had to be carried out and reports that needed to be written, filed and approved. There were many calls to the police, school and social services in New Zealand to request appraisals from them, which was when they discovered that the Child Exploitation and Online Protection team in London had tracked down the individual who'd claimed to be a friend of Chloe's father. It turned out that it was true, for he'd been in prison with Brian Wade; he'd also managed to make online contact with a number of other children who'd already been the victims of child abuse.

Naturally he'd been arrested, and to Charlotte and Anthony's relief the police in London didn't want to interview Chloe.

However, Julia felt it necessary for Charlotte and Anthony to talk to Chloe about the contact, to make sure she harboured no interest in her birth father or his friends any more.

'Ugh, yuk, no, no, no,' Chloe spat when Charlotte put it to her. 'He was horrible and I don't ever want to speak to him again.'

'But you do realise what danger you put yourself in by being in touch with him?' Charlotte prompted.

'I wasn't really,' Chloe insisted, 'because he was in England and I was in New Zealand. Anyway, it's good that he's going to be locked up again. He really gave me the creeps. Can we talk about something else now? Or, I know, shall we Skype Nana?'

As the days and weeks passed while they waited for news from Wendy, Charlotte and Anthony discussed bringing the other children over from New Zealand. In the end they decided that provided it didn't run on for too long they should make this time all about Chloe. She deserved their undivided attention, particularly in light of what they'd almost done to her, so they took her on trips to Bath and London, to Longleat to see the lions, to Center Parks, and to Mulgrove so she could see where Charlotte had hidden her from the police when she was three.

They sailed and rode horses, went for swims at Uncle Ron's leisure complex, watched movies together, played lots of video games that Chloe usually won, and were daily in touch with Cooper and Elodie via Skype. Though it was hard when one of the children cried for them to come home, at least it was reassuring to hear Chloe telling them that it wouldn't be long before they were all together.

'We're going to start having special time,' she told Cooper, 'so I can help you with your reading and teach you some new games.'

Clearly liking the sound of that, Cooper said, 'Then I'll be as good as you at them.'

'Maybe,' she teased. 'I'm going to have special time with Elodie too, so I thought I'd teach her lots of words by using pictures and music.'

'She likes music,' Cooper enthused. 'I play ring o' roses with her and she loves it when we fall down.'

'We'll do lots of that,' Chloe promised. 'We might even let Daddy play if he's good,' she added, with a roguish twinkle.

Giving a hoot of laughter, Cooper said, 'Otherwise Mummy will send him to the naughty corner.'

Though Charlotte ached to hold the other two in her arms again, she couldn't be in any doubt of how valuable this prolonged special time was proving for Chloe. The difference in her was as astonishing as it was heartening; she was so happy that it was impossible not to be happy for her, in spite of the occasional sulks and tantrums that usually occurred when she was tired. Clearly knowing that she mattered as much to Anthony as she did to Charlotte was having a profound effect on her. Her confidence was back, along with her inherent kindness and mischievous humour. She might be a little too outspoken at times, and she was definitely bossy, but she was as loving and entertaining as any near-nine-year-old could possibly be.

'There certainly has been a remarkable improvement in the way she conducts herself,' Julia confirmed after a sixth session with Chloe. 'She still won't talk about what happened when she was small, but I don't think that needs to cause us any concern. She's too young to handle the emotional impact it could have, and absolutely no good would come out of trying to force it. In fact, it could be that she'll never need to revisit it, although I wouldn't be surprised if puberty turns out to be an interesting time for you all.'

'Something to deal with when we get there,' Anthony responded with equal irony.

'Indeed,' she confirmed.

By the time the big day came round Chloe was so excited that she could barely stop talking or laughing all the way to the family court, and as soon as they'd parked she was out of the car, skipping ahead to where Wendy and her team were waiting.

'Everyone's here,' Wendy announced, leading

Charlotte, Anthony, Maggie and Ron through the rotating doors. 'That includes the judge, who you probably remember.'

Charlotte regarded her incredulously. 'Dudley Cross?' she asked, remembering only too well how he'd overseen the unusual proceedings almost five years ago that had resulted in granting her an adoption order for Chloe.

'None other,' Wendy confirmed, 'but I think you might have Anthony to thank for that.'

'I might have made a few calls,' Anthony admitted, 'but as it turned out, by the time I got to Dudley he already knew about the case and had got himself on it.'

Since the circumstances were perfectly straightforward, given Anthony's relationship to Charlotte, it didn't take the judge more than a few minutes to grant the order. However, Dudley Cross wasn't going to allow them to leave without saying a few words, all of which he addressed to Chloe.

'You might not remember me,' he told her, 'but I remember you very well, and what a remarkable little girl you were at the time your mummy adopted you. I've no doubt that you still have that same determination and strength of character, and I hope it stays with you throughout your life, as it will serve you well. You'll hit times when you don't feel as self-assured as you might, because we all do, but what's important is knowing that we matter, especially to those we love. By adopting you – choosing you – both your parents are telling you how much you matter to them, and how much they love you.' With a smile, he added, 'I'm very happy to say that as of today, Chloe Nicholls, you will be Chloe Goodman . . .'

'I already am,' she told him.

Twinkling, he said, 'But now it will be on your birth certificate, so it's official.'

Chloe looked up at Anthony, and as he smoothed a hand over her hair she whispered a reminder about Boots.

So it was that they left the court with a very tatty bear called Boots Goodman, and a journalist from the *Kesterly Gazette* – not Heather Hancock – whom Anthony had invited to come and cover the story of why he, Charlotte and Chloe had been in Kesterly all this time.

Chapter Seventeen

Summer had now yielded to autumn in Hawkes Bay, the harvest was in and the blue skies were constantly cluttered with clouds. Though it had rained heavily for the past two weeks, today felt like a brief return to midsummer as sunshine poured down over the bronzed and golden landscape with an unseasonable heat.

Charlotte and Anthony had brought Chloe home just over a week ago, to be greeted by most of their family and more friends than they'd even known they had. The party had been so unexpected and such fun that it had rumbled on throughout the weekend with more lobsters and scallops being brought in from the bay to throw on to barbies, and frequent trips to the village for more beers.

Although it felt in some ways that they'd been away for a year, everything seemed so familiar to Charlotte that she could have been here her whole life. Tuki River really was home, and now that Mike

Bain and Sara Munds had persuaded their fellow trustees to give Chloe another chance at the school, it was as though they really did belong. People who cared had come together to help them; Sara Munds, with some help from Anna, had been in touch with three child psychologists in the area, each with a different method of therapy, but each with an excellent reputation. All they had to do now was hope that Chloe would engage with one of them, which she might if they were willing to employ the same methods as Julia, and all three had given an assurance that they were willing to speak with Julia and take whatever approach worked best for Chloe. At the same time, Charlotte and Anthony recognised that they must continue working on their own behaviour, and accept that any oddities in Chloe's were just as likely to be a part of her development as her history.

Though things had started off well with all three children being delighted to see one another, helped no end by Olivia Munds having made herself Chloe's new best friend, Charlotte and Anthony weren't foolish enough to think that the adoption was going to solve everything in one fell swoop. However, there had been no explosions since their return, and given how happy Chloe seemed they were daring to hope that things really were turning around. And not only with Chloe, but with the vineyard too, for three large new orders had come in during their absence and, mainly thanks to the new routine Anna and Bob had designed for them – to put the family first while still running the business – they were confident of getting back on top of it all. The big difference this time was going to be that they wouldn't be trying to go it alone.

'Bob and I have taken over the River Retreat cottage,' Anna had informed them during the drive home from Napier airport last week, 'but don't worry, you won't be losing any income from it because we're paying rent. We just thought it would be better for us to be there, so we can still have our privacy and not get under your feet up at the house.'

'Exactly how long are you staying?' Charlotte queried, shifting a sleeping Chloe into a more comfortable position.

'As long as it takes,' Anna replied as though the answer were obvious, and indicating for the road to Hastings, she said to Anthony, 'I know you and Bob worked a few things out before you left, but I'm sure there's still a lot to organise where the winery and vineyard are concerned. For my part, I shall be in charge of the cellar door . . .'

'In charge?' Charlotte protested.

'. . . when you're not there,' Anna finished. 'We'll split the shifts between us and as far as the children are concerned we'll still have Rowan, but you'll be able to spend much more time with them yourself. You too,' she added to Anthony, 'if you're prepared to relinquish some control to Bob and Will, because if recent events have proved anything it's what a very important role you play in your children's lives.'

'All this would be fantastic,' Charlotte blurted, 'if we weren't screwing up your lives. You've got the most beautiful home in the Bay of Islands, all your friends and family are there . . .'

'We've got family here,' Anna reminded her, 'and Bob's really enjoying spending more time with Rick. Whether Rick's enjoying it we've yet to discover, but I think he is.'

'I'm sure he is, but what you're proposing . . .'

'Is to be here as much as possible until Tuki River is properly on its feet. There's no point arguing, Charlotte, we've made up our minds.'

Deciding it would be more than ungrateful to protest any further Charlotte had let it drop there, and only later did she bring it up again when she and her mother were alone and she was able to tell Anna how happy she was that they were going to be spending more time together. Having missed out on almost thirty years, neither of them wanted to be parted again for long.

It was on their fourth night back that Charlotte sent an email to Polly Greenborough, thanking her for her reply and saying how sorry she was that things hadn't worked out the way Polly had wanted for her and Roxanne.

I can only hope that one day soon Roxanne will change her mind about seeing you and you'll find out for certain that you made the right decision, because she really has settled with her special guardian.

She didn't tell Polly any more about her own situation; it didn't feel relevant or kind to speak of her own success, particularly when it was still such early days. The very last thing she needed was to tempt fate to do its worst.

This morning she was making a brief visit to the cellar door before a family day out, having come to see the brochure Zoe had brought for her approval.

Both women looked up at the sound of a car passing on its way up the drive to the house. 'Sara Munds and her daughter Olivia,' Charlotte said to Zoe. 'I should be going or I'll make us all late.'

'Sure,' Zoe replied, closing the glossy brochure. 'So you're happy for this to go viral?'

Charlotte smiled. 'Viral would be good, but until we can achieve that I'm happy for it to circulate. You've done a great job with the photographs and the text. Have you shown it to Anthony yet?'

'Only on a computer. He told me the final say was yours, so that's why I'm here. Sorry, I didn't realise you'd organised a family day out.'

'It's Chloe's birthday, but not to worry. I'm glad to see the brochure, and you before you head back to Auckland. I'm sorry we can't renew your contract, we're not sufficiently in funds to do it again, but you've taught us a great deal about the importance of PR, and pulled together an impressive tastings schedule for the winter months. I'm also told that the last three orders we received came through you.'

With a grimace, Zoe said, 'I can't tell you how relieved I am to have brought them in, and all with the Tuki River label. After what happened with the cleanskins for Australia . . .' Catching herself, she broke off awkwardly.

'What happened with the Australian order?' Charlotte prompted.

'Oh, there were some difficulties, but it's all worked out now. I should be going. I'll be in touch in the next couple of weeks to discuss the interview for *Cuisine* – don't worry about a contract, it's covered by the old one. Are you sure you're OK with the whole family being photographed? You've never been keen on that before.'

'It was different before,' Charlotte told her, starting to close up the cellar door. 'I guess I was being overprotective, especially of Chloe. I'm afraid now that I might have made it seem I was ashamed of her.'

Zoe looked startled. 'I don't think anyone ever thought that,' she assured her.

'But Chloe might have. Anyway, the *Cuisine* article is a good opportunity for us to show ourselves off to the world, in the hope that the world will want to come and see us. I expect you'd call it maximising our assets?'

Zoe smiled. 'You certainly have plenty of those,' she remarked as they strolled beneath the jacarandas towards their cars. 'A great boutique vineyard that really will do well, I just know it, amazing parents, three beautiful kids, and then there's Tony of course.'

Charlotte was regarding the grape-free vines, taking in Zoe's words and wondering what more she might say.

'I wish you and I could have got to know each other better,' Zoe continued. 'I think we might have if you'd felt able to trust me.'

Charlotte studied her carefully.

'You were right not to,' Zoe admitted. 'Your husband is a very attractive man.'

Not much wanting this to continue, but unsure how to stop it, Charlotte opened her car door.

'He turned me down,' Zoe told her.

As her heart flipped, Charlotte said, 'And you're telling me this because?'

'I guess because I want you to know how lucky you are.'

'You think I don't already?'

Zoe shrugged. 'I'm sure you do. And I'm sure I'm not the first woman to try and seduce him.'

'You're the first to admit it.'

Zoe smiled.

Deciding this had gone far enough, Charlotte said, 'Have a good journey back to Auckland, and thank you again for bringing the brochure to show me.'

As she turned the car around and headed towards home she was remembering a little homily she'd read on Facebook a few days ago: *The best revenge is simply to smile and move happily on, leaving karma to take care of the rest.* That being said, it was good to know that Anthony had put her, their marriage and their children before one of the sexiest women alive. If he hadn't, well, she wasn't going to trouble herself with imagining where they might be now, because it hadn't happened and so there was no point.

'Mum! There you are,' Chloe cried as Charlotte came up over the terrace to find her entire family busying themselves about the kitchen. Even Ron and Maggie were there, having arrived two days ago to start their search for a beachfront idyll in Hawkes Bay. Unsurprisingly, Rick and Hamish were in charge of the picnic, while Anna was attempting to coat a wildly cycling Cooper in sunblock, Rowan was struggling Elodie into a playsuit, Bob was loading drinks into a chilly bin, and Maggie was chatting with Sara Munds about properties for sale in Haumoana.

'Look what Olivia gave me for my birthday,' Chloe demanded excitedly, dodging round Cooper to show Charlotte a very pretty pearl and shell bracelet. 'It's my favourite and I'm going to treasure it forever.'

'We got it at a special shop in Napier,' Olivia confided, her cute freckly face pinking with pride, 'and I chose it myself.'

'Then you have excellent taste,' Charlotte assured

her, noting the birthday cards that had been set up around the fireplace.

'I've had eighteen so far,' Chloe informed her, 'which is the most I've ever had. I even got one from Wendy and Julia back in England.'

As thrilled for her as she clearly was for herself, Charlotte hugged her hard. 'Nine today, you're growing up so fast.'

Wriggling free, Chloe ran to get the new smartphone Charlotte and Anthony had dared to give her on the proviso she allowed them to check it each night, and that she didn't use it for the Internet unless one or other of them was there to supervise.

'I just want to take selfies for Instagram like everyone else,' Chloe had assured them, which was precisely what she began doing now, first with Charlotte, then with Olivia, while assuring everyone else that she'd get to them in turn.

'Where's Daddy?' Charlotte asked.

'I don't know,' Chloe answered, putting an arm round Elodie to get a shot with her.

'He was here a moment ago,' Bob told her.

'I think he went upstairs,' Anna said.

After having her fingers slapped away from a tasty-looking vol-au-vent, Charlotte ran up to the bedroom and found Anthony standing on the balcony staring out at the almost perfect day.

'Is everything OK?' she asked curiously.

Turning to her, he said, 'I was thinking of how

lucky we are with the weather, and trying not to imagine how we'd be feeling today, her birthday, if she weren't with us.'

Charlotte's eyes closed as the thought of it buried deep into her conscience.

'Thank god it's turned out this way,' he murmured, folding her into his arms.

'I keep wondering,' she sighed, 'how we even let it get so far.'

'Me too. It was like we lost all sense of what mattered, or who she was and how much she means to us. How could we have done that? OK, she was no angel, there were times when I actually felt scared of her, but she's just a child – our child – and we came so close to completely screwing up her life.'

'But in the end we didn't,' she said forcefully, 'and we can't let our guilt spoil today.'

'No, of course not,' he agreed. 'It just comes over me at times . . . You're right though, we need to change the subject. Tell me what you thought of the brochure.'

Kicking off her sandals, she said, 'Well, it makes us look a lot more upmarket than we are, but I guess that's no bad thing.'

'It's all about the wine,' he reminded her. 'The visuals are just gloss.'

'Of course, and they're gorgeous, especially the ones by the waterfall. I think it's Maraetotara where we've taken the children a couple of times.'

He nodded. 'Yes, I'm sure it is.'

After a moment she said, 'Zoe told me something before she left. Would you like to hear it?'

'I don't know. Would I?'

Charlotte smiled wickedly. 'She said she tried to seduce you, but you resisted.'

Raising his eyebrows in amazement, he said, 'She told you that?'

She nodded.

'It's true,' he acknowledged, pulling her to him. 'I mean, why on earth would I want her when I've got you?'

'We were going through a pretty rough time,' she reminded him. 'You must have been tempted.'

His eyes were searching hers as he said, 'Never enough to carry it through. However, if you were to throw yourself at me the way she did, I can promise you it would have a very different outcome.'

Loving the sound of that, she pulled him down on the bed and started unbuttoning his shirt as she sat astride him.

'Dad! Where are you?' Cooper yelled, banging in through the door. 'Oh, can I play?' and rushing at them he landed with a thump on Anthony's chest.

'I didn't invite *you* to throw yourself at me,' Anthony scolded, hoisting him up as Charlotte climbed free.

'Everyone's ready to go,' Cooper told them. 'They sent me to find you. Dad, you won't forget to pick up Oliver on the way, will you? Chloe said he could come even though it's her birthday.'

'Don't worry, I haven't forgotten,' Anthony assured him. 'Go and get in the car and we'll be right down.'

Moments after the door closed behind him Charlotte was undressed ready to slip into fresh shorts and top, and laughing as Anthony kept trying to grab her when Chloe said from the door, 'What are you doing?'

'Getting changed,' Charlotte answered, wondering whether to cover herself or not.

'It's *my* birthday,' Chloe reminded her sulkily.

Not quite sure what she meant by that, Charlotte continued to dress as Anthony took out his phone to answer it.

'Yes, Maggie, we're coming,' he told his sister. 'That's right, we're taking three cars. You guys go on ahead if you like, we'll bring the birthday girl and Cooper and Elodie with us.'

'And Olivia,' Chloe put in.

'Of course. Is her mother coming?'

'She's gone on ahead, and she's going to set up some games on the beach for when we get there.'

'OK. Now, we're going to miss the tide if we don't get a move on.'

Turning on her heel Chloe disappeared downstairs, leaving Anthony and Charlotte to exchange slightly worried glances.

'Do you think she was upset?' Charlotte asked.

'I'm not sure.'

'Why did she remind me it was her birthday?'

'I can't answer that either, but maybe we don't need to. Isn't it a part of where we've been going wrong, that we keep reading more into things than is probably there?'

Charlotte nodded dubiously.

Minutes later they were downstairs ready to leave, with everyone else either already on their way to Cape Kidnappers or waiting outside in the Volvo. To Charlotte's dismay it almost wasn't a surprise to discover that the car keys weren't where she'd left them.

Her eyes went to Anthony. 'I put them right here on the hook,' she told him.

'Are you sure?'

'Of course I am. After what happened the last time we tried to go to Cape Kidnappers I made sure I knew where they were, and I put them there to show that I trust her.'

Sighing, he said, 'So she did hide them the last time?'

Remembering that she'd tried to take the blame herself, Charlotte had to admit it. 'So what do we do now?' she said, looking at the time. 'I don't want to risk accusing her of anything in case it ruins the day, but if we don't find them in the next two minutes we'll miss the tide.'

Anthony threw out his hands. 'I don't get this

business of sabotaging her own days out. Everything's been going so well. Why would she do it?'

'According to Julia it's about a lack of self-worth and what she feels she does or doesn't deserve. For some reason she doesn't seem to think she deserves these treats.'

Pushing a hand through his hair, he said, 'When are we meeting with the first psychologist? Whenever it is, it won't be in time to find the keys. Bloody hell, how on earth are we supposed to play this?'

'I'll go and look in her room,' Charlotte said.

'Come on you two,' Chloe commanded from the terrace. 'We're going to miss the last of the gannets and it'll be all your fault.'

Glancing at Anthony, Charlotte said, carefully, 'We can't find the car keys. Have you seen them?'

'They're in the ignition,' Chloe cried exasperatedly. 'I put them there so we'd be ready to go. Now please hurry up or I shall get very cross with you,' and with her hands on her hips she stalked off back to the car.

Charlotte and Anthony turned to one another, not quite sure what to say.

In the end Anthony remarked wryly, 'I guess we should go.'

'Yes,' Charlotte agreed, 'I guess we should.'

Acknowledgements

NEW ZEALAND

It's hard to find enough words to express my gratitude to everyone at Black Barn Vineyard of Hawkes Bay who helped in so many ways to make this book possible. From the owners of this magical place, Kim Thorp and Andy Coltart, who so generously threw open the doors; to Dave McKee, the truly inspirational and world-class winemaker; to the lovely Rochelle Palmer who arranged our heavenly retreat (on which Charlotte and Anthony's house is based); to Francis de Jager, the Cellar Door and Events Manager who taught me so much, along with Mary-Anne Walker-Bain who also runs the Cellar Door. Thank you too to those mentioned above who so bravely and generously allowed me to use their names.

If you feel like spoiling yourself, don't hesitate. This place and its exceptional wines, not to mention

outstanding hospitality, combine to make it nothing short of heaven on earth.
www.blackbarn.com

An equally warm and enormous thank you goes to Michael Bain, Principal of Te Mata Primary School in Havelock North. It was a truly magical experience spending time at the school watching the easy, entertaining and affectionate interchange between Mike, the staff and small students.

Another sincere thank you to Lynne Alexander of Springbank School in Kerikeri, who talked me through some education programmes for eight year olds and helped so much to get me into "Chloe's world".

I must also thank Dr Sarah Hampson for inviting me to her beautiful home in the Bay of Islands and talking me through all the medical and social details I needed for the story.

I would also like to thank Becky McEwan of Tauhara Sunrise Lodge at Lake Taupo. This is such a romantic hideaway with all imaginable luxuries that I cannot recommend it highly enough.
www.tauharasunrise.com

A very big thank you, too, to Hannah de Valda, who organised some fantastic interviews for the time I was in New Zealand, and who was such good company during our research chats.

UK

As with the first two books in this series, *No Child of Mine* and *Don't Let Me Go*, Sarah Scully patiently and expertly guided me through the role that social services play in this sort of case. I truly can't thank you enough, Sarah, for giving your time and knowledge so generously.

I must also thank Madeleine Dunham, Consultant Clinical Psychologist, for giving me the benefit of her expertise in working with children. I must stress that some of the opinions expressed in the book are not necessarily Madeleine's, but have come from other sources of research.

Last, but by no means least, my thanks once again go to my dear friend Gill Hall for her invaluable input and for introducing me to Madeleine.

Susan Lewis

You Said Forever

Bonus Material

Susan Lewis

on

You Said Forever

Dear Reader,

What a surprise it was to me when I first started to receive requests for more about Ottilie/Chloe's story. It's such a tragic tale in some ways with so much potential for disaster through *No Child of Mine* and *Don't Let Me Go* that I was extremely touched by how many people stayed with the stories – and then wanted more.

Knowing how warmly you all engaged with this little girl was truly moving. As you can imagine she is very special to me, and it reflects so well on us all, I believe, that we care so much about children who need to be saved.

For a long time I really didn't know where the next book could go. It was clear it couldn't follow on directly from *Don't Let Me Go.* Some years needed to elapse for Chloe to become older and the effects of what she'd been through to start showing themselves.

It was reading about the pressures and challenges of adoption that finally reconnected me to the characters and the issues they were likely to face given the ordeals they had come through. It was heartbreaking in so many ways. I guess it's something we don't hear too much about, the adoptions that don't work out and how devastating it can be for all concerned.

I hope you feel that I ended the book in the way you would want every story for a child in distress to end.

I would love to hear from you to know what you thought of the book, so please don't hesitate to contact me through www.susanlewis.com

Thank you so much for your wonderful support and for your love of this dear little girl.

With my warmest wishes

Susan

Susan Lewis

On writing Hiding in Plain Sight

Imagine wanting something so badly it hurts. Imagine getting that something and it turns out to be nothing like you expected.

For more than twenty years ex-detective Andee Lawrence has tried many times to find out what happened to her sister, Penny, who disappeared at the age of fourteen. No body was ever found and none of the police investigations revealed any signs of abduction, abscondment or abuse. She simply vanished into thin air, leaving her family crushed and bewildered, racked with the fear of what might have happened to her, and tormented by the hope that one day, please god, she might return.

Andee's search for answers has always been weighted with the terror of what she might find, however, the joy of an imagined reunion has constantly played out in her mind. Could someone be holding Penny captive? Was she enslaved to some fiendish psychopath with a fatherly demeanour and elevated social standing that raised him above suspicion? Was she still in the country? Did she have children? Was she desperately willing Andee, or anyone, to rescue her from some unthinkable hell?

Or was she dead?

Then one day the questions are answered.

Nothing could have prepared Andee for the shock of discovery or the way it happened. People she knew and loved had lied to her; covered up truths, protected themselves and failed in their duty both to her and to Penny. No one was who she'd believed them to be, least of all her sister.

Susan Lewis

On writing Hiding in Plain Sight

As the reality of the past years unravels Andee learns the hard way how wise it is to be careful of what you wish for.

Those who've read *Behind Closed Doors, The Girl Who Came Back* and *The Moment She Left* will know how desperate Andee has been for answers, how the fear and heartache of losing her sister has shaped her life. Now, together with Andee, you will finally find out what really happened to fourteen-year old Penny.

Susan

Read and revisit

the Detective Andee Lawrence collection

Susan Lewis

Sometimes the truth is best kept secret

The Moment She Left

THE SUNDAY TIMES BESTSELLING AUTHOR

Available in paperback and ebook

About Susan

I was born in 1956 to a happy, normal family living in a brand new council house on the outskirts of Bristol. My mother, at the age of twenty, and one of thirteen children, persuaded my father to spend his bonus on a ring rather than a motorbike and they never looked back. She was an ambitious woman determined to see her children on the right path: I was signed up for ballet, elocution and piano lessons and my little brother was to succeed in all he set his mind to.

Tragically, at the age of thirty-three, my mother lost the battle against cancer and died. I was nine, my brother was five.

My father was left with two children to bring up on his own. Sending me to boarding school was thought to be 'for the best' but I disagreed. No one listened to my pleas for freedom, so after a while I took it upon myself to get expelled. By the time I was thirteen, I was back in our little council house with my father and brother. The teenage years passed and before I knew it I was eighteen ... an adult.

I got a job at HTV in Bristol for a few years before moving to London at the age of twenty-two to work for Thames. I moved up the ranks, from secretary in news and current affairs, to a production assistant in light entertainment and drama. My mother's ambition and a love of drama gave me the courage to knock on the Controller's door to ask what it takes to be a success. I received the reply of 'Oh, go away and write something'. So I did!

Three years into my writing career I left TV and moved to France. At first it was bliss. I was living the dream and even found myself involved in a love affair with one of the FBI's most wanted! Reality soon dawned, however, and I realised that a full-time life in France was very different to a two-week holiday frolicking around on the sunny Riviera.

So I made the move to California with my beloved dogs Casanova and Floozie. With the rich and famous as my neighbours I was enthralled and inspired by Tinsel Town. The reality, however, was an obstacle course of cowboy agents, big-talking producers and wannabe directors. Hollywood was not waiting for me, but it was a great place to have fun! Romances flourished and faded, dreams were crushed but others came true.

After seven happy years of taking the best of Hollywood and avoiding the rest, I decided it was time for a change. My dogs and I spent a short while in Wiltshire before then settling once again in France, perched high above the Riviera with glorious views of the sea. It was wonderful to be back amongst old friends, and to make so many new ones. Casanova and Floozie both passed away during our first few years there, but Coco and Lulabelle are doing a valiant job of taking over their places – and my life!

Everything changed again three months after my fiftieth birthday when I met James, my partner, who lived and works in Bristol. For a couple of years we had a very romantic and enjoyable time of flying back and forth to see one another at the weekends, but at the end of 2010 I finally sold my house on the Riviera and am now living in Gloucestershire in a delightful old barn with Coco and

Lulabelle. My writing is flourishing and over thirty books down the line I couldn't be happier. James continued to live in Bristol, with his boys, Michael and Luke – a great musician and a champion footballer! – for a while until we decided to get married in 2013.

It's been exhilarating and educational having two teenage boys in my life! Needless to say they know everything, which is very useful (saves me looking things up) and they're incredibly inspiring in ways they probably have no idea about.

Should you be interested to know a little more about my early life, why not try *Just One More Day*, a memoir about me and my mother and then the story continues in *One Day at a Time*, a memoir about me and my father and how we coped with my mother's loss.

Memoirs by

Susan Lewis

Read the true story of Susan Lewis and her family and how they coped when tragedy struck. *Just One More Day* and its follow-up *One Day At A Time* are two memoirs that will hopefully make you laugh as well as cry as you follow Susan on her journey to love again.

Available in paperback and ebook

5 minutes with Susan

Where does the inspiration for your books come from?

I often write about difficult issues, as you well know. I don't necessarily write from experience in these cases but I rely on listening and seeking the experience of others who might have witnessed or been through challenging situations. It's important as a writer to imagine how you'd feel if it happened to you. I enjoy doing it but sometimes it can be quite distressing – sometimes I cry, which tells me it's working. This is how I really bring my characters to life.

Do you have any peculiar writing rituals or habits?

Nothing too peculiar! I'm very strict about the hours I write, starting at 10 in the morning and going through until 5pm or 6pm, usually six days a week. Then, I love to have a glass of wine at the end of the day as I read back over what has happened in 'my fictional world' over the last seven or eight hours, socialising with the characters and often wanting to gossip about them with someone else.

What advice would you offer to aspiring writers?

Remember to listen: listen to the way people speak, to the rhythm of the words you are writing (you're most likely to do this in your head), and always give your characters room to be themselves. They'll have plenty to say if you just let them chatter on to one another, often giving you ideas you hadn't even thought of!

What is the last book you bought someone as a gift?

A variety of children's books for the recipients of the Special Recognition Award that I'm sponsoring for the local secondary school. They've chosen the titles themselves and what a fascinating selection they've made – from *The Diary of a Wimpy Kid* to *The Curious Incident of the Dog in the Night Time* (one of my own favourites).

What's the best piece of advice you've ever been given?

If you want to be a producer you'd better write. I was working in TV drama and this was what I was told to get me out of the Controller's office! I took him at his word and the rest, as they say, is history.

If you had a superpower, what would it be?

If I had a superpower I'd rescue all the children and animals being subjected to cruelty.

What literary character is most like you?

Definitely Emma from Jane Austen's wonderful novel.

If you were stranded on a desert island what song would you choose to listen to, which book would you take and what luxury item would you pack?

That's a hard one. Song choice would have to be Just My Imagination by the Temptations. Book choice . . . *How to Survive on a Desert Island* by anyone who's been thoughtful enough to write such a useful guide. Luxury item: A double-ended stick with a toothbrush at one end and a knife at the other . . . I could give Bear Grylls a sure run for his money!

Have you read them all?

For a full list of books please visit

www.susanlewis.com

Connect with

Susan Lewis

online

Sign up to Susan's newsletter for exclusive content, competitions and all the latest news from Susan.

Want to know more? Visit

www.susanlewis.com

Connect with other fans and join in the conversation at

/SusanLewisBooks

Follow Susan on

@susandlewis